THE FARM ON THE MOORS

(A WHITBY STORY)

Best Wishes

Jenny Hesketh

by
Jenny Hesketh

Grosvenor House
Publishing Limited

The right of Jenny Hesketh to be identified as the author of this
work has been asserted in accordance with Section 78
of the Copyright, Designs and Patents Act 1988

Front cover image copyright GavinD (www.iStockphoto.com)

This book is published by
Grosvenor House Publishing Ltd
Link House
140 The Broadway, Tolworth, Surrey, KT6 7HT.
www.grosvenorhousepublishing.co.uk

This book is a work of fiction. Any resemblance to
people or events, past or present, is purely coincidental.

A CIP record for this book
is available from the British Library

ISBN 978-1-78623-275-5

For Beryl,
for kindly loaning her lovely home to my imagination.

They that know love find many thorns,
They that do not know love never find roses.

CHAPTER 1

In which Lydia has to plot and scheme.
1781.

And so our courtship lumbered on; my dearest Benjamin visited every Saturday afternoon for a couple of hours. We sat in two spindly chairs by the parlour window of my mama's house on Baxtergate and my mama herself sat stony-faced beside the fire watching us, Kraken-like for the entire visit. She had been most against our courtship and had not warmed towards my beloved one bit, though he was always courteous and polite to her. And worked as a respectable curate with the expectation of a full living later that year.

Half-way through, our maid Mary would come in with a tray of tea, which was most welcome, for in these winter months, Benjamin and I were often chilled from sitting so far from the fire. Perhaps it was my mama's way of dampening our ardour?

However, by February our courtship had been going on for more than six months and we were now permitted to hold hands and this gave a *whole* new dimension to our proceedings. For now, we could write messages to each other on our hands.

For example, I could say, "do you think this rainy weather will last much longer Mr Curzon? Or shall it be over by next week?"

Meanwhile, with his finger-tip, he would write on my palm, 'I wsh I ws the lace scarf abt yr neck tucked btwn yr breasts.'

Then he would reply, "I believe we shall have rain only one more day, Miss Franklin and I do hope for finer weather next week, for I have two country christenings to officiate at, and would not wish the infants to be baptized by a sodden curate."

And meanwhile, I would be writing on his hand, 'I also my dearest,' And draw a heart shape on his hand. My Benjamin had the most beauteous of hands, long and narrow, with such a warm strength when they held my own. I dreamed much of their caresses when at last we would be married.

During the long weeks between our blissful Saturdays, I had taken it upon myself to learn Latin, knowing my Benjamin loved to read and study his Latin books whenever he had the time, and imagining us doing this together when we were married. I had asked my Mama if I might learn Latin, but she said no, for she understood there were many unsuitable passages written in Latin, far too vulgar for a young girl to know of. This spurred me on, and of course my Mama was absolutely right, there were many unsuitable passages in that language, which I discovered over the years.

Despite my Mama's protestations, I discovered a Latin primer left behind in my brother Louis' bedroom, and as it was quite a slim book, it slipped easily inside one of my novels and mama never noticed my fervent studies. Thus quite soon I could write, "te amo" and "una in perpetuum" on Benjamin's hand, much to his delight, and his lovely dark eyes would look deep into mine and he would flash me his half smile.

Only rarely was there a stolen kiss for us, until the delightful day when he asked my mama if he might give me my betrothal ring, and though she sighed wearily, she nodded her assent, and he slipped it onto my third finger. It was an antique family ring, which had once belonged to one of his Curzon ancestors, a beautiful deep purple amethyst, with diamonds at the corners and the whole surrounded with seed pearls, set in a mellow old gold. My delight knew no bounds, and in spite of myself, I leapt up and threw my arms about his neck and kissed him. My mama merely twitched slightly and looked away, but even she had to agree that now wedding plans would have to be made in earnest; and in the following days I was caught up in a whirl of dresses and lists, flowers and menus, for a wedding date set for May. All most carefully planned by my mama and excitedly aided by my Aunt Sophia and my cousins, who all lived next door.

So great was my excitement, that I hardly noticed how tired and careworn my Benjamin looked on his next visit. As he kissed my cheek goodbye, he pushed a secret note into my hand, I kept it clutched tightly, smiling in anticipation and thinking it to be a love letter. But he did not return my smile, only kissing my fingers softly and then looking at me so sadly; and as I watched him leave through the parlour window, he laid his head for a moment against his horse's neck and then gazed back at me with the most heart-broken expression before he mounted and rode away.

Now, I knew something was badly wrong, how could I have been such a fool as to not notice this before? I ran upstairs, two at a time to the privacy of my bedroom and carefully opened the crumpled note. It read-

My own dearest Lydie,

I need to talk with you most privately, for my circumstances are to change radically and I fear your mama may no longer consent to our marriage, due to this change.

Is there any chance of you visiting the farm with me, Saturday next, to discuss this with my family? That I might explain myself and you would see how things are for yourself.

Know I always remain your most true and faithful love, and naught will ever change this, but I fear we may have to postpone our wedding until you come of age.

Always your truest,
Benjamin Curzon.

I was horrified, for I was only eighteen and could not wait another three years to marry. Was I not to be married in May? How had I let that slip away from me? I had no notion of what the change in circumstances might be; perhaps the Vicar had decided not to retire and pass the living and house onto Benjamin? Could he have decided to keep him as curate and pass the living on to another? I could not think straight and spent a full ten minutes weeping into my pillow, most unlike me I confess, (though I was near my monthly time).

Then I knew I must step up and make an action plan. I knew that my mama would not let me ride out to Moorhome Farm either on my own or unchaperoned with Benjamin. But in truth, the fates were with me, for my brother Louis was due home from boarding school later this very day, for the mid-term week's holiday. He was the only one who could help me and I was like a cat on hot bricks waiting for his arrival.

* * * *

Louis sat with our mama sipping tea from an elegant pink porcelain tea bowl.

"Dearest son, how we have missed you, have we not Lydie?"

I nodded, quite desperate with impatience wondering if he would ever finish his tea.

"And I you of course Mater." And here he kissed her cheek, "it pains me to ask you Mater, but I am needing a little more money for school."

My mama laughed tolerantly, "what a naughty lad you are, surely you have not spent a whole term's allowance already?"

"Mama I fear I have, though I do try so hard to be careful, but...."

"Of course my darling."

And straight away she was unlocking the bureau and taking out the green tin cash box. She handed Louis two notes and smiling up at her, he helped himself to another two. He stood up and stuffed them into his inside pocket, grabbed a couple of little cakes and pushing them both into his mouth said, "got to go now Mater."

"Oh Louis, surely not so soon, we've hardly talked..."

"No worries, I'll not be long, back before you've blinked." And with his mouth still quite full he kissed her again.

I ran into the hall after him and grabbed his arm, "Louis, you've got to help me, I'm in the most dreadful plight."

5

He shook his arm free, "no time to talk now Sis, I'm in deep shit at The Angel, I owe money and they've turned well nasty about it, the bastards." He glanced at me and I suppose he saw my deep agitation, "you'll have to come with me if you want to talk."

I grabbed my hat and heavy shawl as he called out, "just walking Lydie round the block Mama, to get a bit of fresh air."

And together we ran down the front steps, out onto the street and walked smartly up to The Angel, only three minutes away.

"What's up then Sis?"

"Louis, you've got to help me, I <u>beg</u> of you, if you'll just do this, I'll never ask anything of you again, I've to go out to Moorhome Farm next Saturday, and I need you to chaperone me, for Mama will never let me go on my own."

Our childhood relationship had been based largely on bargains, threats and blackmail, "I'll do absolutely anything you want, if you'll just do this for me."

"Well," he considered, as we turned into The Angel yard, "why not Sis, Uncle says they've some grand horses out there, I wouldn't mind taking a look."

I could hardly believe he'd agreed to it so easily.

"Louis, I'm forever in your debt."

"That I will be remembering," he laughed as he took my arm and swept me into the public bar.

I looked around in amazement, for I'd never been in there before, though of course I'd been many times to the Assembly Rooms above, for concerts and plays. It was cosy and dark with men drinking and smoking quietly at tables.

"Master Franklin, come ter pay yer dues, I'm hoping," said the landlord quite sharply, leaning across the bar.

"Certainly have, my good Sir." Louis thrust two of the notes over the bar. "And we'll take large brandies if you please."

"Miss Franklin," he nodded to me, reaching for a couple of thick cloudy glasses.

"In there Lydie." Louis indicated a little private room to the left of the bar.

"I'll get t' lass ter bank up t' fire," said the Landlord, with a much friendlier tone now, and straight away a pleasant, neat girl came into the little room with a bucket of kindling.

"Pretty as ever Pammy," said Louis admiringly to her.

"Miss Franklin," she said politely to me, reviving the fire, and ignoring my brother. I wondered vaguely how everyone knew who I was.

And so we sat by the cosy fire with our feet upon the fender and I told of my romantic problems and how strict our mama was.

He laughed and laughed and said, "she's a bloody old tartar is our ma." Then suddenly serious he went on, "I'm in a bloody mess Sis with gambling debts, cards and horses and... and a private matter too. I've got to ask you, can you lend us some money, d'you have any money?"

Here I had to shake my head, for though mama let me have whatever dresses and books I wanted, I rarely had any actual money of my own.

"I've got jewellery I never wear though and Mama would not notice it gone."

"Nah, Sis, I can't take that…. But to be honest with you, I'm in a bloody mess with it, I can't take the worry of it." He put his head on one side and looked at me. "If I take your bits, I'll give you my word, I'll not let myself get in this shit again."

And I knew for once he meant it.

"Well, I am to be a vicar's wife, I will have to be quiet and sober dressed; my betrothal and wedding rings will be sufficient finery."

For I was determined, that even if I had to walk bare-foot over a yard of broken glass, I would be married in May, and try my best to be a good vicar's wife for my Benjamin's sake.

"That'll be something to see, to be sure," he grinned.

Then I remembered something else, and feeling inside my glove, I took out a scrap of torn out paper showing an advertisement for special gentleman's watches.

"If there's any money left from the jewellery, would you get a watch like this for my wedding gift to Benjamin, for I cannot buy such a thing myself."

He studied it and burst out laughing, "By Gad Lydie, you're quite a girl!"

"You don't think it immodest to give such a gift?"

He shook his head, "no I don't, I'd be thrilled to get such a gift on my wedding night…that is if I ever find any sweet lady to take me on!"

"You will make sure it's completely plain on the outside of the watch, and you can only see the erotic picture in the secret panel?"

He nodded and put the scrap inside his pocket. "I don't know your Benjamin well, but I think we shall get on. I like him, you know, even though he's so pious."

"I'm glad you like him," and I touched his arm affectionately.

Now, we were the close brother and sister we occasionally managed to be. The fire was very warm as we drank our second brandies and looking into the flames, I could have easily drifted into sleep but for a loud voice saying, "why if it in't Miss Lydia Belle Franklin. A thought it were thee."

I looked up and saw Jacob Curzon standing in the doorway smiling at us.

I said, "Louis, do you know Jacob Curzon, cousin to my Benjamin and to Robert Curzon? Jacob, my brother Louis."

"Only by sight," he said, standing up and shaking Jacob's hand warmly. "Good to meet you, shall you take a drink with us, Sir?"

Without waiting for an answer, he caught the landlord's eye, held up three fingers and indicated "large" with his other hand.

I had not seen Jacob since the previous year, at the funeral of my poor cousin Penelope; she who had been married to young Robert Curzon, the heir to Moorhome farm and all its lands.

"Good ter see thee Lydia, in happier circumstances than last time eh?" he said.

"Indeed," I replied, "tell me how does poor Robert?"

Here, Jacob shook his head and I saw him most moved, "as bad as can be Lydia. He sits in a chair bit' fire all day and does not move from it on a night. He takes barely any food, but he's on the drink, bottle after bottle and swears and curses at any as trys ter stop him. His poor mother can do naught with him and his father just leaves him be...breks my heart ter see him so...but he cannot seem to get himself over Penelope like."

My brother nodded sympathetically, for though he was only sixteen, he had loved our cousin Penelope in quite a romantic way himself.

"Did you know Jacob, that my Benjamin has asked me to come out to the farm to discuss something of importance?"

I looked questioningly at him and he nodded and suddenly seemed very tired.

"Aye, A know that. T'is not for me ter say, for he'll want ter tell thee in his own words like. T'is not for me ter talk of it."

My heart sank deep now, but I battled on, "Louis and I will be coming out to Moorhome, Saturday next."

He smiled, "does our Ben know that? A can let him know if tha want's for A'll be seeing him in t' week."

"Oh please would you."

"Course A will Lydia. But A'll say now, tha'll be reet shocked when tha sees our Robert. It sickens me ter see one so young, brought so low, he cannot get over it and there's none can force him."

There was nothing to say, for I felt myself to be on the edge of a deep Curzon family plot, but knew naught of it and could not guess of it, so I changed the subject and asked, "and how is your dear baby, little Jack, how is he?"

Here, Jacob's handsome face lit up, "grand, aye grand as any lad can be; it's him as keeps me going, cos ter be honest A'm fair wore out wi' all t' extra farm work, for t' Master's not up ter things no more and our Robert's as A said...."

"Shall I be able to see little Jack on Saturday?"

"Aye, A'll get Susannah ter bring him down to t' farm, for Mistress Curzon loves ter see him. She says he's very spit of me at that age, poor little bugger."

He laughed, and on that happier note he departed, with, "good ter see yer both," shaking Louis hand and kissing me lightly on the cheek.

As soon as he had gone Louis said, "how come he's cousin to Benjamin and Robert? For he is not dressed as a gentleman."

For in truth Jacob's coat had been neatly patched and his necktie was shabby and frayed.

"Well," I explained as we sat down by the fire again. "He is the bastard son of Benjamin's other uncle who died many years ago and some dairy maid. So he's had to work like a farm hand all his life, but Benjamin and Robert think the world of him and the three of them are like brothers together. Anyway, he's married to Susannah, you remember her? She was our Aunt's nursemaid, till last summer when they got married."

"Oh yes," he said suddenly realising. "She _was_ a beauty I'd say."

"So, they live in rather a poor little cottage with just two rooms, I believe, on the farm and have a baby called Jack. You'll see it, the whole set up for yourself when we go out there."

"Bloody Hell, the thing sounds like one of your novels, from the lending library, Lydie."

I only prayed that we could have the happy ending that most of my novels had, but I was not at all sure of that just yet.

On our return home I dashed straight into the kitchen, half frightening our maids, Mary and Lizzie, to death. They stared at me open mouthed as I grabbed the sweet-making tin and took a swig of the peppermint oil within it, for of course I could not let Mama smell my alcoholic breath.

"Where are you Lydie?" She called out petulantly.

"Right here Mama." And I walked, as steadily as I could, after three large brandies, back into the parlour.

"Just saying to Ma, I'm taking you out for a bit of a ride on Saturday next. Probably make a day of it, if the weather's fine. Some country air'll do me good before I've to go back to school, eh Ma?"

"Dear boy, you must always be most solicitous of your health."

"Fine, no problem there."

I could not believe our trip to the farm had been so simply manoeuvred. I thought, not for the first time, how easy things were for men, who could do just as they pleased and how hard it was for women to do anything at all. My only fear now being that next Saturday's weather would be inclement, which would scupper the whole enterprise. I could only pray to God now.

CHAPTER 2

In which Lydia and Louis visit Moorhome Farm.
Saturday next.

Whether by fate or prayer, I know not but Saturday dawned a clear bright day, if rather chill.

Louis had recently acquired a new horse for himself, a fine, large, Cleveland Bay; young and rather spirited. For me, he had hired a grey mare, steady but with the sweetest face. I had ridden her a time or two before, so knew her already. I did not often get the chance to ride, but when I did, I loved it more than anything; indeed, I would have been quite happy to spend all day galloping across those fine moors.

My Benjamin had not yet seen me in my new riding habit and I intended to 'cut a dash' in it when I arrived at the farm, for it was a bright rose pink, with a tight jacket trimmed in charcoal velvet. My hat was grey with trailing pink plumes, my gloves of the softest grey kid.

"My God Sis, they'll see you coming a mile off in that," said Louis, as he helped me onto my side saddle, but I knew from his face, that he said it admiringly.

As we turned to set off, our little cousin Chloe ran out of the house next to ours, to pet the horses.

"You're so lucky cousin Lydie, I'd give anything to be riding out today."

And Louis blew her a kiss as we rode away.

We trotted up the hill out of the town, neither of us giving a backwards glance to our poor mama, anxiously waving us off.

Soon, off the muddy road and onto the beautiful winter moorland, Louis shouted, "race you to the farm," and now, at last, I could kick into a gallop. Louis was way ahead of me, having the better horse, though 'tis a poor workman that blames his tools'. I completely forgot about my worries on the subject of my wedding and thought only of my wonderful sense of freedom, as we thundered across the hard, half frozen ground. All too soon, we came in sight of the ancient, long, low farmhouse and we slowed to descend the steep hill down to it.

Now my heart was sinking, not knowing what was going to be said, nor why my Benjamin had mentioned a postponement. But as he came out of the farmhouse to greet me, my heart leapt with excitement. I knew I was flushed from the ride as he lifted me down from my horse and took me in his arms.

"My dearest, you have never looked more beautiful." And he kissed me passionately, for there were no restrictions on our behaviour out here at Moorhome Farm.

A youth appeared to take our horses and Benjamin shook Louis' hand warmly.

"Good to see you Louis, come inside and get a drink."

I took my beloved's arm and we walked through the huge arched doorway into the Great Hall and my delight was at once quashed by the sorry sight that met our eyes. Mistress Curzon, dressed entirely in black sat to one side of the fire and to the other side sat, or rather slumped, young Robert Curzon. He did not move and I could not see if he slept or no.

Suddenly, I wished I had worn a more sober colour; strawberry pink seemed to intrude horribly into their palpable grief. But too late now, and besides I only had the one riding habit.

I swept a deep curtsey and said, "Mistress Curzon..."

"Lydie, my dear, how very good to see thee."

"And you Mistress, this is my brother Louis."

She managed the smallest smile and said, "Louis I have heard much of thee."

"And none of it good I'll be bound," he joked and kissed her hand lightly.

At this point, Robert looked up and I was more shocked than I can say, he was gaunt and wasted, unshaven with great dark shadows under his eyes. He said, "Lydie."

"Cousin Robert, how are......?" As I drew near him I could smell he was unwashed and his linens grey and stained. Around his left wrist was still tied the silk ribbon from his hand fasting with Penelope, now grubby and frayed. I held out my hand to him and he grasped it tightly for a couple of minutes, as he tried to right himself.

Then there was an awkward silence, broken only by Eliza coming in with a tray of bottles and glasses. I took wine as it seemed more ladylike, though I would have much preferred a warming brandy, and a large one at that, for the Great Hall was chill despite the roaring fire in the massive stone fireplace.

Eliza whispered something to the Mistress, who nodded and said, "bring them straight in and let that poor bairn get a bit of warmth."

Benjamin poured more drinks and Jacob, Susannah and their baby came in from the kitchen. Greetings were exchanged and old man Curzon joined us. Louis helpfully pulled up more chairs to the fireside.

Holding Susannah's chair for her, he said, "still a beauty, eh Susannah?"

She smiled and blushed a little, but it was true, motherhood suited her, the extra curves of her figure looked well and her pink and white complexion was as fresh as ever with those delightful dimples whenever she smiled.

The baby was heavenly with his mother's wide grey eyes, Jacob's ruddy good looks and dear little red-gold curls peeping from under his cap. He was bright and smiling as he was passed to me.

"His little hands are like stars," I said, enchanted as he tried so hard to clap them together.

"Well he's our little star, that's for sure, eh Susannah?" She nodded and he went on, serious now, "shall tha' speak first off our Ben?"

Benjamin clasped his hands and looked at the floor, then he sighed and reached across and took my hand in his. "I've decided to give up my church work, though it was the strongest calling for me, I have much searched my conscience and I feel it is the right thing for me to come here and help Jacob run the farm, for Robert's not up to it and Uncle's still bad with his back."

Here Jacob continued, "things are sliding bad and farming's not easy nowadays, yer've ter keep up all t' time. What's tha' think our Robert?"

Robert looked up, frowning, he shrugged his shoulders and said, "A don't give a fuck what the two of yer do. A want nowt ter do wi' it, A wish meself dead."

"Don't say that Robert." Susannah touched his arm, there were tears in her eyes. "Give tha self time ter get well again and get back ter things."

"A know tha means it kind Susannah, but A cannot pull meself outer this blackness, A'd give me life ter see her just once more...." His voice trailed away and he stared into the fire again.

I was bursting to speak, but knew I must wait. My mama had been very reluctant to give her consent to let me marry a vicar but I knew she would never let me marry a farmer, with no actual property of his own, nor any money to speak of and my coming of age was years off yet.

Now my dearest Benjamin turned to me, "Lydie my love, do you think this will change your mama's consent to our marriage?"

"The two of yer'll always have a good home here on t' farm," reassured Mistress Curzon.

"Aye, course yer will, even though our Robert's t' one as'll inherit, it's always a home for all t' family," said her husband.

"No please, please Benjamin, I beg you, do not tell my mama." I clutched his arm in desperation and turned my face into his sleeve for I felt tears welling up.

"But Dearest, I cannot marry in deceit."

Now Louis stepped up, he put a friendly hand on Benjamin's arm, "best not tell our mama, best not, for she'll go bloody off it."

"Surely it is wrong for me to marry and not be honest to all?"

Louis snorted, "there'll <u>be</u> no bloody marriage if she gets wind of this plan, and that's being honest with you."

I was shaking badly now and knew I was making a complete fool of myself.

"I cannot bear not to be married as we planned Benjamin."

Tears oozed down my cheeks as I fumbled for my handkerchief.

"Perhaps tha could tell Lydie's mama after t' wedding instead," said Susannah helpfully.

"I have to give up the church, Lydie dearest, for this farm has been my life, and for the Curzons going back centuries, I cannot stand back and see it go to rack and ruin..."

"Sorry Lydia," said Jacob, mortified. "A've done all A can but A just cannot manage on me own no longer."

"Does tha not like t' idea of a farm life dear?" asked Mistress Curzon, kindly.

I turned to her at once and said tearfully, "oh please do not think that Mistress, I should love to live in this beautiful old house and am most fond of country life.... there is nothing I should like more."

She patted my hand and said, "well, our Ben tha'd be a fool ter throw away a chance of happiness, just for t' sake of telling Lydie's mama something she need not know yet. If tha's ter be wed surely thy first loyalty should be ter thy wife, not her mother?"

"Bloody Hell," he cried. I had never heard him curse before. "Does not one of you have a sense of truth and conscience?"

A silence was his only reply, a silence broken by old man Curzon, who said, "A've worked nigh on sixty year on this farm and give it me all, but A've had it now A've not got me strength and A can't see half of it now any road, so A say let it be decided our Ben's ter tek over, while our Robert recovers his self, and wed yon lass as soon as. Let it be settled now and let's drink to it." He turned to my brother and said, "get them all a drink lad and a large one for me, t' pain in me back's killing me."

Louis did the honours and Mistress Curzon said, "let's make a toast to Lydie and Ben, and promise me yer'll get wed with no more nonsense."

"Yes Aunt, I only wish to do the right thing," he said meekly.

"A know that lad, that's why A'm telling thee what t' right thing is."

Glasses were clinked and I wanted to cry again, this time with happiness, but instead I laughed, for Jacob said, "best get her wed our Ben, for if tha misses out on this one, tha'll like as not never find another lass ter put up wi' thee."

Without any bidding, Tab and Eliza trundled in with great platters of food and the long oak table was quickly set for the dinner. It was plain, hearty food eaten from heavy old pewter plates. The Mistress said a grace and everyone loaded their plates; there was much passing up and down, for the table was over twelve feet long. It seemed that dainty manners were not expected, of this I was glad, for I always had a hearty appetite.

Louis sat beside Mistress Curzon and entertained her with tales of the boys at his school; every so often she said, "eh, they never," or "why the naughty lads," but mostly she was just laughing. Old man Curzon never spoke a word, but I was to understand that this was quite normal for him.

With us all served, Eliza went over to Robert, still at the fireside. She spoke to him as if to a small child.

"Shall tha tek a bit of dinner Master Robert? Shall A bring a plate ovver for thee?"

"Aye, tha can do, and fetch me another bottle please Eliza."

He had drunk nearly a whole bottle of brandy since our arrival and was now wanting another.

"Tha'd be better with some good food inside of thee, Master Robert, instead of t' drink."

"Did tha hear me Eliza?" he snapped.

"Aye, Master."

She disappeared to the bottle cellar and came back dusting off a greenish bottle which she opened and put on the small table beside him. Then she filled a plate with food and put that beside him too, but it remained largely untouched.

It would have been a doleful meal without Louis who now regaled the whole company with stories of when we two were children and all our scrapes, and our endless games with our eight cousins who lived next door to us, (of course he tactfully avoided any which directly mentioned our poor dead cousin Penelope).

After we had eaten, Robert suddenly heaved himself up and dug deep in his pocket. Handing me a jeweller's box, he said, "tek these Lydie, she'd a wanted thee ter have them. A bought them for her Christmas box, but never got t' chance ter give them her."

I opened the lid and saw the prettiest pair of ame-thyst ear-bobs. Amethysts being my favourite stone, I was thrilled, though I would have given my eye teeth to see them in her ears and not mine. Next, he turned to Susannah, unpinned his gold watch and chain, and leaning over towards the baby said, "that's for me godson."

At once Jack grasped the bright gold chain in his little hands.

"Robert," protested Susannah, "tha cannot give away thy fine watch, we cannot tek it."

"A'm not giving it ter thee Susannah, it's for Jack and if he dun't want it when he's older, then he can sell it and get summat he does want." He spoke petulantly and looked at Susannah darkly.

She opened her mouth to protest but I saw Jacob make a silent hushing sign, so she merely said, "tis a most generous gift, A thank thee kindly Robert."

He shrugged, "A've no need of it, A don't give a shit what time it is, day's same as night ter me now."

He turned away from her and slumped back in his chair again.

Once again Louis saved any awkwardness and asked if he might take a look at the horses.

"Aye lad and welcome, A'd show them meself if it were not for me back, go straight through t' kitchen and out in ter t' yard."

Benjamin stood up and offered me his arm and we followed Louis into the great ancient kitchen, which I had not seen before. Huge preparation benches, worn hollow with centuries of chopping edged the room. Two elbow chairs flanked the enormous fireplace which was full of contraptions for roasting meat with spits and pulleys. In the bottom corner was a metal baking oven and a little tank with a tap for hot water. Eliza and Tab were washing up on a flattish stone sink and stacking plates around a pottery bowl full of soapy water.

"Sir, Miss," they nodded as we all stepped out into the chill of the yard.

Deftly my beloved steered me into a white washed dairy with spotless stone shelves and shiny metal bowls and slotted spoons hanging from the ceiling. A pile of neatly folded white cheesecloths sat on the wide, scrubbed window sill.

"God it's freezing in here my dearest," I said.

At once he took off his heavy coat, wrapped me in it and started to kiss me. And kiss me and kiss me, on my lips, down my neck and between my breasts. For the first time I felt his manhood pressed hard against me. I had little idea of what it would look like; of course I had seen baby boys and horses in the street, and also some naughty prints of lovers that my brother had kept under his mattress and could only guess of the rest. For I knew my Benjamin would consider my touching him most improper before our marriage, so I stuck to kissing, though longing most profoundly for the rest. In truth I would most gladly have given my all at that very moment.

He drew away from me, quite flushed. "Darling Lydie, can you be with me on this farming business, I know it is not what you hoped for in me, but it is what I must do, I have prayed much and searched my conscience, and it is clear to me this is the right thing to do for all that I love."

He spoke most seriously, but there was a smudge of my lip rouge on his cheek, giving him a slight theatrical air. I wiped it with my middle finger and then had to lick it and rub it hard to remove it.

"Lydie are you listening to me at all?" He was smiling now.

"Of course I am; I am most particular to listen to your every word always. I love the farm and the splendid house and the moors and everything. I don't think I should have been much good as a vicar's wife, for I am not near as good as you think me, though of course I should have tried my very best at it for your sake."

"I do so love you Lydie," and before I could answer, he started to kiss me again, this time deeply with his tongue and his teeth. I could have fainted on the floor with pleasure but for Louis barging in.

"Come on lovebirds, Sis we need to be getting off home now, it's coming to dark early still and we need to get home before the Mater explodes and starts asking ten thousand questions."

Louis always knew exactly how best to manage my mama.

In truth although it was only mid-afternoon the light was starting to fade in the ashen sky. And so we bid our farewells and galloped across the moors to home.

That night as I lay in my cosy bed with hot stones wrapped in flannel, I thought of all the day behind me. Firstly, of the awful sadness and gloom at the farm and Robert's very clear decline. Then, I could not but think of my beautiful Benjamin and the splendour of his love, these thoughts took me to pleasure myself twice over and even then I dreamed of him vividly and gorgeously when, at last, I fell to sleep.

CHAPTER 3

In which Jacob and Susannah have
some unexpected changes.
That same night.

As soon as we got home to our cottage, Jacob and I went straight to bed, for it was so very cold. We lay in the dark with our baby between us, with blankets and a heavy patchwork quilt over us.

"What's tha think Darling?" he said to me, "does tha think it'll work out like?"

"Mmm, A'm thinking maybe Ben's wanted ter be a farmer all along?"

"He's bloody good at it all, though there's none so good as our Robert when it comes ter lambing and that. A've sore missed him this year wi' t' lambing." He sighed, "no matter how difficult it was, he always brought 'em out alive. Not no more though, he can hardly get out of his chair now."

"Does tha think Jacob...does tha think he might be.... dying?"

"Ter be honest Darling A have thought it; when Penelope first passed from us, A used ter try ter bring him round a bit and he'd be shouting ter me ter fuck off, he'd still his fight and his temper in him. But now he just sits there and hardly speaks. He's lost his will and half of his reason A'm thinking."

I sighed, there was nothing else to say about our poor, dear Robert so I asked about Lydie. "Does tha think we shall get on well with Lydie when she lives out here?"

"Oh aye, she's a good lass reet enough. Ter be honest A didn't like her that much when A first met her last year; she seemed haughty like, wi' all her rustling silk frocks and posh voice. A couldn't get why our Ben were so keen on her, though she's pretty enough A suppose. But now A've got ter know her, why she's a good heart and quite funny too."

"When A worked for her aunt, next door, A hardly saw Lydie, but late at night their Mary used ter come round for a chat and a cup of tea and she'd be telling of all these scrapes Lydie and Louis got into, they were always fighting and breaking things. And poor Mary had to sort it all out before their Mama found out." I smiled in remembering their little mishaps.

"Can't remember did A tell thee? A took a drink wi' t' two of them at The Angel t' other day, Did A tell thee? A'm so bloody tired all t' time, A don't know what A've said and what A've not."

"No-o," I said in disbelief, "Tha's saying Lydie was drinking in an inn?"

"Oh aye, bold as brass, and A know for a fact that Louis' got a bar bill as long as yer arm."

"Well, A'll bet me life on it, her mama knew nowt about it."

My Jacob laid two fingers on our sleeping baby's cheek, "our lad's as warm as buttered toast now, lay him where I am and A can lay with thee."

He sat up, and gently as I could I moved our baby into the space and Jacob rolled over to be beside me.

The baby stirred but Jacob laid his hand across him rocking him back into sleep. He had amazing ways to touch and quiet babies and animals; I hope it does not shame to say he had amazing ways to touch and comfort me also.

Afterwards he always said the same thing, "ave A ever told thee how much A love thee my Susannah?"

And A would say, "nay my Jacob, A believe tha's not."

Then he would say, "Susannah, A love thee more than t' stars in t' sky and t' moon and sun as well."

Usually we would fall straight to sleep, warm and loved, but this night there was something else on both our minds.

"What's tha think t' mistress wanted then? For if it were not much, she'd have said it there and then."

"Aye, A cannot imagine what it might be."

For when we left the farm that afternoon, the Mistress had called Jacob quietly to her and asked him to come in to see her on the morrow, when his main work was done, "And you too Susannah," she had said.

"Hope it's not more bloody work, A'm dropping as it is."

"Nay Jacob, she's so nice wi' us now especially since Jack's been born, A don't think it can be that."

This had been a great change, for most of his life Jacob had worked as a servant and been largely ignored by Master and Mistress Curzon on account of him being the bastard son of the master's brother.

But it was some weeks before we found out what it was she wanted to talk to us about, for the very next morning we got a message to say that the old Master had had some kind of attack in the night and could not rise from his bed; Eliza said one side of his face was all dropped and he could barely speak for slavering.

"It's bloody bad Susannah A tell thee, but A've that much ter do A can hardly put me mind ter it," said Jacob.

Of course, I would have gone down to the farm myself that morning to offer help, but it had snowed overnight and it was too bitter to walk the mile or so there, carrying my baby, so I sent a letter with Jacob saying, it sorrowed me greatly to hear of the master's illness and to offer any help I could give. Then I said I would pray for them and remained their devoted servant, Susannah Curzon.

Night and day I prayed for Master Curzon's health to be restored and prayed, as I always did, that Robert would find his spirit and strength again. But my prayers were to no avail, and three days later Jacob came into the cottage with snow on his tarpaulin coat and in the turn-ups of his hat. He stood in silence for a moment and then said, "Susannah, he's passed."

"The Master?"

He shook his head, "no-o our Robert, our Robert's passed; Eliza found him in his chair this morning when she came down first thing."

"Oh…" I had no words to say and burst into tears at once. Jacob shook off his coat and hat onto the floor and took me in his arms. His body was ice cold against me and it was a long time before either of us felt anything but an icy chill in our hearts.

Robert was buried in the same grave as his young wife Penelope a few days later.

So, it was well into March when Jacob and I did get down to see the Mistress. Though we'd had much snow, it was now all melted, the sun was bright in a blustery blue sky and green shoots were pushing up in our little wind swept garden. I wrapped Jack up as best I could in his white wool hat and coat, so beautifully knitted by Eliza on five spikey needles and tied him to me with a long scarf, for he was quite heavy now. Jacob walked with his arm about my waist and I think it was the first time we had properly smiled at each other since Robert's death. However bad things are, Spring weather always gives a sense of hope in the goodness of God's will. It was a day I shall always remember, for we had the lovliest surprise when we got down to the farm and Eliza showed us into the Mistress' winter parlour.

"Tek t' bairn would tha?" she said to Eliza.

"There's nowt A should like more Mistress," she replied helping me untie him and gathering him into her arms. Eliza was cousin to Jacob on his mother's side and so especially loved Jack, her 'own blood' as she always pointed out.

We sat down in the cosy winter parlour, a small room which was panelled and hung with some tapestries on the walls for extra warmth and lovely plaited rush mats to cover the cold stone flagged floor. A fire blazed and it seemed overwarm to me, but I knew it would be a comfort to the Mistress who was most troubled with painful, swollen joints.

"Shall tha pour drinks for us Jacob," she said indicating a bottle and glasses on a side table, "for my hands shake a bit now."

We sipped our port wines and she said, "yer must be wondering why A've asked yer down here, so A'll get straight to it; A've thought much ovver t' past months of condition of Hill Cottage, A've not laid eyes on it myself for more than thirty year now, but A'm guessing it must be in a bit of a state now with repairs and that?" She looked at Jacob questioningly.

"Well, Mistress, A've done me best wi' repairs but roof's more than two-hundred-year old and windows is in a poor state…."

She nodded, "A'll tell thee honest, A've decided ter tek matters into me own hands Jacob, for me husband'll not rise from his bed again, till he's took out in t' coffin."

"A'm sorry ter be hearing that Mistress, truly."

"Nay Jacob, it's God's will, and tha knows as well as any how things stand between me and my husband."

Jacob did not reply but gave the smallest nod, and she went on, "so A've decided that a bit of rebuilding's needed; a staircase and a couple of bedrooms upstairs, so then yer could use t' downstairs as a kitchen and a parlour with maybe a better fireplace, put in. Yer'll have more room then, A expect yer'll be having another bairn or two?"

She looked at me and I said, "pray God."

"So what do yer think of that as an idea?"

"Mistress, that sounds grand, eh Susannah? A can hardly believe it, it's just what we would have wanted for ourselves."

I could hardly believe my ears too, at our very great good fortune and said, "A cannot thank thee enough for thy kindness and thinking of us so."

In truth, though we had always tried to make the best of things, our home was cold and dilapidated.

She went on pensively, "A came to this farm as a bride when A were only sixteen, best part of fifty year ago, A know it well and every day, since thy father died

Jacob, A've seen tha work like a dog and give it yer all, so it's no more than tha deserves, ter have thy cottage a bit better...So A'll need to send a letter to t' jewellers in Guisborough ter raise a bit of money, can tha write Jacob? For my writing is poor now."

"Nay Mistress, not well, though A'm learning; my Susannah has a neat hand though."

She indicated a small oak desk already set out with writing things and I wrote a letter as carefully as I could, asking the jeweller to call. I think it looked well enough, despite struggling with the spelling of 'convenience'. It must have been the family jewellers, as I had been there once last year with Robert and Jacob. The Mistress signed it in a wobbly hand and after it was folded, I dropped some hot red wax on it and the Mistress lifted a seal from a chain on her waist and I pressed the huge letter 'C' into the wax. How I wished I had such a thing, for after all my name was Curzon too. She asked Jacob to deliver the letter on the morrow and also to ask a builder to call. Then we stood to take our leave.

"One more thing Jacob afore yer go. Tha should have had this years since, but my husband kept it locked away in his box, but as A say, life's nigh on done for him now." Here she delved into her pocket, awkwardly with her stiff fingers and handed Jacob a gold watch and chain. "Tis thy father's watch."

Jacob gasped and looked at it in awe. He pinched the top of his nose with his finger and thumb, which was as near to tears that Jacob ever got.

"Mistress A've not words ter say what this means ter me, all t' jewils in t' county put together could not mean more ter me than this."

He opened it up and saw his father's name and the date of his twenty first birthday engraved inside, (this was also the year in which Jacob had been born, 1749).

"Well tha should have had it afore, but it was not in my power. So let's tek another drink ter yer good future for when my husband passes it'll all come ter our Benjamin, all t' farm and lands. Things'll be a good bit better for thee then, that A do know."

I could see my Jacob was lost for words as we raised our glasses so I said, "for thy very gracious kindness Mistress, our thanks."

"In truth," she replied, "it's no more than our Robert would have done for yer both if he'd lived to inherit. So think of it done in his name." Here she sighed, for the poor Mistress had now buried all seven of her children.

Again I asked if I could do any little thing in return for her kindness. She put her head on one side, "A know tha's busy wi' t' bairn, does tha have any spare time?"

"Of course A do, what's tha thinking of?"

Here she explained that she wanted to refurbish Benjamin's bedroom, for when he and Lydie were married and she had had a length of pink damask sent out, feeling sure Lydie would like pink as she was dressed head toe in it on her last visit, and would I be able to sew bed curtains for them in such a short time, for she feared Tab and Eliza would have little time to spare with their other work....

"A should be most glad to Mistress, for A'm very quick with my work."

Here she smiled, "our Penelope once said if there was ever invented a machine as could sew it would be called a 'Susannah'. She said tha'd made three dresses and sewed up a waistcoat in only three week once."

"Tis true Mistress," I smiled also, remembering that happy time preparing for Penelope's wedding and shortly after, preparing for my own.

* * * *

In no time at all, builders arrived and great stacks of stone and tiles and wood were hauled up the hill by strong dray horses and work began, to re-build our little cottage. As it progressed wooden boxes of glass panes packed in straw arrived, then big sacks of lime plaster and whitewash too.

Living in the cottage was a nightmare of dust and flapping roof tarpaulins keeping us awake at night, but none of it bothered me in the least, for every day was a day nearer to the cottage of my dreams.

The first week in April, the Master was buried with little ceremony and even less grief from his wife, who merely shrugged when I offered my condolences. Eliza said she'd no grievance with the Master and he'd always been fair enough with her. Tab said nothing at all.

After that, some days I sat in the garden with my baby and watched the work progress, but most days I walked down to the farm and sewed the bed curtains and also some matching cushions for the elbow chairs in Lydie's bedroom to be. At the beginning of May, they were finished, Eliza helped me to hang them and then the Mistress came in to admire them, amazed at how quickly they were done. Also in that same week, Benjamin had completed his notice as a curate and moved back into the farm as Master of all, for of course he had inherited after the deaths of his cousin Robert and his uncle.

It was like old times for the two cousins, with much laughter and joking as they worked together. Jacob teasing at Benjamin's lack of strength after years away from farming, "tha's soft as butter now, man."

After the bed curtains were hung and the cushions arranged, Mistress Curzon asked me to come into the end parlour with her. I had never seen that dark shuttered room before where all the furniture was draped with dust sheets. I struggled to open the heavy shutters with rusted catches and then in the light, I saw a most beautiful panelled room with a white, diaper pattern ceiling set with roses; the fire surround was carved with dogs which seemed to have rabbit ears and lion tails.

"Tis a most beautiful room Mistress, does tha niver use it?"

"No, it's niver been used in my time, we've way too much furniture here, it's all more work for t' servants, dusting it and covering it up every year. Am thinking tha'll be needing some bits for thy new parlour?"

"Yes Mistress?" I said in disbelief at my good fortune.

"Does tha mind it being so old, most in here's well ovver a hundred-year-old?"

"No Mistress, I like that, for it gives me t' feel of my Jacob's family being here a very long time; fathers and sons for generations."

And so I became the proud owner of six chairs with high caned backs, a gate-legged table, two Yorkshire chairs for the fireside, four brass candlesticks (like we could ever afford four candles at the same time), a neat little cupboard, some fire irons, a pile of fine table linens and bed linens and the promise of two beds and mattresses from the upstairs.

I thanked her from the bottom of my heart and said everything was exactly to my taste and as I would have wished it.

Later that day, just as I had finished a final coat of whitewash on the cottage walls, it all arrived on the big cart and Jacob and Benjamin unloaded it. My delight knew no bounds and I kissed them both when it was all set out.

"Shall tha stay and get a cup of tea with us Ben in our new parlour?"

"I'd be most pleased to Susannah dear, for I'm quite parched after all that work."

I put the kettle on to boil and put out a cake and scones Tab had kindly given me, for I'd had no chance to bake in recent weeks. Then Jacob went to his heavy coat hanging on the back of the front door and took out a couple of parcels from the deep pockets.

Rather bashfully, he handed them to me, "A got these for thee, so as tha can have a proper ladylike tea party in t' new parlour."

Thrilled, I opened them up to reveal six dainty tea bowls and matching saucers painted with red and blue dots, set as little flowers; the very kind of thing that Lydie's fine mama would drink out of. Of course I hugged him and kissed him again and again until the kettle had nearly boiled over. Then the three of us sat at the new table on the new chairs and drank tea from the new tea bowls.

"Bloody hell Susannah, there's only a swallow in each, tha'll have ter fill them ten times ovver for me," said Jacob but he looked well pleased with everything.

Benjamin seemed far more comfortable than Jacob with a tea bowl, I supposed from his former life as a curate. He looked well and had never seemed happier, but then why would he not? He had just inherited a beautiful ancient house and plenty of good farmland, plus he was about to marry a lady that he clearly loved most dear.

As for me, did I not have a husband I loved true, a charming, cosy cottage and the sweetest baby? But there was one more thing I much wanted; it was far too early to say yet, but I had just a feeling and was so hoping that the old saying was true, "new house, new baby."

We three were so happy that day sitting around the tea table, I prayed God we would always be so.

CHAPTER 4

In which the happy couple are married.
May 1781.

My wedding day dawned, a warm bright Saturday. I felt quite sick with nerves when I awoke, unlike me for I did not consider myself such a person in the least.

"Eh Miss, that A should see this great day, A'm that excited, for thee and for meself too...." Mary was to leave my mama's service and to come with me to Moorhome Farm as my own maid. "A've had me box all packed and ready, three days now, A've just this dress ter put in now, when A gets changed into t' dress for thy wedding. 'Thy wedding,' why A never thought ter see this day, when A first held thee as a little baby."

This was not entirely true, for when Mary first laid eyes on me I was already a contrary two-year-old, my mama having returned to our house on Baxtergate as a widow after an elopement and a disastrous marriage.

"Now Mary," I corrected, "Louis was the baby not I..."

"Well Miss, ter me tha wert' big bairn and he wert' little bairn. A cannot believe it when A see him now, eh he must be nigh on six foot tall ......"

I thought it quite possible that Mary would ramble on all morning, so I gulped down the cup of tea she had brought me and the toast and said, "will you help me dress in a minute Mary, when I've washed."

She emptied the hot water can into my basin while I slipped behind the screen to use the chamber pot. I washed my hands and face, and then my bits and lastly my feet and covered all of me with lavender water which stung a bit but I did not wish to be found wanting on my marriage bed. I hesitated over cosmetics as I sat at my dressing table, for I knew my beloved preferred a natural and Godly look; so just a smudge on the eye-lashes and a tiny touch on the lips and cheeks. I pouted in the mirror and decided I looked well enough.

Mary ran her fingers over my curling rags and started to remove them.

"Mary, I need to ask you an intimate question about marriage."

I saw her reflection freeze in the mirror in front of us; I nearly laughed out loud, when she said, "eh Miss, tha knows A've niver been wed, A cannot answer such, it meks me blush just ter think of it, ... A hardly know what happens Miss."

"No Mary it's not that," for in truth, I had no worries about that and could barely wait. "It's about curling rags, should I wear them every night when I am in bed with my husband? Or should my hair be loosed when... when we are together and then that would mean that my hair would be straight as a stick all day long and I should have to a wear a cap always to cover up."

"A couldn't say Miss," then as she was lacing up my stays she went on, "A think Miss that A see a deal of love in Mr Curzon's eyes and A think when there's such love as that, neither must mind much what the other looks like, so A'd do what tha feels most comfortable with. Yes, that's what A think Miss."

"Oh Mary what a sweet answer, thank you," and I jumped up and kissed her, just as my mama came in.

"Now Lydie don't put your dress on till I've done your hair, dress on last always."

"Yes Mama," I said meekly, having decided to be as compliant as possible on the LAST day in my home. I felt none of the bride-to-be's sentimentality about leaving. Home was boring and restrictive; I desperately missed Penelope, not so much as a cousin but as my very best friend and companion. Although Louis and I had spent a lot of our childhood fighting, I missed him too, now he was away at school most of the time.

My mama was always good with hair so there was no quarrel there. But my mama could never leave be and she said, "Lydie are you sure of this? For he's only a farmer, I had so hoped for more for you... I think it not too late to change your mind?"

I was boiling now; I had foolishly imagined that she would be pleased when I had told her that Benjamin had got his inheritance, and would not be a vicar now but instead was quite a wealthy landowner. But not so, though to be fair, she had not withdrawn her consent.

Fortunately, I did not have to hold back my temper, as just then, my Aunt Sophia came in from next door, with my bridal flowers. And I was at once diverted by how pretty she looked, for it was her first day out of mourning and she was in yellow striped silk with a hat weighed down with matching velvet flowers.

As Mama finished off my hair, she said, "Sister how well you look," and kissed her on the cheek.

She did look well now, for she had spent much time weak and pale from her bereavement and also from a horrendous, near fatal confinement six months since.

"Indeed I do feel so much better," turning to me, she said, "and all the more for seeing you and dear Benjamin so happy."

I smiled and felt more myself again; she had brought me some of her dainty lace gloves for 'the borrowed'. Then she hugged my mama, who was still prickly and anxious, and said, "dear sister, fear not, for where there is true love there is always happiness, as I know from my own marriage, you know how happy I have been with my dearest husband; we love each other more now than ever we did."

And this was true, my aunt and uncle were the most devoted and affectionate of couples.

"Well," replied my mama, lifting my dress from its protective linen bag, "there's naught to be done now, Lydie's a wilful girl and will have her way."

"And you know where she gets that from," laughed my aunt, as they both helped me into my dress.

I shall just mention my dress; it was quite gorgeous, I had chosen a lavender, for it was a colour suitable for the end of mourning and also I loved any shade of purple. It had long tight sleeves and the back polonaise was caught up with striped ribbons in grey and purple silk, tied into large bows. The under skirt was a plain mauve-grey silk, my mama and aunt had beautifully quilted the deep hem, in a pattern of shells and diamond shapes. My wreath, a circlet of pansies, orange blossoms and white ribbons, was pinned to my hair.

Now, my mama wept to look at me, "dear Lydie," she said hugging me, but I felt cross and stiff and could not wait to get downstairs to see my bridesmaids, who I could hear at fever pitch with excitement in the front hallway. (The parlour being out of bounds as it was set out in readiness for the wedding breakfast).

All my seven girl cousins were to be my bridesmaids, dressed in white dimity with purple sashes and carrying little posies from our own garden, behind the house. I hoped the four-year-old twins would behave themselves as they had turned into quite naughty cheeky girls.

There were shrieks of delight as I descended the stairs and the fussing gradually died down as everyone left for the church, two minutes down the road. First the servants, then my aunt and bridesmaids and lastly my mama on my uncle's arm. My uncle had had a fair bit to drink already at the early serving at the Angel Inn, and kept telling me what a grand lass I was.

Soon enough, just Louis and I stood alone in the hallway.

"Well, Sis, this is it, the big day, getting rid of you at last."

I had felt so happy in anticipation, and being admired by everyone, now I suddenly felt on the edge of tears.

"Louis, if only Penelope was here now, if only she could be with me today. Do you think she can see us now?" I looked up at him and he looked back so sadly and bit his lip.

"Don't Sis, and don't be blubbing or you'll set me off. You know I really loved her, don't you? Young fool that I am."

I nodded and he hugged me clumsily, then guided me towards the door.

"Come on now."

I forced a weak smile as I took his arm and we walked down Baxtergate to the new church. But as we got to the church steps he paused and told me the silliest joke about a monkey. Thus, as I walked into the church, I was smiling and Louis was laughing and it was infectious for then everyone was smiling as we walked down the aisle. My Benjamin looked magnificent in a dark blue broadcloth. Jacob beside him, whispered in his ear and then Benjamin was grinning broadly too.

Louis stood to one side and Benjamin took both my hands and squeezed them tight. The vicar improvised a little, going on about a joyous occasion entered into with great happiness, for Benjamin and I were still smiling at each other. So busy were we gazing at one another, that my Benjamin almost dropped the ring, then tried to force it on to the wrong finger, as we exchanged our lovely vows.

Afterwards at the signing, my eldest cousin Jane and Jacob were our witnesses. Jacob signed with a huge flourish.

"Man, that's some signature," said Benjamin.

"Well," he replied triumphantly, "the world's waited thirty-two year ter see me write me name, so A thought A'd better mek it a good 'un. A've been practising all week."

I felt a movement at my shoulder and turned to see baby Jack holding out his arms to me. I was surprised he recognised me, for it was three months since I had last seen him.

"Oh Jack, what a lovely welcome into my new family."

I held him close for a minute or two, for a warm baby is such a comfort, when a little nervous.

Then I walked arm in arm with my NEW HUSBAND, back down the aisle and out of the church into our life together.

The wedding breakfast was spectacular in every way and our twenty guests sat down to hot buttered rolls, eggs, thick ham, kidneys, pressed meats, veal pies, dishes of fruit and lemon flummery, syllabubs and a huge cake covered in white icing. The cake was decorated with a trellis of blue sugar, and on the top our two names were entwined. Of course there was a great deal to drink in the way of wine, brandy and port wine with a good ale and some Geneva for all the servants, eating in the kitchen.

My uncle made a toasting speech saying what a grand lass I was and then what a grand couple we were, I saw my mother purse her lips and fan herself vigorously as everyone drank to our health. My cousin Elizabeth whispered to ask me if I was scared of what was to come, I smiled and shook my head.

"You're always so brave Lydie, I wish I was more like you."

In truth I could hardly wait for what was to come, my Benjamin and I kept exchanging secret glances and touching discreetly. And lovely as it all was, we left as soon as was decently possible, amidst a flurry of compliments and kisses and good wishes. It suddenly seemed conspicuous, Benjamin's lack of family, (for he was an only child, orphaned from the age of ten), just Jacob and Susannah and a couple of his friends from Cambridge-both unmarried curates, were there for him. Sadly, his Aunt found walking any distance too difficult and had stayed at home.

Louis, caught my eye as we turned to leave, he winked and said, "good luck Sis."

I was hot and flushed when we arrived at the farm what with the ride and the excitement and I'd had a fair bit to drink too. My husband lifted me down and scraped two little flies off my face, with his thumb nail.

"Has my trunk arrived yet?" I asked anxiously, as he put an arm about my waist to lead me to the majestic front door.

"Oh I expect so," he said dismissively.

So busy was I staring around me, at this splendid house of which I was now to be mistress, I had quite forgotten tradition and next thing I knew, Benjamin had swept me up in his arms and carried me over the threshold into the hall.

"Mistress Curzon," I said as he set me down in front of his aunt.

"Please call me mother-in-law now dear."

"Mother-in-law, I thank you." I bobbed a slightly unsteady curtsey.

"Shall yer want refreshments? A've little out, for t' servants are still away at yer wedding."

"No Aunt, we have both eaten much already, but perhaps a drink?"

"I've brought you some of our wedding cake," I said, unwrapping it from a linen napkin. I already knew she feared anything from a strange kitchen, so I added, "it has been made in my Aunt Sophia's own kitchen." And then explained about the blue sugar trellis and our names on the top.

"Charming, A thank thee, A can see 'tis a well-made cake." Tactfully, she then asked if we'd like to rest after our ride.

"Please excuse us Aunt," and with this Benjamin grabbed two stem glasses and a decanter of port wine from the table and we ran up the stairs two at a time. In the dark passageway he pushed me against the wall and kissed me passionately, with his hand upon my breast.

"Which room is to be ours, my dearest?"

A dreaded thought had come to me that we might be in Penelope and Robert's old room and that I could not have borne.

"Why my own room that I've always had, it's plenty big enough and my Aunt's had it done out for you. See here." He opened a door almost behind me.

What a delight met my eyes. A four poster bed stood in the middle of the room with rose pink damask curtains and a fine white quilted coverlet. There was a huge old clothes press with the doors left open so I could see my own dresses all laid out and hanging there, with my leather trunk at the foot of the bed. Elbow chairs, with pink cushions flanked the fireplace which was dark like the panelled walls but set with blue and white tiles showing repeat pictures of figures in a garden. There was a corner washstand with pretty soaps and cloths and a little dish of blackish toothpowder, which Eliza made herself; strange as it looked, I had resolved to use this toothpowder, for all the Curzons had sparkling white teeth. Also a dressing table with an ancient spotted mirror resting on it; a desk beneath the casement windows with writing things and some low shelves laden with books. The only ornament was a large copper jug overflowing with pink and white scented roses. The whole room was flooded with the soft smell of lavender, which had been brushed over the floorboards.

"Oh my dearest, how very beautiful it all is."

"I think Susannah made the curtains."

I walked across to look out at the splendid moorland view, all golden and green stretching in every direction dotted with a few cows and sheep. Benjamin stood behind me and kissed the side of my neck.

"You can see the sea from here on a very clear day," he said. I turned to him and then he was serious and continued, "Dearest, will you pray with me before we become true husband and wife?"

"Of course."

We knelt together at the side of the bed, my hands held tight between his and I closed my eyes. Benjamin prayed about this and that and thanked God for our love and asked that our marriage would be long and fruitful. At last, when he had finished, I said "Amen," and started to rise but he held me there saying, "Dearest, I believe there must be no secrets between husband and wife..."

"I too, my darling."

"Then I must confess before we go further... you are not my first Lydie, I know I should have saved myself for this day but I fear I have not and I do so regret it now."

I had not thought of this before, but Benjamin was thirty- two years old; he had been out in the world, I could hardly expect him to be a virgin. In truth, I did not care.

"There were two wenches that Jacob set me up with years ago, though of course I do not blame him, for I had of my own free will, but I am ashamed of it now. Then, when I was at university there were another two, one was a regular for some time, but I do swear Lydie," he looked at me desperately, "I swear on my life, that after I took Holy Orders, I never touched another woman. Truly Lydie I did not."

"Really, my dearest it is of no matter to me, such is a man's life."

"But I should be giving you my purity?"

"Frankly, I already have plenty of purity, I will gladly share mine with you." Boldly I added, "so shall we set to it now?"

He shook his head laughing, "oh Lydie, whenever I am troubled, you manage to make me smile."

"No more than my wifely duty."

At last we stood up and indeed Benjamin did seem very conversant with the workings of a woman's clothing as he deftly undressed me and pulled me down beside him. For the first time I saw his man-hood, I was struck by its beauty, like a great purple orchid, both strong and delicate at the same time.

"Oh, may I touch it?"

"Please do," he laughed, taking my hand.

After that, he covered me with kisses and caresses and asked me if I was ready to be his true wife. Of course I said I was, (my God had I not been ready since I was about twelve).

Nos amare libidine ardeas

Afterwards, he rolled off me grinning and flushed and told me he was consumed with love for me. Then I remembered, that with all the excitement I had forgotten to give him his wedding gift. When I showed him the watch he was puzzled for a moment, because of course he already had a watch (his father's), then I showed him the secret panel which lifted up to show an enamelled picture of a naked lady and gentleman at their 'amours', with Cupid flying above them, the whole surrounded by a circle of pink enamel covered with tiniest gold stars. He laughed and laughed between kisses, and insisted it was the nicest gift he had ever had, and promised that he would look at it every day at noon and think of our two loving hearts.

The weeks that followed were the happiest I had ever known, the freedom to do as I pleased every day, and riding out onto those beautiful moors with my divine husband, on those long summer evenings. Sitting on the bracken, and later the purple heather, watching the distant sparkling sea. Benjamin taught me the name of all the plants and birds that lived on that secret moorland. Then home to bed in our pretty bedroom, where he would love me in every way imaginable; I could hardly believe that we were to be allowed to do this wonderful thing as often as we wanted for ever and ever.

CHAPTER 5

In which hopes and dreams are realised.
1782.

And so my wish came true; on the second of January, on a mild, starry night our little girl was born, we had decided long since that we would name her Penelope if she was to be a girl. There was no chance to send for the midwife, for it was barely two hours, start to finish and Jacob saw to it all as easy as if I had been birthing a lamb!

Lydie and Benjamin came up to see us the very next day. He smiled to see the baby but would not hold her, Lydie on the other hand was positively weepy, for she had already said to me privately, more than once that she considered herself barren and she clutched the baby to her as if she could never put her down.

"Thy turn next, eh Lydia?" said Jacob, brightly.

"I do not know Jacob, I pray God," she replied, staring hard at the baby. I saw she was biting her lip, which is what she always did when she was trying not to cry.

"Early days yet, A'd say."

"With my first husband, we were married more than two year afore A fell, though he was away at sea some of that time," I said encouragingly. "Jacob's right it's

4 8

very early days." I knew she had already discussed all this with the Mistress, who had said the same, for Lydie had only been married seven months.

She nodded and gave me back the baby. Then she took little Jack onto her lap, and perhaps he sensed her sadness for he took her face in his baby hands and kissed her and everyone laughed.

Benjamin glanced at the empty fireplace, "take whatever wood you want man, don't stint on that, anytime. Get a cartload brought up if you need it."

Indeed, our life had much improved, far more than we could ever have dreamed of; not only a beautiful and spacious rebuilt cottage but Benjamin and Lydie had shown us the very greatest generosity. Lydie rode up to take tea with me most days and never came empty handed.

Sometimes it was meat or eggs, a big cone of sugar or a bundle of candles. If ever I remonstrated, she would snort and say it was small recompense to pay for the amount of tea and cake she took in my parlour. After she had been married a few months she would bring cheese or butter made by her own hand in their dairy. For Lydie had taken most well to farming life, taking charge not only of the dairy work but of the chickens too, and the feeding of the pig recently slaughtered for the Christmas. She was quite happy to clean out a stable or a sty if need be and many a time when she came up to see me she had dirty nails or mud on her skirt. This often made me smile to see her, remembering the fine young lady she had seemed before her marriage, so slender and elegant, always dressed in expensive fashionable clothes. Her greatest love of course was her horse; quite against all advice, she had insisted on having that great black mare that had belonged to poor

Robert. Both Benjamin and my Jacob had said the horse far too strong and spirited for a lady but she merely said she was spirited too, so they'd be well matched. I was always a little afraid of the great beast but Lydie rode her well and talked to her and kissed her as if her horse was a little child.

Eliza came up to help me with laundry and cleaning for a couple of hours each day, for the two weeks of my confinement. She adored the baby and little Jack, for, as she pointed out every day, they were of her own blood, as she was first cousin to my Jacob, on his mother's side.

Although she was a great help and talked non-stop about what she'd said to Tab and what Tab had said to her, and what everyone at the farm had said and done; there was something very closed about Eliza. For all her idle chatter, I felt I knew nothing whatsoever about her. Sometimes, when she thought I wasn't looking, I saw her staring at me, though I had no clue as to what she was thinking.

Lydie, however was quite different, despite the difference in our stations, our education and my initial doubts, she was easy and open, with her lively ways, good humour and kindly warmth.

It was only a few weeks later when she burst through my cottage door and before she even sat down she was asking, "Susannah, how will I know if I'm with child?"

"Well tha might feel a swelling in thy bosom, or to make water more often or being sick when tha wakes in t' morning…"

"My mother-in-law said just the same things and Eliza had to let out my stays last week, she gave me a funny look but I thought naught of it then," she spoke excitedly. "And I was sick yesterday and this morning and I feel fine now."

"Did Benjamin not notice that?"

"No-o, he's always up long afore me, anyway he knows naught of babies, he'd only notice if I was a sheep or a cow. So do you think I am Susannah?"

She had a softened, flushed look that so commonly goes with the condition, and I confidently said, "why yes A believe tha'rt, Lydie. A'm so pleased for thee, for A know how much tha wanted it."

"Mother-in-law thought so too," she said triumphantly.

"That'll be a goodly surprise ter tell Benjamin eh?"

"Bloody Hell, is this it? Am I with child at last, after so long?" She sat down carefully and touched her stomach, "when will it move?"

"Eh, not for a few weeks yet, with quickening tha feels like it's a real bairn then. Afore that A don't think they seem like they's real."

Now she was laughing and joking, every few minutes she was touching her stomach and asking a hundred questions about how babies made their entrance into the world.

"I have wanted this so very much, all my life. I can still barely believe it," she said, lifting little Jack onto her knee.

Whilst I made the tea she sang him a song, which she made up as she went along, and every time she said 'star', Jack had to put his hands above his head like stars.

"Up so high I see a star,
If I could catch a star,
I'd put it in a jar,
So then I'd have a star,
To give to my mama," and so on.

When she had drunk three cups of tea, eaten two large pieces of ginger cake, and kissed the sleeping Penelope, she decided she must return to the farm to tell Benjamin of their good news.

And thereby hangs a most amusing story, which I would know naught of, but for Tab repeating it to me a few days later. At the time, Tab was cleaning out the fire in the Great Hall and Benjamin was at the long table with his account books and Lydia came in, almost tripping on one of the dogs.

"Bloody Hell..." says she.

"My dear, I wish you would not curse, it is most unladylike."

"Well husband," says she as bold as anything, "I have spent eighteen years being ladylike, so I'm going to spend the next eighteen being unladylike and then see which I like the best."

Poor Benjamin just sighs for he never speaks back at her. Anyway, next thing she reaches across that great table and touches his arm and says, "but one thing I do promise you husband, I will not curse in front of our child."

Then he looks up smiling in disbelief and says, "no Lydie, no?"

And imitating him, she goes, "yes Lydie, yes and... yes."

Then he pulls her across the table to kiss her and then, this is the funniest bit, the Mistress comes in and she sees them, (well she knows about it already) and says, "A see he's been told then," with a twinkle in her eye.

So poor Lydie's trying to right herself, but can't very easily for she's stretched across the table so she says, "I do beg your pardon for my behaviour mother-in-law."

And the Mistress says, as dry as anything, "nay 'tis Benjamin's table now, he must use it as he pleases, A just hope yer'll have cleared yerselves off afore t' dinner's ter be set." And off she went!

* * * *

Lydie was as well as could be for her carrying time, running about and doing all her farm work, and riding her big horse for a couple of hours every day. I knew that when Benjamin was out of the way, she would ride astride, and not side-saddle, as was proper, which did shock me a bit.

It was decided that when her time came, we would all go and stay at the farm for a few days, so that I could help with the lying in, which might be long with it being a first baby, and then I could help Lydie get going with the feeding in the early days. I was most excited about this, knowing we would be sleeping in a four poster bed, in one of the beautiful old bedrooms, where Curzons had slept for centuries. I thought I should feel like a princess at the very least. My Jacob thought it all a pile of old junk and he'd rather be at home, and know "what were what," as he put it.

When the day arrived, one of the hired lads rode up to tell me it was time. Luckily Jacob was at home, so I quickly packed up our things and he carried Jack on his shoulders and I rode on his horse with baby Penelope and our bundle of clothes.

"Hope this won't tek long Darling," he said when we arrived, "A like me own bed."

"We must help where we can, Jacob."

He nodded and we walked in through the kitchen door.

"Best go straight up there Susannah," said Tab anxiously.

"She's teking it bad, is the young mistress, and t' midwife's with her now," said Eliza taking my baby in her arms.

So I ran upstairs as quick as I could and was greeted with terrible groans coming from Lydie's lovely bedroom. I peeped around the door and saw Mrs Vye, the midwife sitting by Lydie, rubbing her back. Everything for the birth was set out neatly on a table at the end of the bed.

Then her spasm came and she screamed out loud, "oh no, oh no, I cannot bear it, it is so bad. Susannah is it always as bad as this?" She clutched my arm hard and laid her head on my shoulder. Moaning as it passed, she said, "Susannah is it nearly over?"

I looked at Mrs Vye, who said, "a bit to go yet Mistress."

Poor Lydie screamed well into the night, naught would ease her, not walking, nor crouching, nor squatting. Mrs Vye, was so kindly and encouraging, telling Lydie how well she was doing and how it would all be worth it in the end. Eliza brought up regular trays of food and drink as the afternoon wore on and every time she came in, told us how badly the master was taking it, blaming himself for Lydie's terrible pain.

When I went downstairs to feed Penelope, Benjamin was sitting with his head in his hands and Jacob was teasing him, "get up there man and see thy son born." But poor Benjamin seemed as distraught as Lydie.

At last, at nearly mid-night, it was time to push and Eliza and I knelt on the bed and held up her shoulders, and though she screamed start to finish, in only a few minutes Mrs Vye was holding up a little girl. Ironic, you might say, but the baby never cried at all and just looked around in a surprised way.

Every mother is filled with joy when first she holds her little one, but Lydie's ecstasy knew no bounds.

"Oh I have a baby, a beautiful baby," she said over and over again, completely entranced. Mrs Vye came to take her saying, "lets clean her and dress her ready to meet Papa."

"No, no, Mrs Vye, I cannot let her go, I shall dress her myself if you please."

"Well, it is not usual Mistress," she replied doubt-fully. Never the less, she cleaned the cord wound as the baby lay in Lydie's arms, and I fetched the little clothes, all laid out in readiness. Mrs Vye rolled tiny twists of linen and put them behind the baby's ears, in the armpits and in the creases of the thighs, which I had never seen done before, but seemed like a good idea. Together we dressed the little one in the exquisite layette, embroi-dered for Curzon babies of a previous generation, none of whom had lived long enough to wear the fine caps and gowns.

Eliza took away the various basins and buckets of bloodied rags and the afterbirth (which was always a treat for the dogs).

I tidied Lydie's hair for her, as her arms were full of the baby, and Benjamin was summoned.

Literally shaking, he rushed to the bedside, "my dearest, dearest Lydie, please forgive me, I never knew the pains would be so bad, how can you ever forgive me for causing you this," and he took her in his arms as if he would never let her go. He seemed not to notice the baby.

"What?" said Lydie blankly, "oh did I make a lot of noise?"

"Aye," said Jacob, who was standing in the doorway, out of politeness, "aye, we thought ten Christmas pigs was being slaughtered in here, didn't we Ben?" he joked.

"Did it hurt a very great deal my poor, poor dear?"

"Oh I can hardly remember now," she said vaguely, "I suppose it did, but then I'm always a terrible coward with pain. But look at our beautiful baby, Benjamin."

He looked down and smiled, "indeed she is beautiful... shall we call her Lydia, after her beautiful mother?"

"Good God no, Lydia's a horrible name, I would not inflict it on anyone, certainly not on our darling baby. What was your mother's name dearest?"

"Hepzibah."

Lydie frowned doubtfully; myself, I was amazed they had not discussed names before. My Jacob and I had always names planned, for boy or girl, months in advance of my confinements.

"Shall you hold her Benjamin?"

Here Benjamin was very hesitant, "Lydie every baby I have ever held has bawled its head off, you know that."

Of course, Benjamin had held many babies, to christen them in his work as a curate, before he inherited the farm.

"But she will not, for she will sense a father's discipline at once."

Tentatively, he cradled her in his arms and of course she made not a murmur. "She is so very beautiful," he said in that wonder, which is always felt at the first sight of a new-born.

I said, "what about Belle then? That would be after Lydie and also does it not mean beautiful in the French?"

They both turned to look at me in amazement as if I had just revealed all the secrets of the heavens.

"Oh yes Susannah, you always know exactly the right thing. What think you husband?"

"It is just the right name for her, thank you Susannah, thank you so much."

"Aye well that is a pretty name," said Mrs Vye, "A've never brought a Belle into this world afore."

As she was putting on her outer clothes, Lydie begged her forgiveness for screaming so much, but she only said, "nay Mistress if tha cannot cry out on t' childbed then when can tha?" With that she patted the baby's head and said jokingly, "see you in a year's time, for a little lad next time, eh?"

"Pray God," replied Lydie most seriously.

Benjamin, still shaken, looked from one to another in a kind of mild horror.

* * * *

A couple of days later, I was sitting with Lydie, I had brought Penelope with me knowing she would need feeding soon. We were chatting quietly, when we heard a loud voice from down below and someone coming noisily up the stairs. I had no idea who it could be, but Lydie smiled broadly at once, "why it is my brother come to see us."

And at that very moment, Louis Franklin burst into the room. He had grown a tall lad, over six foot I'd say and already a little heavy. Though he was not so handsome, with his pale eyes and mousy hair, there was something very likeable about his boisterous ways and easy manner.

"Where is she then, me new niece?" He strode to the bedside and at once picked her up letting her head flop back.

"Oh Louis, do be careful, she cannot support her little head yet," said Lydie crossly.

He rearranged the baby awkwardly in his arms, (though she seemed to mind not at all).

"By God Sis, she's a beauty and no mistake, how come such a lubbock as you's had such a beautiful little treasure?"

But Lydie only laughed. Belle was swathed in a shawl so next he said, "has she got arms and legs, unwrap her and let me see."

"Of course she has arms and legs, she's a baby."

Lydie took her and opened the shawl. Now he knelt down by the bed and made soft blowing noises on the tiny hands and feet. "How did her little nails know to grow exactly the right length?"

"Why, that is God's own miracle Louis," I said.

He looked up, seeming to notice me for the first time. He walked around the bed and took Penelope's fat little hand in his fingers, "And who is this sweet young lady?"

"This is Penelope…"

On hearing the name his face contorted for a moment, "well if she's as lovely as her namesake and as pretty as her mama when she grows, won't she be something to see?" He kissed her hand as if she had been a fine lady.

I knew that Louis had loved his cousin Penelope in a romantic way and was still cut by her death, not two years since.

Lydie lifted her baby to her breast and I started to feed my Penelope, keeping my spare hand to cover myself, for you never quite knew where Louis was looking. But he was diverted now, when the door creaked open and my little Jack toddled in. Seeing a stranger he hesitated.

"So who is this fine boy, can it be baby Jack, grown to such a big lad?"

Jack nodded shyly. I was impressed that Louis remembered his name for he had not seen him since the wedding, last year.

"Tell me Sir," he went on, "do you ride a horse yet?"

Jack shook his head sadly.

Laughing, I said, "Jack is not yet two."

"Never too soon to learn Jack, if you'll come to me I'll show you how I first learnt to ride; my sister Lydie here taught me when I was much your age."

"Did I?" she said puzzled.

"Indeed you did Sis. Shall you come to me Sir and I'll show it to you."

He held out his hand to Jack and lifted him gently on to his knee, to sit astride, "ready now Jack? The lady goes a nim, nim, nim, the gentleman goes a trot, trot, trot and the farmer goes.... a gallopy, gallopy gallop," and like every baby before him Jack shouted with laughter and cried, "again, again."

"That's right, indeed we did do that," smiled Lydie.

After a few repeats, Louis turned Jack to him and spoke seriously, "now young Jack, I've only one piece of advice for you, never fight with your sister there," he indicated her with his thumb, "because girls always win. I know because I used to fight with my sister and she always used to win. We chaps fight by rules but the girls don't, so they can beat us every time."

Jack stared at him mesmerised and Lydie laughed, embarrassed, and said, "it is true we used to fight all the time as children, though I've no idea why, have you?"

"Not a bloody clue, Sis."

I was amazed, for I had had a quiet, orderly childhood and would no more have thought of fighting with my brother than walking to the moon.

Then Benjamin walked in, "how good to see you Louis, I thought I heard your voice."

"And you Bro, and you."

"Shall you come down and take a drink."

"Mmm, only if this fine lad will come too?" Jack nodded enthusiastically. "So let us leave the ladies to their milking parlour."

And he lifted Jack onto his shoulders; ducking under the ancient door, he missed the top of Jack's head by only a hair's breadth.

"Fancy your Louis being so good with little ones," I laughed.

"Well, although there was only we two, remember we had eight cousins living next door, all younger than us."

All I could hear now were gales of baby laughter as Louis was obviously doing a funny walk down the stairs.

A couple of hours later, Louis came back to bid us farewell, "Sis, I won't see you for a bit," he spoke quietly and sheepishly, without his usual bravado, "for I'm off to be a soldier and I'll be away a good while."

Lydie looked shocked, "what's our mama said?"

He snorted, "not told her yet, I'll tell her at the last minute when it's too late to change things. She'll bloody explode, I do know that, for she's wanting me to study to be a lawyer."

"And that's not for you?"

"No way, I'm wanting a bit of adventure."

"Take care Louis, please take care."

He laughed and said, "you know me Sis, luck of the devil."

With that he was gone and Lydie had to bite her lip hard, for a minute or two.

Then she said, "he saved my life when I was a little girl, you know."

I already knew this story, for Mary had told me of it, late one night in the Walker's kitchen, but I let her tell it anyway.

"I must have been about nine, I think, well me and Louis climbed out of his small bedroom window, that faced the roof ridges, where there was a narrow lead gulley between the two roofs. It was slippy with moss, but we were so excited with the thrill of it, we did not notice and both of us climbed up the tiles to the ridge and we could see for miles and miles. Then of course, I lost my footing and fell down the space at the end, and had Louis not caught hold of my skirts, I would have fallen, maybe thirty feet or more into the yard below. Well, all my skirt ripped away from my bodice, but still he hung on to me for dear life, even though he was quite little still, and somehow I managed to get a footing and scramble back up. We were scared then, as you can imagine. Poor Mary had to spend the rest of the morning sewing my dress back together so as my mama wouldn't find out and beat us both. So, anyway Mary got my dress mended and Mama never found out. But of course with all the sewing, Mary hadn't got her own work done and my mama slapped her and called her an idle slattern, and poor Mary never said a word, nor gave us away. We felt bad about it, but Mary just kissed us both and said she was glad we were safe and that Louis was a plucky lad."

"There tha'rt Lydie, if he were that brave and strong when he were only a little lad, A'm thinking he'll mek t' finest soldier now."

She nodded thoughtfully.

CHAPTER 6

In which Lydia looks after her little sons.
1783.

When my Belle was only a year old, I gave birth to twin boys, who we named (somewhat unimaginatively) Benjamin and Robert. Of course by then I thought I knew all about babies. Belle was such a sweet, easy little girl, I loved to watch her grow and speak her first words and try to walk. Night feeds were naught but pleasure sitting in the soft moonlight rocking her; bathing a daily delight, playing with her in the warm water. And thus when my twins arrived I thought I knew everything, and babies were my true vocation. It started well enough, they were both a decent size for twins, though Robert was the smaller being the second born. I was quite entranced with them and my Benjamin so proud that now that he had twice as many sons as Jacob. Susannah helped me with special positions to feed both the babies together.

As the early weeks passed little Ben seemed to settle more, and Robert less. I longed and longed for sleep. Mother-in-law, suggested a wet nurse, but I so wanted to care for all my children myself and anyway my husband would not have heard of such a thing.

Eliza suggested a good spoonful of brandy but Dr Buchan's trusty book "Domestic Medicine", which my husband read and followed as avidly as his bible, strictly forbade any spirits for infants, not even a swallow of wine. I also agreed with the instructions in the book, for although the good doctor was highly critical of most parents, he seemed to have such a sympathy and understanding for little ones. I thought he must be a very kindly, clever man indeed.

And so I struggled on rocking, wrapping warmly and singing softly to a roaring baby Robert, while his brother slept quietly at our side. One night we went to bed in good time, for my Benjamin had to rise early to go to Pickering the next day on business; Robert cried and cried, and my husband put his pillows over his head for a while then leapt out of bed and said, "I can stand this no longer," and went to sleep in another room.

Now, I was as unhappy as my poor baby, tears rolled down my cheeks and I felt a hopeless useless mother. At dawn I fed them both again and little Ben quickly snuggled back to sleep. When Eliza came to bring me hot water and tea and help me dress, Robert was still wailing pitifully.

"Dear me, Mistress, what a carry on, is he ailing?" she touched his forehead, "nay, there's no fever there. Let's hope he dun't work his self into fits or owt like that."

The thought of that horrified me and I bathed his dear little face in cool water just in case.

As soon as I was dressed, I carried him down to the kitchen, desperate for another cup of tea, even though it was still early. Jacob was standing there eating a large piece of toast folded over some bacon.

"Bloody Hell Lydia, he's got a pair of lungs on him."

"Jacob, he's been crying all night, I don't know what to do to quiet him."

"Tha wants ter swaddle him Mistress, A've told thee afore, t' old ways is best," said Tab helpfully.

But Dr Buchan's book advised strongly against swaddling of any kind, besides Benjamin and I had already decided we didn't want our babies tied up and helpless.

"Perhaps a tiny spoon of brandy, just this once?" tried Eliza.

Jacob laughed and said, "By he's a naughty little lad, eh?"

He stuffed the last of the toast in his mouth, "give him here, A've got a bit of a way with 'em."

With that he laid Robert face down across the palm of his hand, his little arms and legs dangled helplessly but at least he was quiet now. He put his other hand across the baby's back and swung him up to shoulder height and down to his knees in great sweeping movements, several times, then he turned him onto his back in the crook of his arm, whereupon Robert sighed and closed his eyes in sleep.

"There tha goes Lydia, it always does t' trick does that."

"A've niver seen t' like," said Tab.

"Eh, it's a miracle ter see it," said Eliza appreciatively.

"Thank you, Jacob," I said sighing with fatigue and relief.

"A got that worked out when our Jack were little and wouldn't sleep."

"I cannot imagine dear little Jack ever crying for more than a minute."

"Bloody Hell," snorted Jacob, "our Jack could give it right enough when he were tiny." He looked at me very directly and said, "always remember Lydia, A can turn me hand ter anything, tha's only ter ask."

"I'm so grateful, thank you... that's how I got my name you know Jacob."

"How's tha mean?"

"Well I don't remember my papa at all, but apparently I made so much noise as a baby, that he called me the 'bell' and the name just stuck. And when I was little and learned to write my own name, my Aunt Sophia suggested I put an 'e' on the end to make it sound nicer."

Jacob laughed and laughed, "well A niver, A've niver heard that afore. So tha's no need ter worry about this noisy lad then, for look how well tha's turned out, eh?"

I looked at my dear little boy, "thank you so much."

"Don't be thanking me, for A'm going to ask thee ter do summat for me in return."

"Of course Jacob, what?"

"Give this naughty lad and his brother ter Mary for t' morning, and put tha riding things on and A'll saddle up thy poor horse that's been ignored for weeks. Tha can tek her out for a good ride and then go up to ours, A know Susannah'd be more than glad ter see thee. Then t' two of yer can both tek a cup of tea and talk about whatever yo women talk about."

"Oh I couldn't, what if the babies needed feeding?"

"Then Mary could mek them a cup of pap, that A do know."

I hesitated.

"It'd do tha good Mistress, get some roses in thy cheeks. Tha's been cooped up too much recent like," said Tab touching my arm.

Suddenly Jacob looked down at my skirts, "is tha all reet ter be riding now, is tha… well now?"

"Oh, yes, yes I'm fine."

Indeed, it was the most pleasant thought to me, to be riding my Star again. For though I'd been out to see her almost every day, I'd not ridden for more than two months and I longed for that freedom and thrill.

"Yes, I will," I said with determination, "thank you Jacob."

"Good lass," he laughed, giving back my baby.

I took him gingerly in my arms, dreading him waking again.

Ten minutes later, I was dressed in my navy blue riding habit and running through the kitchen and out into the yard. My darling, darling Star was skittish and prancing, with excitement and having been unexercised for so long. I hugged her tossing head and could have wept with the joy of it. Jacob had to hold her bridle with his full weight to keep her still enough for me to mount. As I gathered the reins, he let her go and we were off on a heavenly moorland canter, quickly turning into a full gallop. Happiness washed over me, the heavy, steady thudding of her hooves against the hard, autumn ground, the sweet smell of my beautiful horse, I could have ridden away for ever. But I knew I must not over tax her as she had not been out for a long while, so I eventually turned towards Hill Cottage.

Susannah came out and watered and baited her for me.

"So how are things Lydie," she asked as we went into the cottage, arm in arm.

"Absolutely fine now," and I explained about how Jacob had helped me with little Robert and what a marvellous ride I'd had.

"Our Jack were like that in t' early weeks and Jacob were half dead wi' work, for if tha remembers then, t' old master were not up ter much and poor Robert had given up entirely, so Jacob were doing t' work of three. He'd come in on a night exhausted and our Jack were carrying on, so he fathomed out that swinging thing, and it always worked like a dream." She laughed, "but one things for sure, for good or bad, bairns stop crying in t' end for they grow out of it, then they start talking and they're asking questions all t' time. Does tha know our Jack must ask a question every minute of t' day. Of course his father thinks he's t' cleverest bairn in t' world. A've not t' heart ter tell him they all ask questions all t' time when they're three!"

Susannah had the neatest and cleanest cottage imaginable, scrubbed or polished to the highest degree. Everything always in its place; their few books on a little shelf, sewing things in a basket, pot plants growing neatly on the window ledges, pots and pans tidied away, Penelope's little sleepy blanket folded on a chair and always the huge old bible, open at the ready, on the gate-leg table. The children too, were just as clean and orderly at all times, playing quietly with a pile of home-made bricks on this occasion.

"Susannah, you have such sweet children," I said lifting Penelope onto my knee, I think I felt naked at that time without a babe in my arms.

"Where is Belle," asked Jack seriously.

"At the farm Sweetheart with Mary and the babies."

"Why?"

"I'm not sure Jack, shall I bring her with me next time I come?"

"Want to play with Belle," said Penelope.

"Why is thy dress blue?" asked Jack touching my skirt.

"I am fond of blue, Jack."

"Why?"

"Stop asking questions our Jack and let thy Aunt get her tea."

Susannah had out her dainty little tea bowls, and in truth I could have drunk a gallon, so I asked if I might have a cup of water as well.

"Of course, A'm not thinking, with tha nursing t' two of them. Jack can tha fetch a cup of water and carry it very carefully. See if tha can do that grown up job well."

And my water was brought to me without a single slop.

Always there were fresh baked cakes; today it was my favourites: - Fat Rascals, still warm and buttered. The children loved them for they all had a little face on them made with almonds and cherries.

"Look Pennikins, this one looks like you, it's got dimples in its cheeks."

She stared at it most studiously, touching it with her finger tip, and then agreed it did. I took my fill of tea and cake; the little parlour was very warm, and I hardly knew how it happened but I drifted into much needed sleep.

I awoke with a jerk to find Penelope had covered my lap with her sleepy blanket.

"Oh, how long have I been asleep?"

"Not too long, tha looked like tha needed it Lydie."

Susannah was sewing now. Jack was sitting to the table trying his hardest to copy letters with a stub of pencil and Penelope was nursing a rather ugly wooden doll.

And thus I departed this scene of loving harmony, with the warmest of hugs and kisses. (Also, resolving to try to find a really pretty doll for Penelope's next birthday).

Of course the minute I arrived home, I ran straight up to the nursery, where, thank God, another peaceful scene was awaiting me.

"They've not stirred once Mistress, and Miss Belle has been playing quiet as a mouse so as not to disturb them," said our ever trusty Mary.

And by the time my dearest husband returned we had retained that calm: our little boys were smiling for the first time and Belle was clumsily cuddling them, much to their delight.

"Forgive me dearest wife, for leaving you so this morning."

"I think you've been talking to Jacob, have you not?"

"In truth, he has remonstrated with me, and I intend to mend my ways and show myself the supportive husband and devoted father."

"My dear," I said jokingly, "even Dr Buchan would be proud of you." For the dear doctor recommended an active role for all fathers, in his most enlightening book.

"I'm just not very good with babies as you know, and Jacob quite puts me in the shade with that one."

"Not so, speak to one of your sons."

I had to smile inside myself then, for instead of speaking in a baby talk, he politely said, "my dear son Robert, how are you now?"

But it was of no consequence for Robert rewarded him with a huge, gurgling smile, as did little Ben when asked the same question.

So a bad night ended in a happy day for all of us. Of course I did so love being a mother, which was as well, for Benjamin and I had another five children after these three. I should like to say that Susannah and I had many healthy children and lived happily ever after with our devoted husbands, but this was real life and not a fairy story.

CHAPTER 7

In which Susannah's life is not what she thought.
1789.

After our Penelope was born, I had three miscarriages, all in the early months, but this year, I was with child again, and at last all seemed well. The child moved strongly, Jacob and I were most hopeful, until one evening when my pains began in earnest.

I managed to get my children to bed on the promise they could read for a while in the summer light. They had a little shelf of chap books given them by Benjamin and Lydie on birthdays and as their twelfth night gifts each year.

At last, I could lie on my bed and give myself over to the spasms. My Jacob showed me such kindness, touching me in his special way so I felt little pain and my dog lay quietly at my side throughout. We both counted the months two or three times but no matter how we counted, it still was far too soon.

Neither of us suggested fetching the midwife, we feared the worst, for I had felt no movement since morning.

He cared for me most tenderly, cleaning me and soothing my anxiety, sucking his lip to hide his own. As darkness started to fall, I silently gave birth to a tiny, perfect girl, who never drew a breath. Jacob pinched the top of his nose and laid her beside me.

"What a beauty she is…" his voice trailed away as he held me close.

"She would have been our little Rebecca," I said tearfully, for that was the name we had chosen for a girl. I looked at him desperately, "she cannot rest with God, she never drew a breath nor was baptized…"

"Nay Susannah, as soon as God sees her dear little face and hands, why He'll want ter tek her straight off, A know He will."

I so much wanted to believe this.

"Dress her in summat nice and A'll mek her a little grave in t' garden, then she'll always be near us."

I nodded, too sad to speak. He passed me some baby clothes out of the chest at the foot of our bed, (I was surprised he knew where I kept them).

And while he dug the grave, I dressed the mite, rolling back the sleeves to show her little hands with no nails yet and wrapped her in a shawl for she felt cold already.

"A've set out a chair for thee," said Jacob coming back in, "and those two are well fast asleep."

Weakly, I got out of bed and he carried us both down the stairs in his strong arms, out of the cottage and into the balmy, moon-lit night. He sat me in the chair and took our little Rebecca and laid her in the cold ground, pulling the shawl across her face so the soil would not fall directly on her and covered her with dark earth.

"Say some Godly words, for tha knows A know none."

He stood by the grave, his hands clasped, as I murmured a prayer or two and begged God to take her soul.

Then, he carried me back to bed, burnt the soiled rags in the little bedroom fireplace and lay beside me, holding me close that long night. For all the horror of it, Jacob had cared for me so lovingly and kindly that it never occurred to me once that he did not love me true.

And what happened two weeks later came all the more of a shock to me, believing myself a much loved wife.

So by then, I was feeling much more myself. It was a bright morning, the children were out gathering some kindling sticks and I had just filled a big bowl with warm water to rinse out some bits of washing, when the dog growled and there was a sharp knock at the door. I wiped my hands on my apron, greatly surprised for we never had visitors at the cottage other than Lydie and her children who just walked straight in without knocking.

Cautiously, I opened the door and there stood a low, shabby looking young woman carrying a baby.

She looked past me, "Jacob in?"

"No he's...."

"Yo his wife like?"

I nodded, I suddenly felt afraid. She looked me up and down and said, "don't want ter shock yer, but this is Jacob's bairn, A can't keep him no more. Me husband's back from sea, he's been away for more than a year, for t' whaler was stuck in t' ice ovver t' winter and he's come home looking near dead, three fingers froze off and thin as a stick, but knowing this one weren't his straight off. Sez he'll keep me on but A've ter get rid of t' bairn."

I clutched the side of the door to steady myself, my stomach lurched in my fear.

"So Jacob'll have ter tek him now."

In shock I could not reply.

"So shall yer tek him or shall A lay him on t' step."

Hardly knowing what I did, I reached out for the baby and she said with only the faintest flicker, "he's called Hugo, A've called him Hugo."

She pulled her cheap shawl about her and as she turned to go she said, "tell Jacob it's Sally, he'll want ter know which one of us has fell," and she walked away without a backward glance.

I had to put the baby down suddenly and ran out the back of the house to vomit on the ground. When I came back in, I had to compose myself quickly for my children were coming through the door with a basket of sticks and I had to pick up the baby.

"It's a bairn," said Penelope in her simple direct way.

I avoided Jack's very direct gaze and said, not too shakily, I hope, "yes it's a bairn, shall we wash him and mek him clean and comfortable?"

"Oh Mother, can we bath him," she cried in delight.

By chance the clean water in my washing bowl was still warm.

"Our Jack, will tha put that bowl on t' floor for me, careful as tha can, for it's quite full. Penelope run upstairs and fetch me some of t' good soap from my drawer."

I reached up to the drying rack and took down a towel and together the three of us crouched on the floor around the bowl and I undressed the poor baby from his stinking damp clothes.

"Ugh Mother, he smells horrible," said Jack wrinkling up his nose.

"Nay Jack, we'll soon have him fresh and cleaned, just tha wait and see."

There was not a rag on his body worth keeping and I threw them all on the fire. His little body was caked with dirt and was quite sore. I wondered if he'd ever been washed in his whole short life, though he'd obviously been fed, for he was a sturdy little boy. I lowered him into the water and showed Penelope how to wash his face in plain water and then how to soap her hands and wash the rest of him. Jack trickled water gently over him to make him smile. If my children had had all the toys from the finest of shops, they could not have been more amused than they were bathing this baby. I wrapped him tight in the towel and told Penelope to sit very still and hold him while I fetched some clean baby clothes.

Together we dressed him and I heated some milk to make a pap, I put a few drops of brandy in, to warm him and brace him. He drank it down hungrily. I was aware of time getting on and Jacob would be back for his dinner soon.

"Now children, A want yer ter listen carefully, A want yer ter run down to t' farm and ask your Aunt Lydie if yer might have yer dinners there today. And A want yer ter ask if A might borrow some sugar from her."

"But Mother there is plenty of sugar in the sugar box," said Penelope helpfully.

For the first time I snapped, "Penelope will tha do as tha's told for once."

"Yes Mother," she said meekly, "may A kiss t' bairn afore we go?"

"Of course my Lambkin," and I felt ashamed of myself for snapping. "Now hurry along and don't forget ter ask thy Aunt Lydie them two things."

"No Mother."

Jack stared at me, I knew he knew more than he was letting on, but he said nothing as he took his sister's hand to walk down the hill.

I sighed with relief, for it would not be long before Jacob would walk through the door, I had little time to plan my strategy. I rocked the baby a bit more and, thank God, he quickly fell asleep. I wrapped him up and laid him in the wide wash basket, where my own children had lain as babies and I could hear Jacob's horse coming up the hill. I felt sick with fear as he opened the door and held out his arms, as he always did and said, "darling wife."

I backed away from him, my throat was too choked to speak.

"What is it Darling?"

Still I could not get out any words, so I pointed to the sleeping baby.

"What...?"

"That...that," I swallowed hard, "that is thy son Jacob."

The darkest flush spread across his face, "what's tha mean 'my son'?"

"Some woman, called Sally brought him over, her husband'll not keep him, so she's brought him here..."

He gasped and turned away from me, shamefaced and I knew it to be true, for up till then, a corner of my heart had hoped that it was all a terrible mistake. But clear as day, Jacob could not deny it.

"How could tha Jacob, how could tha do this ter me?" I was finding my voice now and shouting.

"A didn't know she knew where A lived," he said brokenly.

"Well, that weren't hard were it? Is tha t' Curzon that lives like a lord with his fine wife in that great farmhouse? Or is tha t' bastard son as has next ter nothing and no money, and lives with the stupid little nursemaid, who spends all day baking and trying ter mek a nice home for him? Bloody fool that A am. No Jacob that weren't hard."

I knew I had hurt him deeply with these words, but I could not stop myself now.

"Susannah…"

"No Jacob, tha's broken my heart, A cannot forgive thee ever, how could tha do this? A'm humiliated beyond all…"

With this I raised my hand, and though I had never hit anyone before, I slapped him as hard as I could across his face. Clearly it was hard enough for he put his hand to his cheek and gasping, he staggered back against the wall.

And at that very moment Lydie walked in.

"Oh," she said, stopped in her tracks, but as always, she quickly righted herself. "Do excuse me, I only came to ask if the children might stay overnight with us, for we're planning a bit of a treat for them all… They won't need anything; I've only come for that blanket thing that Pennikins must have to sleep with." Neither of us said anything. "Ah, I see it there."

And she strode across the room to where Penelope's sleepy blanket lay upon the chair. Her eyes fell upon the baby and she started as if she had been slapped herself, but said nothing and picked up the blanket.

"Thank you Lydie," I said weakly.

She nodded, said she had to go and then I heard her horse trotting away.

"Susannah don't leave me, A'll do anything ter right this, but don't leave me."

"How can A leave thee Jacob? Ave nowhere ter go, A've no family ter tek me in and A'm too ashamed ter go ter Ben and Lydie's. For shame it is, me being here and knowing nowt of what tha's up ter, scattering thy bastards half across the county no doubt."

I wrenched my betrothal ring from the thin chain around my neck and threw it through the open door and onto the ground outside.

"Susannah..."

"Tha'll have ter get rid of him Jacob, A cannot bear t' shame of it."

"A will Susannah, there's a woman on Church Street as teks bairns in that's got no mothers, when t' fathers have gone ter sea and that. Teks them in for money. A'll tek him there right now and tha'll never have ter look at him again."

"A'll mek him ready then," I said more quietly. I went into the scullery and fetched a deep soft basket which could be fastened to the saddle and lined it with a large piece of flannel. I tore off a strip of the flannel and wrapped it around his sleeping head under his cap for warmth. I lifted him into the basket as carefully as I could, so as not to wake him. Jacob was already on his horse when I went out to fasten the basket onto the saddle with the pannier hooks. As I moved away, he reached out and touched my hand.

"Do not touch me, now or ever."

With that he rode off, slowly down the hill.

Shaking, I sat on the doorstep trying to calm myself, but I could not for a thousand thoughts were buzzing through my throbbing head. I thought of his tenderness when we had buried our own stillborn baby and how he had pushed a scrap of paper into her tiny clenched hand, on it he had pencilled 'Rebecca Curzon'. I thought of the happiness of my children when they had bathed the baby that morning accepting him without any suspicion or question. I imagined if things had been other with my first husband, twelve years ago, suppose he and our baby had lived and I had died. He would have had no-one to care for our little son and would have to have left him with the gin soaked hag in the town for Lord knows what. I remembered the fine lady who helped me that same terrible day twelve years since, when I thanked her, she had said, the best thanks I could give was to pass on kindness to another. I repeated those words out loud and my conscience before God spoke to me, for little Hugo was alone and friendless in this world, and in need of my kindness, for he clearly had no other to give him such. An indifferent mother and a father who could not even look at him.

I jumped up and shouted to Jacob's distant figure, but he was too far away to hear. I took the deepest breath I could and shouted again, "JA-COB".

This time he turned his head and saw me, I beckoned him, with my arm to come back. He was too distant for me to see the expression on his face, but as he turned the horse, his hand dropped protectively over the basket and my broken heart stirred just a little, to see his tenderness.

He rode slowly up the hill to me and before he could speak, I said, "Jacob, A will look after thy bairn as best A can, for he is brother to our own children, but A do ask that tha niver speaks ter me nor touches me again, for my heart is broken and A believe can never mend."

"Thank you Susannah," he said, and after that remained true to my request, neither speaking to me nor touching me.

"Tha'd best get thy dinner, though A expect it's burnt to cinder by now." I said unhooking the baby basket and carrying it inside.

Jacob hardly touched his dinner and soon returned to work.

Next, I could have timed things to the minute, how long it would take Jacob to get back to the farmyard, how long it would take Lydie to see him and saddle up. And to the minute, I heard the sound of her horse. Now everything released inside me and as she came through the door, I sobbed in her outstretched arms, so glad of any comfort for my lonely, lonely heart.

"Cry all you want Susannah dear, then you must tell me what terrible thing has happened."

"I am so ashamed Lydie," I wept.

"Nonsense Susannah, there can be no shame nor secrets between us, for I consider you my dearest friend, besides we are cousins by marriage. I knew there was something amiss when Pennikins asked for sugar, for you are such an efficient housewife, I could not imagine you running out of anything ever."

"A'm ashamed of myself, for A hit Jacob so hard, he fell against the wall."

"Well if you did," she said with her customary loyalty, "I don't doubt that he thoroughly deserved it. But tell me, do I really see a baby there? Can it be?"

"Oh Lydie, the humiliation of it, it is Jacob's bastard son... he's called Hugo. A never thought he would do such a thing, A thought we were so happy as husband and wife." I looked at her for reassurance.

"I too, Susannah, I too." She stared at the baby who was beginning to stir. "Bloody Hell, I don't know what to say, what is going to happen?"

"A've decided ter look after him as best A can, for he's brother ter my own bairns."

"I don't know Susannah, you're a wonder on this earth, that is the truth, there's not many would do that willingly."

I lifted the baby and we both sat down in the elbow chairs by the fire.

"Shall tha tek him Lydie?"

"Good God no," she leaned back in her chair and folded her arms firmly across her chest, "but hold him up so I can see if he really is a Curzon."

I turned him around to face her, and though he had his back to me, I could tell by his movements, he was smiling at her and I knew Lydie never could resist a baby.

"Why, just look at him," she laughed, holding out her arms for him, "just for a minute then." She cradled him as if he were her own and shook her head, "I don't know, as they say, 'he's more like Jacob than he is himself'."

We drank plenty of tea and I buttered some slices of ginger cake. Lydie kept dropping tiny crumbs of cake on his little tongue, as he lay in her arms and we were much amused to see him licking his lips in such delight.

"Now you're not to worry one bit about Jack and Pennikins, for they're having the greatest fun. Mary's going to make fudge and peppermints with them, she's got seven of them around the kitchen table already, even little George, and the whole place is aboil with sugar stickiness and God knows what," she laughed, "And Tab and Eliza are having twenty fits about the mess to be cleared up. So we'll give them their lessons tomorrow: Benjamin's starting Latin with them, God help him, then I'll bring them back here for dinner time."

"That's so kind of thee Lydie, A do thank thee."

"Tis the very least I can do. And if the worst happens… know that you'd always be welcome at the farm. I do know that Benjamin would say the exact same."

Here she kissed the back of Hugo's neck and departed.

Now I had a few hours to finish my washing, sort out some baby clothes and do a bit of baking for the tea. The baby, or Hugo as I had to get used to calling him, was as good as gold, whenever he cried, I made him some warm pap, but my breasts ached and ached, for it was such a short time since we had lost little Rebecca.

Jacob and I did not speak as we ate our tea and when bedtime came, he looked at me but I turned away, picked up the baby and went upstairs, closing the door firmly behind me. I know not where Jacob slept that night or for many more nights, I imagined he slept in his chair or took some of the horse blankets and laid on the floor, I cared not.

I fell asleep, more quickly than you might think, that first night and I was heavily asleep when Hugo awoke crying, hardly thinking, I took him to my breast. After that he slept, soundly, for a long time, but I lay awake, wondering what God's plan for me was. Why did it fall to me to feed the wrong babies? Years ago, my own baby with my first husband had died and poverty forced me to leave my home and wet-nurse the Walker twins, now I had lost my little girl, who was so much wanted, and here I was suckling my husband's bastard. Plenty of tears rolled down my cheeks that night.

Lydie brought back my children the next day, as promised. She was well out of breath after walking up the hill, for she was with child again, and she sat down by the fire to catch her breath.

Jacob arrived a moment later, "Lydia," he nodded.

"Jacob," she replied icily, but did not look at him. I put the dinner on the table for the three of them, but first the children ran to look at the baby.

"He's still here," cried Penelope in delight.

"Is he our brother?" asked Jack directly.

A stony silence fell upon us all, for none could reply until Penelope said, "Yes he is," and planted a large kiss on his sleeping forehead.

"Sit ter yer dinners both of yer," I said, and they joined Jacob at the table. The three of them sat very close.

"Father, A've started ter learn me Latin today, and A'm enjoying it so much. Dominus, domine, dominum, domini, domino…" said Jack.

"But tha's a clever lad our Jack, A niver thought in me whole life that a son of mine'd be learning his Latin. Well done lad." He ruffled Jack's red gold curls and Jack flushed with pride.

"Father, look A've made some peppermints and some fudge, all myself." And Penelope pushed a twist of paper towards him. Jacob tried one of the sweets at once, even though he was still eating his meat.

"Bye tha's a clever lass, our Penelope, A've niver tasted such good sweets, there'll be nowt as good as these in all t' fine shops in York," he squeezed her hand.

Here she was overcome and jumped up and put her arms around his neck. "Father A missed thee so much last night, even though we had the lovliest time and played with Belle's best dolls and made sweets with Mary."

Clearly moved, Jacob said, "get thy dinner now, while it's hot."

Jacob truly believed his children to be the cleverest, most beautiful children in the world and always spoke to them like this. In happier times I would often say that they only had to blink their eyes or draw a breath for him to think them the most wondrous of all children.

In spite of herself Lydie had to smile and catch my eye at this little scene. She refused a cup of tea and was soon on her way.

* * * *

And so we carried on for several months like this, Jacob and I never speaking or looking at one another, nor did he ever look at or touch little Hugo. And the mite would look so longingly at him, especially when Jacob was playing with Penelope and Jack, but he was never rewarded with even a glance.

As for me? Well, fool that I was, my heart began to soften. Sometimes when I was alone I used to rehearse a little speech until it sounded just right.

One evening as dusk was falling, it seemed to be the right time. Jack and Penelope were to bed early, for they were tired having been out riding all afternoon with their Aunt. Hugo was fractious with his teeth, Jacob sat staring into the fire, so I walked over to the wash basket and picked up the fussing baby and put him in Jacob's arms, giving him no time to protest, as he had never held his son before.

"I cannot do everything Jacob," I said and carried on clearing away the tea things.

Then I sat opposite them. He was rocking the baby who was drifting into sleep, I reached out to take him and Jacob shook his head, "a minute more, he's not off yet."

It was the first time he had spoken to me in six months, and a few minutes later, he laid his sleeping son back in his basket, covering him warmly, for the nights were turning chill now.

"Jacob A would like ter speak with thee and A would ask that tha listen ter me till A've finished?"

He sat opposite me and nodded.

"Jacob, tha dug a deep and horrible hole for me, which A could not see and one day tha pushed me into it and A fell so hard, A hurt myself badly."

Here he put his head into his hands.

"But Jacob A'm feeling different now, my brother and my first husband lie at the bottom of t' sea, A've buried two bairns and lost three more that never even grew into life. Our cousins Penelope and Robert barely got t' chance of a life together. So now A'm thinking, life's too short for bitterness between us."

He looked up at me. And I went on.

"A'm thinking if tha would give me thy hand, tha could pull me out of that deep hole now…"

Before I could say more, he grasped both my hands and his warmth shot up my arms. He pulled me onto his knee and held me close for a long time. Neither of us spoke until at last I said the boldest words I have ever spoken, "Husband, will tha come ter bed with me?"

We stood up and he turned away from me, walking towards the front door, where his heavy coat hung. He delved into the inner pocket and took out a small box, handing it to me, he said, "Susannah will tha tek my ring again?"

Astonished, I opened the box and saw my betrothal ring, which I had flung out of the door six months since. But now the ring had been made bigger and the coloured stones were cleaned to a bright sparkle. As I turned it in my hand I saw that inside he had had the words, 'beloved wife,' engraved in tiny letters.

"A've had it made bigger so as tha can wear it on thy finger, proper now."

I slipped it onto my finger above my wedding band, where it sat perfectly.

"Jacob A thought it were lost forever," and I put my arms around him.

"Nay, Darling, A thought A were t' one as were lost forever."

CHAPTER 8

In which old Mistress Curzon has two young visitors.
Next day.

We had hardly got breakfast finished, and my husband had only been out in the yard at his work a few minutes when he rushed back into the summer parlour where I was sitting with my mother-in-law.

"You'll never guess what, they have settled their difficult matter between them. It seems Susannah's forgiven Jacob and he's as happy as can be, joking and laughing like his old self."

"Why how glad I am to hear it," I smiled, pleased for I knew now, that for all his faults, Jacob loved Susannah deeply, though I had found this so hard to understand at first. Months since my husband had remonstrated with me very sharply when I had spoken out against Jacob. He had gone on to say that he and Jacob were as brothers and we must do our best to help him in his trouble and leave judgements to God. I had felt quite ashamed of myself, for my husband rarely spoke angrily to me or corrected me.

"Aye, 'tis best not to bear a grudge, though 'tis not always easy," said my mother-in-law.

My husband kissed me on the cheek and went back to his work, and so we two were able to discuss it a bit more.

"A hard thing to forgive, I am not sure I could forgive my Benjamin for such a transgression."

"Nor I, A don't know if tha already knows this, but my husband kept a mistress and three bastards, over at Ruswarp. And A tell thee A niver could forgive him, not that it meks no difference; in this world a man does as he pleases and a woman has ter put up with it whether she minds or no."

"I am so sorry mother-in-law; I never knew of it." I was quite shocked, to be honest.

She shrugged and picked up her knitting. "A would not have known myself, but Tab told me, not from spite, but fearing I'd hear it from another. So A do admire Susannah, for Our Lord does require that we forgive."

"Susannah is God's own angel on this earth," I said with feeling.

We had not talked much more, when Eliza popped her head around the door, "Mistress," she said, addressing my mother-in-law, "our Jacob's two eldest are here asking ter see thee, shall A bring them in?"

"Why yes," she answered most surprised.

Next thing, Jack and Penelope were shown into the parlour.

Penelope began, with, "Mistress." She gave the deepest curtsey, and on nudging Jack, he shuffled his feet and gave a small bow. "Mistress," she went on, "A do beg thy pardon, for interrupting thy work but we have something of great importance to ask thee…"

"What is it dear, please ask."

"Mistress, we have no Grandmama, and we are come ter ask if tha would agree to be our Grandmama, knowing that it is much ter ask of thee. But it would mean a great deal to us."

Here she nudged Jack again, who repeated, this. Then they both stared at her anxiously.

"Why my dears, A should be most pleased ter tek yer both as my grandchildren and of course yer'll call me Grandmama as the others do. But yo two will have special responsibilities, as yo two will be my eldest grand-children, and as such would have ter watch out for t' younger ones."

"Oh yes Mistress, we would, we do thank thee most kindly... but there is one more thing that we must trouble thee with."

"Yes my dear?"

"Mistress, we have a new brother Hugo, who has no Grandmama either, and we would wish that tha would take him on too, as thy grandson."

"Well now, A don't know," she said this with mock doubt, "A have not met Hugo, what kind of a little boy is he?"

"Oh Mistress, he is the sweetest little boy, always laughing and making games with us." Here Jack smiled broadly at the thought of his little brother and Penelope went on, "and he only ever cries if things are really horrid for him."

"Well, in that case, A shall be happy ter have little Hugo as my grandson too, though A shall expect yer ter bring him down ter see me soon, that A might get ter know him."

"Oh Mistress we shall, we do thank thee with all our hearts." Here another curtsey was swept.

"Now, both of yer give me a kiss, then run along ter t' kitchen and tell Eliza yer ter get a bit of Moggy cake afore yer lessons start at ten o clock."

Penelope hugged her, in her effusive way and gave her the warmest kiss, Jack bowed low like a gentleman and brushed her hand with his lips.

As soon as they were out of earshot, we laughed and laughed at the droll little scene, all the more amusing because they had been so very serious and so very polite.

Later on, that same morning, the two of us went into the kitchen to check on the bottling jars, I had my new baby Frederick in my arms as well. Jacob saw us from the yard, and stepped into the kitchen, how well and like his old self he seemed, after his reconciliation with Susannah.

Grinning, he said, "well Mistress, tha's had a busy morning A'm hearing, getting three more grandchildren in one go, eh?"

"A'm pleased ter tek them Jacob, such goodly well-mannered children tha's got."

"A'm glad ter hear they remembered their manners." More hesitantly he added, "it's good of thee ter tek on our little Hugo as well."

"A shall look forward ter meeting him, A hear he's the very spit of thee Jacob."

"A don't know that that's much in his favour Mistress," he said, laughing again. "He's a bit troubled with his teeth at minute but A know that my Susannah'll be bringing him down soon, now that we've...er... made things up."

"A'm truly glad ter hear that, for tha's a good wife Jacob, remember that, especially when tha's in town on a market day." She wagged her finger at him.

"Aye, there's no man has a better wife than me, and A've learnt me lesson, fine well on that one." He glanced at me, "has that bairn doubled in size since last week?"

"I think he might have done." I spoke with pride, for I had born Benjamin a fourth strong healthy son, (as well as our two dear daughters).

We spent some time sorting out the bottling jars, checking for leaks and stacking them neatly in the pantry, all with baby Frederick tucked under my arm. That year we had done plums, gooseberries, pears, and peaches mixed with apricots; there were plenty to last over the winter, though we would not start eating them until the apples were done and there was a whole roomful of apples carefully laid in neat rows in one of the attics.

Then, we had reason to laugh some more, my mother-in-law and I. As we walked back through the Great Hall, quietly so as not to disturb the morning's Latin lesson, we espied a scene of such disparity; Jack was sitting up straight and alert listening to my Benjamin's every word as was Belle, meek beside him, little Ben was scratching his head and rubbing his eyes, his twin brother staring out of the window, Olivia, too young for Latin was studiously copying some letters with her tongue sticking right out.

"Bless them," silently mouthed mother-in-law.

Just then Penelope leapt up and stood before her uncle.

"Yes, Penelope dear, what is it?"

"Please dearest Uncle, though A thank thee most much for thy very great kindness in trying to teach me Latin, A believe it is not for me, and if thou will excuse me, when it is the Latin hour, A would prefer to sew in the parlour with my new Grandmama. A do thank you kindly dear Uncle."

Here she circled his neck, kissed him on the cheek and ran ahead of we two to hold the door open for us and followed us into the parlour. I think my husband was too stunned to speak, he certainly did not let any of the others escape lessons over the coming years, whatever their excuse.

So Penelope joined us in the parlour, and bold as ever she said, "now Aunt Lydie, A know tha does not like sewing, but myself, A'm already a neat stitcher, so if tha will say what needs ter be done, A shall gladly do it for thee."

Of course with six children, I always had plenty of sewing and mending to be done, more than enough to keep Pennikins very busy over the years!

CHAPTER 9

In which there is a surprise visitor at the farm.
1790.

In the Summer I visited my mama in Baxtergate. I did not visit as often as I should, for I always seemed to have a baby to feed or it was some vital time on the farm, like harvest or some horse was about to foal. Anyway, little Frederick was at long last weaned and I could leave him and George with the trusty Mary for the day.

In truth, we so rarely went out, it took me some time to find decent, clean clothes for the older children to wear to go into the town. Mostly, as my mama would have said, they lived and ran around like gypsies, in plain serviceable clothes, which suited our country life. When they were not having their lessons with myself or their father, they spent all day riding, helping with the animals, playing in the haylofts, running about the fields or climbing trees in the orchard. To be honest, I had no idea what they did most of the time as I was so busy myself, and if there was ever a quiet moment, I liked to shut myself in my bedroom with a book. Indeed, I had even come to look forward to my very regular confinements, as after the worst was over, I could spend a delicious two weeks in bed reading.

At last, we seemed to be ready and I had packed up a basket of butter and cheese that I had made as a gift for my mama. I felt drained before we had even started out, the twins squabbled and pushed all the time, often ending up fighting, Olivia was one of those very sensitive children, who get over excited and then start crying, as she had done twice already, that morning. Only Belle remained calm and neat at all times, thus being my mama's favourite grandchild.

"I'm sick of them all Jacob," I said crossly as I climbed onto the front seat of the cart to sit beside him.

"Nay Lydia, surely not."

"In truth I am, they fight and cry all the time."

"Are they not children?" He was laughing at me now.

"Well I do tell you this, if any one of them rolls out of the cart on the way, they are to be left at the side of the road and not picked up."

And we set off.

Straight away I felt bad for my harsh words, for when I looked around at them, they suddenly looked so very sweet. Robert was showing little Olivia a magic trick with his handkerchief and she was quite entranced; Belle was sitting with her arm through Ben's and they were talking quietly about some of the cows like true farmer's children.

My mama WAS pleased to see us, in her stiff, slightly disapproving way. When I told her I had made the butter and cheese myself, she merely said, "surely you have a dairy maid for such things?"

Jacob departed and said he would return from his deliveries in a couple of hours. I left the children with Mama and slipped next door to see my Aunt and Uncle, who were delighted to see me. They suddenly seemed old; my poor Aunt was quite an invalid now, after some kind of awful prolapse "down there" which kept getting a fester, (I resolved to look it up in Dr Buchan's medical book when we got back home). Despite all this, they insisted I bring my dear children round to see them, though I warned them of their boisterousness. Uncle kept saying what a grand girl I was and how grand my children were.

As I was going out, my cousin Chloe, now nineteen, ran up behind me, "please Lydie, will you take me back with you to stay for a visit, for I am so bored here, and me and Margaret are always arguing. I'll help with the little ones and do all your sewing, for I know you dislike it, please Lydie, please."

"Now there's an offer, for I've a pile of mending as high as your head. Of course you can come Cousin, no one will mind will they?"

"Oh no, I'll tell Mama and Papa at once and get my things ready. Thank you so much Lydie."

I thought what a very pretty girl she had become, yet disconcerting how like her poor dead sister Penelope she looked, with the same hazel eyes, long golden curls and dainty, curvy figure. I felt for her, remembering my own boredom at around her age, before I married. Quick as a flash, she had a little trunk packed, though it was a good while before we were all ready to depart for home. Robert persuaded Uncle to take him down to the harbour side to look at the ships and they were gone some time. Ben, rather nastily said, "I hope Robert sails away in one of them ships and dun't come back."

"Ben please say, 'those ships' and 'does not' instead of 'dun't'." I said firmly, with still the vain hope that my sons would grow up to be gentlemen.

"Yes, mama," he replied and promptly disappeared with my youngest cousin, Daniel to see some spaniel pups.

As to Belle, she went out with my twin cousins Christiana and Clementina to the sweet shop, on their own. I feared for my dear little Belle, for my cousins had turned into two quite naughty, bold girls and Belle was rather an innocent.

Thus, when Jacob returned to collect us, there was only Olivia left, (sitting on my mama's knee, weeping about something or other) and Cousin Chloe at the ready with her trunk.

"Bloody Hell tha's not sent them all off to t' orphanage?"

"No, but many's the time I've thought of it," I laughed.

My mama shuddered with disapproval, not at my thoughts of child abandonment, but at my speaking so lightly with Jacob, who she considered to be a low servant.

Eventually, we all climbed into the cart, plus two wriggling spaniel pups and drove slowly home over the moors in the most beautiful of summer evenings.

* * * *

Chloe was true to her word, and almost straight away, when we got back home to the farm, she started on a pile of mending, not seeming to mind at all. She was more skilled than I had imagined and was soon cleverly altering Belle's favourite pink and green print dress which was outgrown but that she could not bear to part with. What a useful girl she had become and she was quickly a great favourite with everyone, with her gentle ways and charming good humour.

"Eh," said Tab, "it could be t' young mistress come back ter us, she's that like."

When not sewing, Chloe was out riding; and we had the greatest fun riding out together across the purpled moors. Of course, she much admired my Star and I let her take her out sometimes, for she was a competent rider. Most of all she loved Star's offspring, eight-year-old Belle Star (born the same year as my daughter), five-year-old Morn Star and the last one, who was all black, with no star markings, and I had named Storm Star. We spent some time sitting on hay bales in the stable, while I explained about the coupling and gestation of horses and she was so impressed that I had overseen the birthings of all the foals. Though to be honest there had been no complications, and as with most animals, Star had done it all herself. Anyway, there was always my husband or Jacob nearby in case of difficulties.

"You are so lucky Lydie to have all this, I would give my eye teeth to have my own horse and ride about all day."

I sighed for though I was sometimes cross and tired, most of the time I thought myself the luckiest person alive, especially in having a loving husband and six healthy children. Often, in anxiety, I feared losing it all, for my cousins Jane and Elizabeth had both died on the childbed and poor Susannah was always having a miscarriage. Not to forget my dear mother-in-law, who had buried all seven of her children. I feared dying myself and leaving my babies motherless and alone.

"Why not take Star out now, for I've to see to the children's lessons today, can you saddle her on your own?"

"Indeed I can, and I'll be as smart as a pin in your pink habit, Lydie."

I had given her my pink riding habit, which, as she was quite a lot shorter than me, she had skilfully altered to fit. I considered myself too old now to be wearing bright pink anyway. My plain, navy blue habit being both more serviceable and more suitable for me.

The children's lessons were in full swing when there was the sound of horse's hooves at the front of the house; when I peeped out, why I could hardly believe my eyes, for there on his fine bay, in full red army uniform, was my brother Louis who I'd not seen for eight years.

"Ben, run and get your father at once, tell him we have a visitor."

"Who is it Mama?" asked Belle.

"It is your Uncle Louis, come back from fighting."

Then there were gasps of excitement all round, as I ran outside to greet him.

Benjamin rushed out from the barn, in his shirt sleeves, "why Louis how good it is to see you, come inside and get a drink."

He called to one of the hired lads to take the fine bay horse, and with one arm around me and the other around Louis, he walked us back into the house. "Now children, no more lessons today."

There were whoops of delight from all except Jack, who looked mildly disappointed.

"Tell, Brother-in-law how many children do you have now?"

"Six, two daughters and four sons."

"My," said Louis impressed, "what a lad you are Bro."

"Not so much a lad," laughed my husband, "more a middle aged man."

"Sis, get the little ones, are they with Mary? Get her to bring them down, for I've some gifts for them all."

He looked around him trying to make sense of everyone, so I quickly introduced them all and sent upstairs for Mary.

When she came downstairs and saw Louis, she literally threw baby Frederick into my arms and ran to him. He hugged her so tight he lifted of the floor.

"Eh Master Louis, Master Louis, A cannot believe it is thee, after all these years. How fine tha looks in thy uniform, and how tha's grown."

"Sadly in every dimension Mary," he laughed, in truth Louis was quite stout now. "Now let's get a look at me nephews, get them lined up in order, you too Jack lad." He delved in his army bag, took out a bundle of wooden toy swords, beautifully made and painted to look like metal, and handed them out. Then he gave Belle and Olivia little purses made in curious beadwork patterns of red and blue and mustard yellow, which he had brought from the Americas.

"Made by native Indians," he said and turning to Penelope, he went on, "Miss Penelope, I do fear you find me wanting, for I did not know you would be here…"

"Sir, may A call thee Uncle Louis?"

"Of course my dear," he said ruffling her hair lightly with his thumb.

"Uncle Louis, A see there is a spare sword, A should be most pleased to have that if A may."

"Of course you may…"

"Girls don't go to battles," sneered young Ben.

"Well, there I must correct," said Louis, "there are women and girls on the battlefield, far more than is commonly thought."

"Really?" said Penelope, her eyes shining with fascination.

"There's some selling food and drink, that spend all day walking around the soldiers with refreshments, for a battle's always in the middle of nowhere. And others that dress wounds and give kindness to the dying. A few I've known of, dress as men and fight and shoot the same as men. And..." here he sat on the low bench beside her and looked her in the eye, "some women cannot bear to be left at home, so follow their husbands into battle to help them reload and so on. And this I saw with me own eyes, a few years back in the Americas at the very end of the war, a soldier of ours, was shot down by a filthy Yankee, and quick as a blink before the Yankee could bayonet him, his faithful wife picked up his musket, reloaded it faster than any man and shot the Yankee in the... below the waist."

"Was the filthy Yankee dead?"

"Course he was, for she'd shot brave and true. And our soldier was only wounded and had his dear wife to dress his wound and he lived on to tell his tale."

Now, Louis picked up his horse whip and demonstrated a few key moves for the swords, he was extraordinarily agile for such a heavy man, and soon a proper little battle was taking place, with Penelope as bold as any.

"Don't lag back man," Louis shouted to baby Frederick, who had only just learned to walk properly and was holding his sword upside down. Louis grasped him around the waist and manoeuvred his sword for him, charging about the room with loud battle cries.

For a second Frederick looked as if he might cry with fear, but changed his mind and decided to shriek with laughter instead.

"Will they be hurt Mama?" asked Olivia, fretfully.

"No dear, it's just Uncle Louis having a bit of fun." But I lifted her onto my knee in case she started weeping.

Jack being the eldest, was of course the most adept with the sword and Belle stared at him the whole time with deepest admiration, fingering her beaded purse.

After some minutes Louis caught sight of Eliza hovering in the doorway from the kitchen, with a tray of dishes waiting to set the dinner.

"Battle over, to the mess men," he shouted, putting down Frederick and wiping the sweat from his own face.

"Thank you Eliza," I said.

"Now then Sis, I haven't forgotten you." Here he delved into the inside pocket of his uniform jacket and pulled out a leather jeweller's box. "I know I've reason to be grateful to you for helping me out with your bits, that time."

I opened the box and gasped with delight, for it contained a beautiful, expensive bangle in gold, set with amethysts and pearls. I could not try it on straight away, as I had to separate my sons, Ben and Robert, who seemed intent on poking each other's eyes out with the toy swords. Then, I said, "fancy you remembering I like amethysts," as I snapped it on my wrist.

"I remember you helping me out of deep shit, that's what I remember. I expect you know, Benjamin, that when I was a young fool, poor Lydie had to help me out and sell all her jewels to save me, and she sacrificed some good pieces, two or three from our Father's family I think."

Benjamin looked puzzled for I'd never mentioned it to him.

"Oh yes, I got meself up to me eyes in debt with horses, cards, the drink and some wench that said she was with child, but then wasn't, thank God. Could have been the debtor's prison for me, stupid young pup that I was." He laughed ruefully.

Then, just as we were waiting for the setting of the dinner, Chloe arrived back from her ride. Louis gasped to see her, "by Gad it's me cousin Chloe, for a second I thought you were Penelope come back to us."

"No-o," she said petulantly, "everyone thinks me like her, I may look like her, but inside I am quite different."

He had hold of her hand now, "and tell me Cousin Chloe, how is it that you are different inside?"

"Well, for a start, my sister did not like horses, but I adore to ride, as much as I can."

"Perhaps you will ride out with me while I am staying here Cousin Chloe?"

She lowered her head and looked up at him flirta-tiously, smiling she said, "perhaps I shall, Cousin Louis, perhaps I shall."

With that she released her hand, turned on her heel and swept upstairs, letting her long pink train trail behind her.

I do swear that Louis' mouth hung slightly open as he watched her.

After dinner, Louis spent the afternoon chasing the children around the house, which was the greatest fun for them, as we had two staircases and a whole floor of hardly used attics to race through. The battle cry for all (except little Frederick, who couldn't get the words in the right order) was; "Tis my delight, those French to fight," and Louis told us he knew for a fact that we'd be at war with France in a year, or two, at most. The afternoon ended in a raucous game of hide and seek, in which Louis and Chloe were the seekers and finished up with Robert's nose bleeding, Olivia with her dress ripped from waist to hem and George crying from his finger being trapped in a door. Jack and Belle seemed to disappear entirely, so I don't know where they found to hide.

At tea, Louis sat by my mother-in-law and entertained her with stories of army life in America and India. She laughed and laughed until she had to wipe away tears with her handkerchief, she clearly thought my brother quite the lad.

Louis' stay with us was a most jolly affair, every night we were drinking and playing cards till late; Susannah and Jacob joined us on some of these evenings, to add to the liveliness.

One such evening, after several drinks, I overheard Louis and Jacob talking quietly about little Hugo.

"By God man you're a fool, with a lovely wife like that," he looked across at Susannah sitting by the fireside.

"A know it, A were a fool and ter be honest, A thought A'd lost her ovver it all."

Louis was sympathetic and said it could happen to anyone, he went on, "She's still a beauty; you know when I was a lad, before I went away to school, I used to have the top bedroom at home and I'd lie on me bed thinking about her, lying in her bed on the other side of the wall in me Aunt's house. And imagining what she looked like... I hope I'm not speaking out of turn here? But you know what it's like when you're young?"

"A bit of polishing the old rifle eh Louis?" joked Jacob. "But A've learnt me lesson, A'll not be teking no more risks again."

"Mind you I've had a scare or two meself in that direction," my brother continued, "but I've had the luck of the devil in most things. Never got caught with that, cheated death more times than I can remember, never got the whores' pox, touch wood." Here he touched the table with both hands, and laughed.

It made me think I knew naught of Louis' private life, how many whores he'd had, if he kept a mistress, if he'd taken native girls as I think it was common for the officers to do. On the other hand, my intimate life was there on a plate, for all to see; an untouched virgin until my wedding night and six children fathered by my husband. Such it was for a man, to spread his seed where and when he pleased.

Louis had only two weeks of leave, every day he said he must get in to town to see our mama, but he never did. Each morning, while the children were at their lessons, he rode out with Chloe; as the two of them were cousins, I could see no harm in this. However, on the tenth day of his visit, I was most surprised to find them kissing in a deep embrace at the foot of our main staircase, she standing up on the first step as she was quite small in height.

"Brother, surely you do not take advantage of our cousin," though it appeared to me that Chloe was giving quite as good as she got in this.

"Sister, I do not, for Chloe has done me the honour of agreeing to be my wife."

I had not expected this and said, "but Chloe dear are you sure of this, for you have only spent a short time together."

"Why Lydie," she laughed, "what a thing to say. I saw Louis every day, for the first nine years of my life, there is no man I know better, except my dear papa of course."

"I plan to go and see Uncle tomorrow, and get his consent, as Chloe's not of age yet. I've to sail for India, with the Company, in a month's time, so we're wanting to marry soon, eh Darling?"

"Oh yes please," said Chloe as if she had been offered a chocolate.

"Then of course I'll have to tell the Mater, God help me."

****

Of course all the parents were delighted by the news and the wedding took place three weeks later, with Louis on special leave. Both mamas cried copiously, not at the beauty of the wedding, but because the happy couple left for Mysore the following day and none of us saw them again for nine long years.

CHAPTER 10

In which all are tested to their limits.
1792.

The November of 1792 was the wettest month I can ever remember; heavy rains were mixed with cutting icy winds, almost every day. Everywhere was swamped with mud, and for this reason the animals were brought into the barns earlier than usual. Also, the previous Summer had yielded a bumper harvest, so there was plenty to feed them.

Towards the end of the month, it was about nine in the evening and I sat with my husband (my mother-in-law, to bed long since) in the cosy winter parlour by a roaring wood fire. We talked a little of this and that, but my dear Benjamin could not settle, every few minutes he got up and paced around the room, looking anxiously out at the cruel night with rains lashing at the window panes.

"What ails husband?" I said a time or two. But he simply shook his head, shrugged his shoulders and said he knew not.

"Dearest wife would you mind if I smoked?"

I had to smile, for even after eleven years of marriage, he would always ask me this question out of courtesy before taking his pipe.

But he had hardly finished, before he strode to look out the window again, though there was naught to see but blackness. I stood behind him and put my arms around him.

"Fear not husband, our dear children are all safe in their beds and our beasts safe inside too."

"I just feel something bad, like an instinct, but I know not what."

I laid my head upon his shoulder; I had planned to tell him I was with child again, but it did not seem the right moment for that. Instead I said, "shall I read to you dearest?" and I reached for "Tacitus", for despite all, I had kept up with my Latin studies.

"Why yes, indeed I should like that."

So we sat down by the fireside again and I began to read, though I had not finished a page when we heard a banging. We looked at each other. "Is that the wind?"

But no, it was not the wind, and the banging got louder and it was clearly someone at the front door. Benjamin jumped up and ran into the hall to open up. I, more circumspect and always fearing the Frenchies, grabbed the two pistols off the wall.

As he drew back the great door bolts, Susannah fell forwards into the hallway and Benjamin only just caught her in his arms. I don't think I have ever seen anyone so wet in my life before or since; her clothes were soaked and clinging to her, hair straggled across her face and trailed like long rat tails down her back.

I threw the pistols onto the hall table and went to help her up. "Susannah, what has happened?"

Here she could not speak, so out of breath she was, gasping she flailed her arms and all I could hear was, "the horse…"

"The horse?" I repeated, wiping her face and pushing back her sodden hair.

She shook her head, shaking with the cold now, she grasped Benjamin's arm and taking a deep breath, said, "Jacob's horse has come back without him..."

"What?"

"Jacob went into Guisborough after dinner...and he didn't come back... and his horse has just come home, come home without him." She looked searchingly into Benjamin's face.

"Dear God," said Eliza who had appeared from the kitchen.

"Then I shall go out at once and find him. Eliza get two of the lads and the horses saddled, right now."

"Yes Master."

"Wife, I shall need blankets, brandy, ropes..."

"And splints?" I asked hesitantly.

"And splints, and bandages....and rags. Fear not our dearest Susannah, I shall find him and not return until I do. Where's the dog?"

"Went with him and's not come back."

"Good, if he's got the dog with him, we'll find him all the better."

Susannah sank into one of the hall chairs. In next to no time all the necessaries were bagged up, and two of the lads were at the front door with three horses at the ready. Fortunately, we had really good hired lads at that time, who had been with us some years. They stared at the weeping Susannah sympathetically, as my husband secured the saddle bags.

Already in his outdoor things, he turned to me and I tied an extra muffler about his neck, I handed him his pistol and powder flask.

"God speed, my love." I kissed his cheek and with that he mounted his horse and the three of them disappeared into that wretched night. I prayed in my head that Jacob had not been taken by the Press Gang. Oh God, I begged he had not.

"Now Susannah," I said as brightly as I could, though in truth, I was choked with fear. "Let's get you dried and warm. You feel like something out of our ice-house."

"My children are alone," she looked at me plaintively.

"Do not fret on that, I shall go and fetch them myself, this very minute. Eliza, get Susannah some dry clothes, get the fires banked up, warm the spare beds, have hot possets at the ready...oh and anything else you can think of."

"Yes Mistress," and she took Susannah's arm firmly, to lead her in to the warm kitchen. "Will tha be all right Mistress, riding out into t' night alone?"

"Of course I shall Eliza, I'm only going up the hill and back," though in truth it was a most treacherous night.

As I was saddling up Star and old Bessie for the children to ride, I saw Jacob's tarpaulin coat hanging there. Dear God I thought, he's out there in his ordinary coat, he'll freeze on a night like this. I put the coat on myself, and indeed it offered me great protection against the weather.

I could hardly stay steady for the icy wind in my face, as my horse climbed up the hill, but at least it would be behind us coming back. I crept into the dark cottage lit only by the fire embers, on the table was their great bible lying open and by it a candle stub, my heart ached for poor Susannah, seeing it there. Upstairs, I took a moment to look at the children, Jack asleep on a narrow bed, Penelope and Hugo, their arms wrapped around each other, asleep in the other. Now, I must break their idyllic peace, and shake them awake. Jack sat up rubbing his eyes and staring at me in astonishment.

"Jack sweetheart, Father has not come home tonight and your Uncle Benjamin's gone out to look for him. So you three are to come down to the farm and sleep there."

"Is Father hurt?" he said at once.

I bit my lip, "it may be that he is hurt, we do not know yet, but you must be a brave lad and look after your mother, for it is what your father would expect, for you to be the man of the family, till he gets back."

"Yes Aunt Lydie."

"Now dress as quick as you can and put on your warmest clothes."

Penelope was stirring now; I saw her clothes neatly folded at the end of the bed and I helped her to dress. It gave me a lump in the throat to see her standing there so brave and quiet, holding Jack's hand with her sleepy blanket clutched to her. I lifted little Hugo and wrapped him in a couple of thin blankets and still sleeping, I carried him downstairs. Jack held him while I mounted, then handed him up to me.

The slapping rain had woken him, "Hugo, we're going on a bit of a ride, you'll be very cold and very wet, but you're to be a good quiet boy and not cry. Can you do that?"

"Not cry," and he clutched me anxiously with his fat little hands, but true to his word he never cried once.

Jack mounted the silent steady Bessie, and pulled Penelope up behind him.

I think we presented a sorry, wet sight when we arrived back at the farm; Eliza and Janet (our new serving girl) rushed out at once.

"Take these three Eliza and get them warmed and fed, I'll dry the horses and be back in a few minutes."

I handed her little Hugo. Sitting by the kitchen fire was Susannah, wearing my bed-gown and a heavy shawl.

"Thank you Lydie," she called, as she held out her arms to her children.

Leading the two horses across to the stable, I suddenly felt sick and achy, but I put it down to nerves and being so chilled. Putting the horses in adjacent stalls, I reached up for their drying towels, and was doubled up with wracking pain and something hot and thick sliding down my legs.

I squatted down on the straw covered floor, holding onto the stall post, moaning out loud. Why, oh why had God chosen this moment to send me a miscarriage, on this night of nights, when I needed every ounce of my strength to help my family? I moaned again.

"Mistress, Mistress, what is it?" came a voice, and it was Janet, our new serving girl. She knelt down beside me.

I waved my hand dismissively, "simply, I was with child and now it seems I am not."

"Let me help thee t' house, Mistress."

"No, no there's no time for that, I have to dry my horses."

"That's why A came out, me father's an ostler and A were brought up wi' horses. A know how ter rub them down proper. A can do that for thee Mistress."

"Well Janet, if you'd run across to the dairy and bring me all the clean cheese cloths you can find, I'll sort myself out and then it would help a great deal if you could dry the horses for me." She stood up and I added, "make sure no-one sees you and tell no-one of this please Janet."

"Yes Mistress," she said meekly.

I remained squatting, not wanting to stand up in case I stained my dress, and thus I bled onto the straw like one of our beasts, until the cheesecloths came.

Indeed, Janet made an excellent job of drying and baiting the two horses, in truth I could not have better done it myself. And I cleaned and sorted myself as best I could.

"Please, Mistress, tha needs ter rest."

"Thank you Janet for your kindness and not a word to anyone."

Shakily, I walked back into the kitchen, not too wet for I had been wearing Jacob's big coat and sat with Susannah by the roaring fire. Taking two good glasses of brandy straight down I felt more myself.

It was past eleven o'clock now and the two of us sat dozing and talking for the next six hours.

"Lydie, do you think God is punishing me in some way?"

"Of course not, I think some good things happen and then bad things happen, not for any reason I don't think." I knew this would not fit with Susannah's deeply held religious beliefs.

She began to weep silently, "A fear my Jacob's dead, why else would he not come home?"

"Let not your mind run on the worst, save your strength and pray God for his safe return. I know Benjamin will not rest until he is found."

"A know A've not been a good wife ter my Jacob."

"Come Susannah, you've been an exemplary wife in every way, what makes you say that?"

"When A found out about little Hugo, A said cruel and terrible things ter Jacob that hurt him and that he's never spoke of since." She took a deep breath, "A did not speak ter him nor let him touch me for six month, and all that time that A showed him no love, he was steady as a rock for me."

"Any woman would be angry, Susannah, do not blame yourself."

"All that time he was so patient and steady, A asked him not ter speak ter me and he did not. Just watched me and saw when A needed help and every morning when A came down, he'd cleaned t' fire and fetched all t' wood and water for t' day. When he went into t' town, he'd try ter guess what A'd be wanting, and leave me packets of pins and threads and such on t' table. Sometimes he'd buy me bits of ribbon, in pink, knowing it was my colour."

"Come now dearest Susannah, bear up." I had a lump in my own throat from listening to her.

"A was cruel and spiteful for t' sake of it, and A brought my Jacob low and A hate myself for it... Perhaps he strayed because A did not love him enough, being married afore?"

"No, Susannah, I fear it is just the way all men are sometimes."

The night wore on and my bleeding was not too bad, I had no time to think of my poor lost baby, only annoyance at my weakness. I was worrying about blankets, hot drinks and what to say to the children if the worst happened. As that terrible night dragged on I had to face the idea that Jacob might be dead, for who on God's earth could survive a night so treacherous as this on the icy moors? I still feared the Press Gang could have taken him, and that, to me, seemed just as bad. The rain did not let up all night.

The sky was beginning to lighten, though it was not yet dawn when, at last we heard the horses at the front of the house. We ran through, Eliza too, (I believe she had not slept all night) and opened the front door. I stood there biting my lip in dread. The men dismounted and Jacob was in a blanket slung between two of the horses. Benjamin did not speak and started to unrope this crude stretcher, as the two lads supported Jacob's weight and he was lowered onto the sodden ground. The men took up three corners of the blanket and Susannah and Eliza together took up the fourth. It galled me to stand back, but I did not want any strain to start my bleeding again. The dog was with them and ran straight to the warmth of the fireside, and shook herself vigorously.

"Lay him on the big table," said Benjamin backing into the great hall.

I pushed the chairs out of the way and still on the blanket, Jacob was heaved upwards. He let out a dreadful groan as his body hit the table and in the candle light I could see the full horror of it. There was a blood caked wound on the side of his head, his right leg was splinted and crudely tied with bandages and his whole body was soaked to the skin and covered in mud. He was shaking badly with the cold.

"He's in a bad way," said Benjamin, still gasping from the lifting, "his leg's broken near the hip."

Then, he turned to the older lad, James, and bade him fetch the bonesetter and the doctor, with instructions to tell them it was a matter of great urgency.

Susannah had her arms about Jacob's neck and was desperately kissing his face, as she drew away a little, he clutched on to her arm though he was quite unable to speak.

"A'm here Darling. Always here," she said.

I did not quite know where to start, but knew his wet clothes must be removed.

"Eliza, scissors and the gutting knives."

I put blankets over chair backs close to the fire to warm and together we started to cut off Jacob's clothes, gently pulling them from under him. Eliza deftly cut his boots open, having spent years butchering our animals for meat, she could do this well, but never the less he moaned with agony as we removed them. When he was near naked, I had to look away, such was the beauty of his strong golden body and for some inexplicable reason I thought of the night my cousin had died years ago and Jacob had taken me in his arms to comfort me. But there was no time to let my mind run on such things now.

We wrapped him in the hot blankets and I chafed his hands and Eliza his frozen feet. He seemed barely conscious.

Benjamin appeared again, changed and dried, but still with a drained ashen look about him. He shook Jacob's shoulder lightly, "can you hear me man?"

Jacob shuddered, gasped and quite suddenly opened his eyes, looking about him and realizing where he was. He tried to speak but his lips were cracked and his mouth too dry. By now, Eliza had a cup of warmed milk and brandy at the ready and indeed it seemed to restore him a little. He took Susannah's hand and kissed her palm. She was weeping again but this time with relief.

"Bloody Hell, pain's bad in me leg."

I slopped some more brandy in the cup and helped him drink it. As he raised his head, Eliza stuffed a pillow and a towel under it and then started to bathe his head wound and I fetched some fresh Agaric for it.

When I slipped upstairs to fetch a dry shirt for him, I could hear the children's voices as they started to wake. (By this time we had seven children, for little Francis had arrived a year ago). So I went into the nursery to kiss them all and bid them stay there till after Janet had brought them breakfast.

Mary mouthed, "how is he?"

I mouthed back, "bad," and saw her kindly eyes fill with tears.

I knew I could not keep the older children away, Jack stood at the top of the stairs looking at me expectantly, he was holding Penelope's hand tightly.

"Go downstairs quietly and you may speak with Father, but he is very tired and...." My voice trailed away remembering his terrible pain, "do not be upset by what you see, for the doctor and the bonesetter will be here soon to make him well again," and I prayed God I spoke the truth.

Arrayed in a clean shirt and with his head wound cleanly bandaged, Jacob began to look more himself and talk a bit. He had no memory of what had happened, only of lying on the dark moor in the drenching rain, drifting in and out of consciousness.

"Our Robert were there wi' me for some time."

We all exchanged glances.

He drew a breath, "A know yer think that's me knock on t' head talking, but A tell yer he were close by me, A could feel t' weight of his body at me side, he kept saying, 'hang on man, it's not tha time yet'."

No-one said anything.

"Dog were on me other side, laying against me and A had me hand on her back and her hackles were right up when our Robert were there."

"Dogs do always know if there's a spiritual presence like," said Eliza uncertainly.

Then Benjamin spoke quietly, "I cannot explain it in any rational or Christian way, but Robert came to me too, some time since."

"You never told me that," I said in surprise.

He shrugged and went on, "I couldn't explain it, it was a bad calving, with the uterus twisted and I could not for the life of me get the legs and the cow was half dead by this time, well I heard Robert's voice as clear as if he was there with me, telling me to go at it from the other side and twist in the opposite direction, so I did and I got the legs roped straight off and it was fine. Cow and calf were as fine as could be."

"Aye," nodded Jacob, "he's maybe with us all t' time, we just don't know of it."

It seemed an age before the bonesetter arrived, though it was only a little after eight and the doctor arrived shortly after. Both of them sighed and shook their heads and agreed it was a bad leg break, being so high up on the thigh. A half bottle of brandy and a gag were needed for the setting of the leg.

I took Penelope and Jack into the kitchen and held them tight against me, but they could still hear him cry out as the bone was straightened. "I promise he will be more comfortable soon," I said desperately. "I promise."

The doctor bled him to get rid of any poisons, and left a bottle of laudanum for the pain. He said, lying on the moor all night would have killed most, but that Jacob was a strong man and that would stand him in good stead.

Eventually we set up a bed in the end parlour, where there was not much furniture, and poor Jacob was carried there. After rambling a bit with the laudanum, he fell to a deep much needed sleep, and Susannah would not leave his side even then.

At last, a very late breakfast was set, at which my husband and I could barely keep awake.

"There will be no lessons today, for Papa and I need to rest."

"Indeed there shall be lessons," said mother-in-law stepping up, "for I shall take them myself, and our Jack can teach t' hour of Latin just as usual. I think him quite good enough, eh lad?"

"Yes, Grandmama," he said proudly.

"Our Robert, fetch out pens and ink and t' books and such."

And, as my dearest husband put his arm about me to lead me upstairs, our older children and their cousins sat smartly at the table to take their lessons. They all knew that Grandmama would think naught of giving a sharp rap on their knuckles with the ruler, if they slacked in attention.

As we approached the bedroom, Eliza was coming out with the slops bucket and the basket containing my much bloodied linens. She looked at me questioningly and I made a silent hush motion, she nodded and said, "does tha need owt Mistress?"

"Thank you no Eliza, only to sleep."

We climbed under the covers fully clothed, I thought we would talk a little, but Benjamin put his arms about me and said, "Amor sempiternus" and at once we fell to the deepest dreamless sleep.

When we finally awoke, we went down to find Jack and our sons hard at work, feeding, cleaning out and milking the various animals.

Over the coming months, it was decided that Jacob and his family would live at the farm for the foreseeable future, to make things more manageable for everyone. He and Susannah remained in the end parlour, now their bedroom, Jack took one of the small attic bedrooms, where he could work at his studies quietly, Penelope shared with Belle and Olivia, and of course Hugo joined my own little ones in the nursery, supervised by the trusty Mary.

Jacob's recovery was long and drawn out, it took him a good while to wean himself off the Laudanum, for he needed it to dull his terrible pain, yet knew it to be affecting his mind. Lying in bed, they were long days for him, having been used to such an active life, so to entertain him I brought in all nine volumes of "Tristram Shandy".

"What," he marvelled, "all the one story?"

"Yes, I think you will be most amused by it, it being one of Benjamin's favourite books, and also written by a Yorkshire man."

"Well, say no more, A'll mek a start on it at once."

"Tis my bet Jacob, that by the time you've finished it you'll be up and about again."

He looked at me sadly, "not sure about that Lydia, but A'm determined ter not let meself get downhearted ovver it."

One time when I brought him some beef tea, I thought he must be getting better, for he said, "Bloody Hell Lydia, A'm not one of thy babbies, what about a mug of ale?"

I had to laugh, then I saw he was up to the page that Mr Sterne had left blank for the reader to fill in his own description of Widow Wadman.

"So come Jacob, tell do, how do you see Widow Wadman, the most beauteous of all women?"

"Eh, that's easy enough," he glanced across at Susannah, who was folding some clean clothes. "Why Widow Wadman has long, chestnut curls, the finest of figures and the pinkest of cheeks with pretty dimples in them when she laughs."

"What's tha on about now, Jacob?"

"Tha'll have ter read t' book thyself Susannah and find out."

Another time, I suggested he learn some Latin to fill in his long hours of idleness, but he simply roared with laughter, saying he couldn't speak bloody English proper, never mind a foreign tongue. He said he'd thought many a time of not saying thee and thou, and reet and neet but he never could stop himself nor change his ways!

Nothing suffered on the farm in the coming months, for we had strong sons and faithful servants, but our lives were never quite the same after that terrible night. Contrary to the doctor's prediction, Jacob did walk again, after several months he suddenly heaved himself out of bed onto crutches, and despite grinding pain learned to walk again, but he always limped for the rest of his life. Benjamin, though only injured by cold and strain that night, began on a slow decline, of chest troubles and eventually breathlessness at any heavy activity. He gradually found farm work exhausting and needed more drink and tobacco just to get through the day.

Jacob's memory of that night never came back, but over the coming months we managed to piece together the story, from others who had been with him at the Fox Inn.

Apparently, it was the Press Gang. They had entered the inn by both doors, so there was no escape. Unlike the other captives who had protested violently, Jacob had seemed to go with them quietly. Until they were lined up in the coach yard, whereupon Jacob had suddenly taken a chance, turned and run for his horse, disappearing into the blackness of the night. Of course, he was chased by two of the Press men on horseback, but when he was thrown, his captors must have lost sight of him and chased the riderless horse for some way in the darkness. And somehow the dog had managed to follow and find him, without drawing attention towards him. Then, she saved the day by barking ceaselessly when she heard Benjamin calling out Jacob's name on the moor, guiding him to her semi-conscious master, having lain against him for hours, giving him a scrap of warmth to keep him alive. Well, she was made much of by us and lived years more with no ill effects at all.

CHAPTER 11

In which Susannah enjoys the first day of Spring.
1796.

I always loved the first day of Spring, somehow it seemed to remind us of hope in God and all his wonders. This year it was the day before Palm Sunday and I loved that day too, thinking of our dear Lord in his last week. I was so looking forward to going to church on the morrow for that special service, my favourite of the year.

Every year, Eliza said she liked the orderliness of this time of the equinox. With there being equal amounts of light and dark, you could get all your work done in daylight without wasting candles and take your rest at night in proper darkness. My Jacob always joked about this, for Eliza was often worried about wasting candles and as he would point out, it was not as if she had to buy them herself!

I looked out of my bedroom window at the beautiful gardens, bursting with daffodils, the trees with their tight green buds and early blossom. All so lovely, and in my heart I was so glad to have this beautiful bedroom at the farm, for Jacob and I had never returned to Hill Cottage after his dreadful accident. Though he never said, I believe Jacob would have liked to go back, but Lydie and Benjamin were always most insistent that we stay, and of course the children all loved being together and having that great house to play and run around in. For myself, I liked to be there in the Curzon family home, where my Jacob's ancestors had lived for three hundred years, I felt it our rightful place.

Much as I had loved our cottage, there were many days when I had found myself lonely up there, when Jacob was working and the children away at their lessons and so on. Here, there was always someone to talk to or something going on. Often in the mornings, I would sit in the Great Hall with my sewing, while the children had their lessons, for though I had learnt to read well enough as a child, I had never been to school and I learnt so much from listening in to Benjamin, and also from Lydie who taught the little ones. If there was one thing I always thanked God for in my prayers, it was that my children were having this kind of good education. I will confess how little I knew, for the baby Octavia was more than three months old before I found out that her name meant eighth child in the Latin!

But for all my hopes, I never could have dreamt of what happened only a few days ago. The older children were at their Latin studies, when Benjamin turned to my Jack and said, "I think it time to start on your Greek after Easter, for you'll need Greek to take you on to Cambridge Jack."

"Am I to go to Cambridge University Uncle?" I could hear the absolute astonishment in Jack's voice.

"I see no reason why not Jack, you're quite clever enough. It's just a case of keeping up with your studies on a regular basis."

"Should you like that Jack dear?" asked Lydie from the other end of the long table, where she was helping George, Hugo and Frederick with their arithmetic.

"Indeed I should, Aunt Lydie, more than anything," turning to Benjamin, he went on, "I mean to study as hard as I can Uncle, every day."

Of course young Ben was set to inherit all, in the fullness of time, and sometimes his twin was a bit left out, so I called across, "and what of thee young Robert, what path in life shall thou chose?"

"I should like to go to sea Aunty Susannah, and see foreign lands and different things…"

"Bet yer'd bloody drown afore yer saw anything," mocked his twin brother.

Before Robert could reach under the table to kick him, Benjamin put his hand quietly on his shoulder and said, "son I believe that to be a good choice for you, I think you would do well…"

But at once Lydie jumped up to put her arms around Robert, "I should miss you far too much Dear, for you'd be away for months on end, and there's such dangers at sea."

Robert grinned and shrugged off his mama, considering himself too old to be cuddled. And no more was said of it.

That night as we lay in bed, I told my Jacob of the whole Cambridge thing. He smiled broadly but said he was not surprised and in truth ever since Jack had been a tiny baby, he had considered him the cleverest child in the world, and frequently said so. Myself, I was beyond proud to think of such a thing for our son, for my own family were plain fisher folk or servants as far back as any could remember.

And so back to today, the first day of Spring, I was just putting some daffodil buds in a blue and white jug when Lydie burst into my room, with little Octavia in her arms.

"Guess what Susannah, Benjamin has suggested we keep Palm Sunday at home tomorrow, it'll be so much nicer than going to church…"

"Now Lydie, are you sure that was Benjamin's idea and not your own?" I had to laugh at the look on her face, as I had clearly hit a note of truth.

"Well, possibly I did just help the idea in to his head, just a tiny bit," she replied guiltily, "but don't you think it will be good to not be stuck in church half the day when the weather is so fine?"

To be honest I had been looking forward to that special Palm Sunday church service, especially to the taking of communion, which we could not do at home. But I did not say this, instead I remarked that it would be nice for the Mistress, for us all to be together, as she was never mobile enough to attend church herself.

"There you are Susannah, I knew you'd agree with me." She plumped herself down in a chair and went on, "I cannot wait, tomorrow I intend to have two eggs on some thick fried ham for breakfast, in fact I might have three eggs."

Poor Lydie never stopped thinking about food during the Lenten fasting. Benjamin would not allow eggs, butter or roasted meat during this time, except on Sundays when the restrictions were broken for the day. The rest of the week it was plain boiled meats, bread and vegetables. As a result, there was a glut of eggs and they sat in two great baskets in the pantry awaiting the baking of the Simnel cake and the other Easter celebrations. I was to make the cake myself this year and Eliza would be hard boiling the Pace eggs and colouring them pink and gold with beetroots and gorse flowers, to decorate the Easter table next week.

"Anyway, what I came in to tell you," she went on, "is that Benjamin and Jacob are in the rick yard loading up the guns, they've set up some targets and they're going to practice shooting with the boys, if you want to come and watch?"

"Yes, A will," I said, putting in the last of daffodils. "These'll soon be in flower, it's that warm today."

"Mmm," she replied, putting her arm companiably through mine and her baby on her hip, as we walked along the corridor. "You know, last night I got really worked up worrying about the French coming and killing us all; they could land anywhere on this coast and we're so vulnerable out here, away from the town. But Benjamin said… you know how steady he is and always puts my mind at rest, anyway he said that if we were always well prepared there was naught to worry of. So that's how this shooting practice came about."

I nodded sympathetically, I knew Lydie feared greatly for her children. For myself, Jacob had quite reassured me that no way would General Napoleon be bothering to sail so far North, when they were up to their eyes with things in Europe.

Benjamin, Jacob, the older boys and two of the hired lads were lined up in the rick yard with flintlock muskets at the ready. Jack, young Ben and Robert had often been out game shooting over the years and all were competent with a gun but the point of today's exercise was to improve their speed and accuracy. Planks of wood were leaning against the hay bales, they had crude faces painted on them and hearts, where the lads had to aim for. Lydie stood well back from the noise, with little

Octavia (who was nearly ready to start walking), in her arms. They all lined up and then the bright spring air was filled with the smell of smoke and the sound of gunshots.

Benjamin was way the best shot, beating my Jacob every time with his sure and steady aim.

"Bloody Hell man, there's none ter touch thee," moaned Jacob. Then he vulgarly said to Benjamin in a low voice, "that's why tha's eight children and A've only the three."

Benjamin flushed very slightly and laughed out loud.

Penelope, ever loyal, said, "Father once shot a highway man and saved everyone's life."

"Think A've lost me touch since them days," replied Jacob ruefully.

They all shot another few rounds. I kept my arm firmly around Hugo, who was dying to have a go, but would have to wait another two or three years before he was strong enough to hold the heavy guns and take the recoil, even though he was a big, sturdy lad for his age. He and George kept saying that little Lenten rhyme, while we were watching;

One, Tid, Mid, Miseray,
Carlin, Palm, Pace egg day.

I knew it had been going around in Hugo's head all week, that rhyme that I had taught them all, to remind them of the different Sundays in Lent.

I noticed that so far, Jack had stood back from it all. I saw Benjamin wink at him and Jack grinned back knowingly.

"Come on Jack," he said at last, "show them how it's really to be done."

Now Jack stepped before the targets and Benjamin took out his watch. In no way was he a gambling man but he said, "I'll lay any money Jack can do four shots in a minute."

"Surely not?" I said in surprise. For the thing to be done was that the cock had to be rotated to half cock, the paper cartridge bitten open, the flash pan primed with a little powder, the rest rammed down the barrel with the shot, the ramrod replaced, full cock set, the gun levelled and the trigger pulled. To do all this four times in a minute seemed impossible, for I knew that even well trained soldiers in the army only managed three a minute.

"Go to it son," Jacob said with pride.

And of course Jack did eight shots in two minutes flat, with the same steady aim as his Uncle Benjamin.

Everyone clapped and cheered, young Ben slapped him on the back and said, "well done Coz, bloody well done."

Jack turned and caught Belle's eye for a second and she gave him her very lovely smile; in that moment she seemed most thrilled and her cheeks quite were pink with excitement. I wondered to myself if there was anything between them; I hoped not, for Jack had another six years of studies ahead of him and needed no romantic distractions. Though I own they would have stood as a most handsome couple.

"Oh Mother, when can I shoot? Please, please let me," begged Hugo.

Laughing, I let go of him, "not yet awhile Hugo tha needs ter be a bigger boy yet."

Jack came over to us and put his hand on Hugo's shoulder, "I promise to teach you myself, soon as you're old enough to hold the gun steady, I'll be bound you'll be able to shoot as fast as me in no time."

"Want to, want to, want to…" he said jumping up and down, but he accepted it well enough and hugged our Jack, for Hugo still had the same pleasing happy nature he had had as a baby when he first came into our lives. A minute later he was smiling, and joking with Frederick, the two of them were great friends, being close in age.

"Reassured then wife?" asked Benjamin, putting his arm around Lydie and the baby.

She nodded and touched his cheek. But I knew nothing would ever totally reassure Lydie, so great were her fears and anxieties concerning her children, even though she could use a pistol well herself and always kept one in the box crib beneath her bed, primed at the ready, and another two by the front door.

CHAPTER 12

In which life changes like a snap of the fingers.
1798.

Only the week before, Jacob had said to me, "Lydia, tha wants ter get t' doctor ter tek a look at him."

"Why?" I asked, though I knew what he was going to say.

"Well, he's so breathless, sometimes he has ter sit down ter get his breath, before we've hardly started. A know we're all getting older now, but our Benjamin's gone down-hill a deal, recent like."

In truth, I had seen a change in my dear husband over the past months, his dark hair had suddenly greyed completely, he was always exhausted, drinking and smoking, less for pleasure and more to keep himself going. Some nights recently, he had gone to bed as soon as work was done, sleeping heavily, yet still tired on the following morn. I could not recollect when we had lain together last.

"His colour's not so good neither, we Curzon's all have a ruddy flush, but he's, like an ashen grey."

I frowned and touched Jacob's arm, "d'you think he might be really ill, Jacob?"

"Don't fret on it, but there's no harm in calling t' doctor, eh?"

But when I mentioned sending for our doctor, Benjamin quite snapped at me, saying he could not be expected to be a young man forever and there was naught ailing him that a good night's sleep would not cure. Then he lit up his pipe, and did not speak to me for some time after.

I consulted Dr Buchan's medical book, but found it rather confusing on his symptoms, then next day I was diverted by the fact that both Francis and our youngest, Octavia, were covered in the flattish pink spots of measles (the others had all had the measles before these last two were born). I was much occupied with nursing the two of them, well knowing the danger of blindness if this was not properly done. And also, as Dr Buchan recommended in his informative book, the importance of keeping them quietly amused so that they did not dwell too much on feeling poorly. So most of my time was spent putting cooling cloths on fevered foreheads, holding hot little hands and reading endless stories.

The following week my little ones were much better, both had thrown off their fevers and had returned to the nursery to be under Mary's care again. I went into the kitchen, where Benjamin and Jacob were sitting side by side at the great scrubbed table discussing a newspaper in front of them. Eliza was fussing round, pouring mugs of ale and there was nothing out of the ordinary in this little scene, but life can twist and turn at a snap of the fingers.

Benjamin looked up at me with the most distraught expression, and gasped "Dearest wife..." These were the last words he ever spoke; he clawed at his chest, his head rolled back and his arm fell limp to his side. There was no other sound from his slightly parted bluish lips.

"Eh Master," cried Eliza, going to him at once. She loosened his neck bands, put two fingers on his neck and then laid her head upon his chest for a moment or two.

She shook her head, "Mistress, A think he's...." her voice trailed away and I stood frozen to the spot in disbelief.

Janet was there then, "Mistress, put a glass under his nose ter see if there's a bit of breath yet."

I wondered how I had no notion of what to do to tell if a person was dead or not, yet my servants knew exactly what was wanted. She reached into the dresser cupboard and passed me one of the good clear glasses. With shaking hands, I held his poor head and put the glass sideways under his nose, but no breath came to mark it, all I saw was a smudge of blood in his nostril.

"Oh husband," now it hit me, I clasped him desperately to me and the useless glass rolled unbroken onto the floor. "Benjamin, Benjamin, my dearest..." I said over and over again, as I sobbed into his poor lifeless body.

Jacob stood behind me, I thought he would reach out to comfort me, but when I at last turned around, he was shuddering with tears and his fists were clenched tight.

"Lydia, A cannot bear it, he was as a brother ter me, A'm lost without him," he wiped his face on his sleeve and shook uncontrollably, for some minutes.

And so my beloved husband had died, not yet fifty years old. I can say little more of it, for this time of my life is so blurred and confused. I retired to my bedroom for days on end, with only my two young spaniels for comfort, it shames me much that I left my children to grieve on their own, such was my own despair.

Sometimes Francis or little Octavia would creep in, lie on the bed with me and sleep wrapped in my arms, but I hardly saw the older children at all.

It overwhelmed me that I had lost my life's love. My truest love, who had loved me in every way it is possible for a man to love a woman; he was fatherly to me, a fatherless girl; brotherly in the great good fun we had together riding and reading books, and most of all, he had loved me as an ardent and devoted husband, and would no more. I wished I could be more certain of the afterlife, or at least feel his spiritual presence near me, but I could not. I felt nothing but an empty comfortless grief.

Memories of his firm kindness and devotion to his children brought me to tears many times, his great desire to be fair to them all, and the way they would cluster around him vying for attention. The way he would listen to them so seriously from their very first lispings to their reasoned mature speech.

After more than a month, my mother-in-law took things in hand, "Lydie A fear A must speak sharp with thee, do A need ter remind thee, tha's eight children that need caring for? Tha's forgetting they're grieving too and need their mother."

"I cannot, dearest mother-in-law," I replied weakly.

"Well, A know tha can Lydie, tha needs ter help thy children, they've lost their father, as much as tha's lost a husband."

I sighed and felt the tears coming again. She handed me her handkerchief, for my own was quite soaked.

"What's tha think our Benjamin would say ter this carry on, if he could speak ter thee? Would he not expect thee ter be tending thy children?"

I nodded.

"Tha thinks A don't know t' grief tha's feeling, but A do, A know it better than t' back of me hand."

Blinking back my endless tears, I said, "you're right, I must do this for my dear husband's sake."

Eliza, who had clearly been listening at the door, then came in with a can of hot water. "Shall A help thee dress Mistress?"

"Thank you Eliza," I said, filling my washbowl and looking for the soap, for I own I had not washed for several days.

Finally ready, I opened my bedroom door and there in the passageway stood my eldest son, my dearest Ben.

He held out his arms to me and smiled, "at last Mama, you've emerged. Might I walk you down to breakfast?"

"Oh Ben," I could have wept as I held him in my arms, he looked and felt so like his father and was already almost as tall, but I did not, for I'd firmly decided I'd cried enough for the moment. Instead, I swallowed back my tears, took his arm, walked downstairs to breakfast and picked up the threads of life again.

And so I did my best to step up and be the mother my dear husband would have expected me to be, but looking back on this time I fear I did not do it well.

There was much work to be done, and as usual in times of crises, Jacob alone had to organise this, hampered now by his bad leg. It was coming to the busiest time of year and thus it was fortunate that Jack had not left home for Cambridge yet. My own sons were good strong lads and none of them shirked from hard work. All of them wore black arm bands, which I later found had been sewn by Mary, the girls wore black cotton dresses (which I supposed Susannah must have made).

"Where's t' dogs been then? A've hardly seen them for days."

"They've been sleeping on my bed Jacob."

"Eh Lydia, we'll never get them trained for the shoot if tha fusses them like that."

"I'm just so lonely Jacob."

"A know Lovie, A know," he stared at me thoughtfully. "Shall A tell thee of first time A ivver saw Benjamin?"

I nodded, not ever having thought about this.

"We'd have been ten then, for there were only a few days in age, between us. It were t' day of me father's funeral and me and me mother had walked t' mile or so ter t' church in heaviest rain tha'd ivver seen. Mother's skirts were all sodden and sticking to her and there were such an icy wind we could hardly walk against it. Any road, we got ter t' graveside and stood like two drowned rats, while t' vicar were saying his words, me mother had her arm around me, as much ter hold herself up as ter comfort me. After t' coffin were lowered, A looked across ter t' Curzons, all smart in black broadcloths and silks, course they was dry as bones with servants holding a big tarp sheet ovver them all. Then Ben caught me eye and give me that friendly half smile of his and that were such a comfort ter me just then. A din't see him again for another three month, by which time both his parents had died and he came ter live at t' farm. We was allus more than cousins, more like brothers though, reet from first off, niver a disagreement in t' best part of forty year. Allus having a laugh and a joke together we was. A feel like A'll niver laugh again now." He sighed sadly.

"He always spoke of you as a brother," I said, touched by this little scene he had painted.

He nodded and gazed at me for a moment before he turned and walked away.

CHAPTER 13

In which Susannah finds herself with child.
Later that same year, 1798.

My Jacob and I still longed for more children, we rarely spoke of it now, but it was always there between us. Such hope, when I was sick and my courses stopped, then cruelly dashed when yet another little one was lost. After Penelope was born, I had three miscarriages, then little Rebecca still born, then two more miscarried, late enough for me to know they were both boys. Then, nothing for several years until this year, shortly after poor Benjamin's death, much to my surprise, for I was forty now, I found myself with child again.

Due to my age, I thought this would be my last chance. But all seemed to progress well enough. We would lie on the huge old bed in our lovely room at the farm house, on the long summer evenings and feel the baby moving about as lively as any, Jacob's hands touching me, as we tried to guess where arms and legs might be. He would rub my back every night, telling me that if I felt good, the baby would too, but he never lay with me for fear of harming that most precious little one. I was tired though, more tired than I'd ever been in my life. Lydie insisted I see the doctor every two weeks and as soon as he saw my swollen legs, he told me on no account should I rise from my bed (except to relieve myself). He bled me several times, but I remained flushed and bloated. Dandelion tea was recommended, which took a bit of getting used to, I can tell you, so bitter and yellow.

At one time, I'd have been bored staying in bed all day, but now as my time drew near, I was all out to stay awake in the day. To amuse me, Lydie had provided "Clarissa", but I found it heavy going, I did not share Lydie's love of novels, much preferring the uplifting nature of the bible with it's beautiful words.

"Try reading 'Pamela' instead," said Lydie, trying to be helpful, "at least it has a happy ending."

"Oh Lydie, now tha's spoilt it for me, there's no point in reading it, now tha's given away t' ending!"

"I suppose not, sorry."

"And t' way tha said it, it sounds like 'Clarissa' ends sadly. So tha's give that away too!"

I had to laugh, for Lydie often spoke before she thought. So I gave up on reading 'Clarissa', and just lay on the bed staring at the snowy white ceiling with its rose patterns and wondering how the flowers were stuck on to it, when it was first made. Then, I would stare at the fireplace and its strange animal carvings-the dogs with the lion tails and rabbit ears, and imagine myself showing them to my new baby.

At the end of Summer, my son Jack left home to start his studies in Cambridge and of course I had plenty of time for silent weeping, for I missed him so much. Yet what mother would not burn with pride, for all my family had been plain fisher folk and my own son was studying to take Holy Orders at a great university. I could hardly imagine what a university would be like, but Lydie spent a good while sitting with me and talking of all she could remember of Benjamin's university days, for he had often talked of that time with her. Her kindliness did much to put my mind at ease and it did not seem to sadden her to talk of him, but rather she said she welcomed it. Of course in my delicate state I had not been able to help him prepare for his departure, but Lydie did all that too, mostly single-handed, organising the clothes he would need and getting him the right books, all packed neatly in a studded trunk. Eliza had filled a large lidded basket with cakes and cheeses and a jar of her special black toothpowder, and she too shed many a tear at his departure.

At the end of November my waters broke and Dr Myers was sent for, arriving within the hour. Lydie and Eliza were busily setting out everything for the birth. Eliza banked up the fire and closed the heavy shutters, even though it was only early afternoon.

"A'm so hot," I moaned.

In the farthest distance, I heard Dr Myers say, "I fear there is some fever there."

A few minutes later he gave me a bitter draught to drink and I knew not whether I waked or slept, for my vague thoughts merged with my vivid dreams. I felt little pain, for Jacob touched me in his special way, but I wondered why he looked so worried as I drifted away into a hot drowsy world. A long way away I could hear people telling me to push, they seemed to be shouting yet I could hardly hear them, so loud was the throbbing sound in my ears.

When at last I came to, Jacob had his arm around me and was pinching the top of his nose, the doctor took my hand and said, "so sorry my dear", and my mind sank away into another place.

I know not how many days passed then, maybe two or three or many more.

I seemed to be a little girl again in the baiting shed helping my older brother to bait the lines. I was sitting on a high stool and my feet could not touch the ground. There was a tiny fireplace in the baiting shed, so small it looked as if dollies should be sitting around it. In it, burned scraps of driftwood and despite it being such a little fire, I was pouring with sweat.

My brother was warming his hands, for baiting was a cold job in winter months, "eh, tha's that dainty wi' t' baiting Sister, tha's a real help ter me."

He reached out and patted my knee, his hand was badly marked on the back with a star shaped scar, from a harpoon accident. I touched it with a childish fascination and flushed with pride at his compliment. I opened my eyes, to see my son Jack beside me, along with Penelope and little Hugo.

"Eh, Jack what's tha doing here? It cannot be t' Christmas break already."

"No mother, I came back early to see how you are."

He leaned down to kiss me, I took him in my arms and thought it was my brother again.

"A love ter help thee wi' t' baits," I said.

When I opened my eyes, I was surrounded by anxious faces staring at me.

"No A'm sorry, for a minute A thought A were a child again, in t' baiting shed, but only for a minute though," I reassured them, and promptly fell into a sleep of yet more mysterious dreams.

The doctor seemed to have gone now, I felt so hot and said so. Lydie whispered to Eliza to go to the ice house and bring anything that was left there, then she looked at

Jacob and silently indicated with her head that he should leave the room.

"Come children," he said reaching out to them, "let us leave yer Mother for a few minutes."

Now, Lydie bathed my burning face in tepid water and washed my hands with rose soap, she gently smoothed my damp hair. "Shall I brush and plait it for you, for it's all hot around your face?"

I nodded weakly.

"Your hair's so beautiful, not a single grey hair," she said tying it in place. "I'm still jealous of it."

Then she went to the foot of the bed and turned back the sheets, I felt some shame, for my discharge was brown and foul smelling now, but I was too weak to do it for myself. Her hands were cool and competent, cleaning me and putting fresh linens there and under me. She moved so quietly, still as slender and graceful as she had been as a young girl, twenty years ago, with no mark of the eight children she had borne.

"Thank you so much Lydie," I murmured.

She poured the dirty water into the slops bucket, burnt the soiled linens and washed her hands.

"It's nothing Susannah, I only wish to make you comfortable, shall you take something to drink?"

She held some wine and water to my lips for me to sip.

Now I knew I must speak before I lost more strength, "Lydie, tha's my dearest friend and A need ter ask thee ter watch ovver my children when I am gone, and mek sure they stay on t' right path of life. A feel A can go in peace knowing tha's there for them."

She looked as though she might protest and tell me I'd soon be better, but instead she said, "you need not ask it Susannah, for I think you know I love your children as my own."

I thanked her and touched her hand for a moment. She bit her lip and turned away.

Eliza appeared with some small lumps of greyish ice, wrapped in cloth, they were held against my forehead and against my wrists and gave me the greatest comfort, for a short while, helping me to sleep again.

When I awoke, I tried to move but I could not, for to one side of me sat Jacob and Hugo, both holding onto my hand, and to the other side sat Jack and Penelope with her sleeping head on his shoulder, again both tightly clutching my hand.

"Jacob," I struggled to speak, "Jacob, my Jacob A need tha ter mek me a promise."

"What Darling?"

"When A'm gone, A want thee ter tek another wife."

"No Darling, A could not, not ever. A cannot mek that promise."

"Jacob, look at me, this is my last wish, the last thing A'll ever ask of thee. A want thee ter promise ter wed again, as soon as is decent." I was gasping with the effort of speaking so much. I drew in all the breath I could, "promise me…"

He glanced across at Jack, who gave him the smallest nod.

"Is that what tha truly wants?"

I could not speak much more, but I looked deep into his eyes and nodded, squeezing his hand. My breathing had taken on a hideous rasping sound.

"Then A promise it, for thy sake." He kissed the palm of my hand. He sighed and in a shaking voice said, "my Susannah, have A ever told thee how much A love thee?"

"Nay, my Jacob...." I could not finish the words.

"Susannah, A love thee more than t' stars in t' sky and moon and sun as well...and yet more still." I felt his tears upon my hand.

I closed my eyes and felt like I had drifted up to the white ceiling amongst the white roses moulded there and was looking down at the bed where I saw my three dead babies and five piles of bloodied rags. But when I blinked, I was back in the bed with only the dark red velvet bedspread covering me and my family sitting to either side of me, as before. I looked around at that beautiful room, as if seeing everything for the first time. So quiet and peaceful it seemed in the half light, with glowing embers in the grate and two candles burning. I closed my eyes and saw the brightest light, so dazzling I could not see the faces of the people in front of me; yet when I opened my eyes again, I saw only the dim room and heard only the heavy breathing of my sleeping children around me. Jacob and Jack watched me intently as I drifted away. This time when I closed my eyes, a strong hand emerged from that piercing brightness, I saw a star shaped scar on the back of it and now I found I could reach out and grasp it firmly in my own.

CHAPTER 14

In which quite a lot happens.
1799.

So I grieved my husband and Jacob grieved his wife; whereas I had left my children largely to their own devices and shut myself away from the world, Jacob's mourning was quite different. Every evening when work was done he would sit in the great hall, with either Penelope or Hugo upon his knee, one arm tightly around their waist and the other hand holding their head upon his shoulder, no tears, no words, only a loving silence. When Jack came home for the Christmas break, he and his father would sit side by side at the long table; Jack with his head in his hands and his father's arms holding him tightly about his shoulders.

"A good way ter grieve, is that," said my mother-in-law admiringly one evening, after that first lonely Christmas, as we sat in the winter parlour, talking of it.

"Tis my regret, I did not help my own children when their father passed, but I could not think straight at that time, I could only shut myself away," I said.

"Tis of no matter, for they had each other, everyone is different when there's a passing. Years ago, A thought my husband cruel, for he never gave me a single kind word nor a touch when any of our children died. Yet now, A know he did not know what ter say, his grief was probably as much as my own."

I did not know what to say myself, so I reached out to her. She patted the back of my hand, and shrugged her shoulders and said, "Tis of no matter now, for 'tis water under t' bridge Lydie."

And thus, without any celebrations of any kind, we slipped into that last year of the century, 1799.

* * * *

It was one of the first mild nights of Spring, in early April, when the heaviness of my heart had lifted a little. There was a wonderful silence enveloping the house, for all were abed, except Jacob who sat at the long table in the Great Hall with a single candle and some quarterly bills in front of him. He looked up, but said nothing as I passed through to the kitchen to make hot drinks. I made two coffees with sugar and plenty of brandy to cool them and carried them back into the hall. I placed one on the table beside him.

"Sit with me Lydia," he said, as I was turning to go. "A need ter ask thee summat."

I sat down clasping my warm cup. He looked so serious, I said, "Is it about Jack? And the monies for his university? Benjamin had that all provided for in his will..."

"No Lydia, it's not that, it's summat else A wanted ter ask thee." He put his hand around my wrist, "tha knows tha's my best friend, A wouldn't want owt A said ter change that..."

"Of course not Jacob, what is it?" I had no idea of what he was going to say, I hoped to God he was not planning to leave the farm or anything of that sort, for I had rarely seen him so serious and could not have managed for half a day without him to run the farm for me.

He placed his other hand over mine, "Lydia, A wanted ter ask thee afore, but A couldn't get ter t' right moment… Lydia A'm asking thee ter tek me as thy husband."

"Oh," I gasped in astonishment, "oh Jacob."

"Shall thee at least think on it, please say tha'll think on it."

Now he was uncertain as he looked deep into my eyes. All kinds of things flashed through my mind; his holding me so close when my cousin Penelope had died many years ago, the utter beauty of his body as his clothes were cut from him on the terrible night of his accident, his tenderness with his children, but most of all his infinite supply of good humour and his unfailing kindness to me and everyone else.

"No, no Jacob I don't want to think about it, my answer is yes…yes I would like to be your wife."

Slowly a broad smile spread across his handsome face.

"Lydia, did tha really say yes?"

I nodded, smiling too much to speak. We both stood up and he took me in his arms, holding me tightly and breathing in my scent, he murmured, "by God tha's made me a happy man, the happiest."

I could smell his hair, his skin, his linens and I was intoxicated and longing for him to kiss me.

As I turned to him, he put two fingers over my lips, "Lydia, let our first kiss be under t' stars."

Taking my hand, he led me through the darkened kitchen and out into the stable yard. We stood there, under that exquisite starry sky and he kissed me so softly with his broad sensual mouth, drawing me closer to him as he kissed me more deeply, I felt warm and faint with the pleasure of it. He cupped his hand behind my neck and looked into my eyes.

Stroking my face, he said, "Lydia, can A show thee how much A love thee, or would tha rather wait until we are wed?"

"Jacob," I said kissing him lightly on the cheek, "I believe there to be no time like the present."

Smiling, he led me back into the house and I added, "but please may it be your room and not mine?"

"Of course Darling, of course."

He picked up the candle from the table, leaving our coffees there, undrunk. The spaniels stood up expectantly and Jacob laughed, "A'm not sharing me bloody bed with them two."

He shut the bedroom door firmly in their faces. I think I had not been in Jacob's room since the time of Susannah's death, but I resolved to put that from my mind, as well as any thought of my poor dear husband. The moonlit room was chill but Jacob quickly nudged a little fire into being, I wondered if he had brought in the logs for this purpose, or whether they had been there since the Winter. He sat me in one of the fireside chairs and sat down opposite me; taking my feet in his hands, he caressed me, gently removing my stockings. I felt myself go hot and weak inside.

"Thy little feet are cold Lydia," he kissed them and chafed them into warmth, kissing me so softly on my ankles, inside my knees and upwards. "Shall we ter bed Darling?"

I stood up shakily and gazed at him in delight, for he had removed his shirt and I could feast my eyes upon his beautiful golden body. Turning to me and holding out his arms, he stared at me very directly with the smallest smile upon his lips. He looked more beautiful than a god in that soft candle-light, and as we lay in bed, he loved every inch of my body. He used his lips, his tongue, his teeth, his nails and hands to find places I hardly knew I had, until it almost became too much, so great was my longing for him. At last he pushed my knees up, and rocking me from side to side, entered into me, thrusting to my very depths. I could feel the sinews in his arms almost bursting against my hands.

"Say my name Lydia," he was gasping now, and beyond himself, "say my name."

I waited a moment, and sighed, "oh Jacob, my Jacob, my love...."

Thereupon, we both stiffened, and truly pleasured together. He shuddered and rolling off me, said, "by God tha's a fine woman Lydia, the finest... At last tha'rt my own." Still breathless and up on one elbow he looked at me and said, "Lydia, my Lydia, tha knows A love thee more than worlds." Taking my hand, he kissed the inside of my wrist.

"And I you," I said, putting his hand to my lips to return the kiss. After I had caught my breath, I asked, "Jacob, did you ever think of doing this, afore now?"

He lay back on the pillow and grinned, hesitantly he said, "course A did, A'm a man aren't A? 'Course A've thought of it."

Fortunately, he was too much the gentleman to ask me the same question.

Then he was serious, "but tha knows A'd niver have done owt against our Ben, niver, nor against Susannah.

My God, A learnt me lesson fine well on that one, when our little Hugo came along. But A cannot help me thoughts can A?" He pulled the blankets up over us. "A'd have given me life for our Benjamin, if A could, but A cannot, all A can do is tek his place as best A can. And try ter care for his children and keep t' farm going till young Ben comes of age and teks ovver proper." He sighed, "A'll niver be half the man he were though."

I was warm and sleepy now in his arms, "shall we tell our children tomorrow?"

"Aye, best had."

"Do you think they'll be pleased for us?" I asked innocently.

He shrugged, "A think thy Robert'll be remembering his father…."

How right he was, I had no notion of what a 'Pandora's Box' I would be opening, but we were both too tired and too happy to speak any more of it.

* * * *

Next morning, I awoke cradled in his strong arms, as I was to awake every morning for the rest of my life. For a second I had to think what was happening, then I remembered with a rush of happiness, that I was going to MARRY Jacob Curzon. He was still asleep and breathing heavily, so I could stare like never before, at the lovely flush of his face, in the early morning light.

Suddenly he opened his eyes, "dreaming of thee my Lydia, and now tha's here, with me."

He drew me to him and kissed me slowly, but I could not respond, for I could hear the sounds of morning and the farmhouse springing into life.

"Oh shit, I can hear Mary with my hot water." I leapt out of bed, wearing only my shift, ran down the passage way, just in time to catch Mary ascending the stairs towards my old room.

With as much dignity as I could muster, I said, "Mary, I shall require my water in Mr Curzon's room this morning."

She turned towards me and could not have looked more shocked if I had shot her in the leg with a pistol.

"Mistress," she stuttered coming towards me.

I looked her straight in the eye, "Mary, I shall require my hot water in Mr Curzon's room every morning from now on, for Mr Curzon and I are to be married shortly."

With shaking hands, she put the water can on the wash stand, and hardly able to glance at the tousled bed and Jacob's barely covered body, she blurted, "my best wishes, A'm sure Mistress."

Then she ran from the room, with that explosive look that servants get, when their only relief is to pass gossip on to another.

"A'll give it five minutes and no more," laughed Jacob making little attempt to cover himself up.

And sure enough, in minutes, there was a sharp knock on the door, and Eliza burst in.

"Mistress, our Jacob," (I had to smile at her curious form of address), "congratulations, and Mistress tha'll niver find a better nor a kinder man than our Jacob, that A do know."

With that she bobbed and departed.

"Well, my Lydia, there's ter be no pleasuring this morning, now t' cat's owter t' bag like."

I started to pull together my yesterday's clothes. There was a gentle tap at the door, and when I opened

THE FARM ON THE MOORS

it, Janet stood there meekly, with some clean undergarments and my wash things piled neatly in her arms.

"Why thank you Janet, how thoughtful," for she had brought everything I needed.

"All t' best Mistress," she said quietly.

"Thank you Janet."

I dressed as quickly as I could, wanting to be the first to tell my mother-in-law, I pushed my straggled straight hair under my cap, I regretted not having curled it, but I'd become slack about putting in curling rags since my widow-hood. I ran upstairs to her bedroom and knocked on the door.

She called me in, and there was Eliza, helping her to dress. I saw at once by her face, she already knew what I was going to say.

"Well Lydie, is there summat tha wishes ter tell me?"

She had a twinkle in her eye, so I thought she must not mind much.

"Jacob has asked me to marry him, and I have accepted."

"Aye, A thought as much, way he's been looking at thee recent like."

I was surprised and said so.

She laughed, "me eyesight's not what it was, but A'm not bloody blind Lydie. A've seen him looking at thee in that way, for weeks. A'm surprised he's not spoke up afore now."

I knelt on the floor in front of her and she kissed me.

"A'm pleased for thee Lydie, yer both deserve a bit of happiness after all that's passed."

"We plan to tell the children at breakfast."

"Aye well, little ones should tek it well enough, and not think one way or t' other. A'm not so sure about t' bigger ones though, it's more difficult for them to see a mother or father replaced."

Now I felt full of doubts, but never the less half an hour later, we were all sitting to breakfast around the long table, grace was said and I looked across to Jacob.

He stood up, rather formally and looking kindly around at all our eleven children, including Jack who was still home for the Easter break, he said, "yer Aunt Lydia, yer mother, has agreed ter be me wife and made me a very happy man, so we'll be getting wed in a few weeks' time..."

Here his voice trailed away for Robert stood up and with a thunderous dark look at me said, "what about me father, yer've forgot him pretty quick."

I was stunned and ill prepared for this, but mother-in-law stepped up and said, "now our Robert, thy father's passed from us a year now and none of us can bring him back, thy mother deserves bit of happiness, and thy Uncle Jacob's a good man."

Robert kicked away his chair and ran off through the kitchen.

The awful moment was diffused by my eldest son Ben saying, "nowt wrong with Uncle Jacob, I'm all for it Ma," and he loaded his plate with food and started eating.

Jack and Hugo both embraced their father fondly.

"Are we to be bridesmaids Mama?" asked Olivia.

"Of course, you girls and Penelope too; tomorrow I think we'll go to Guisborough and choose some materials, I know Mr Mcrae always has unusual things at his shop." I hoped my voice was not shaking.

Belle looked at me coldly, then she looked at Jack sitting opposite her, who gave the smallest nod and stared at his plate. The other girls were all over excited, and Penelope got up from her chair to hug me in her affectionate way.

"Dearest Aunt Lydie," she said.

Mother-in-law said, "tha wants ter get summat really bright and special, with thy first wedding being a bit ovver-shadowed with bereavements like."

"Shall we still call you 'Uncle Jacob'?" asked Frederick, who was an exacting child who liked to know the practicalities of a situation.

"Aye, best had lad," replied Jacob who seemed a bit cast down now.

"I think you boys all have good Sunday jackets you can wear," I said, my mind running overtime on the practicalities. My husband and Susannah had always been most strict about regular church going, and Jacob and I had kept it up half-heartedly, weather permitting, ever since, so all of us had 'Sunday clothes'.

"And what about thee Mistress?" asked Jacob, "what fine dress shall tha be wearing?"

"Nay, Jacob," she laughed, "tha knows how A'm fixed, A've not left this house for thirty year with me bad joints and poor walking."

"Well that's it," he was grinning now, "if Mistress in't coming, well t' weddings off, A say. There cannot be a wedding without thee there."

Ben looked up from his enormous breakfast and said, "Yer could hire one of those little carriages, and me and Jack could link hands to carry yer to it, for we're both of a height, eh Jack?"

"Yes Grandmama, we could do it easily, and carry you into the church, when we get there, no trouble."

"Well, A don't know," she said, though she was clearly enchanted by the idea.

"We could put pillows and blankets in t' carriage ter mek thee comfortable Grandmama," said Penelope who was ever practical, like her mother had been.

"All settled then," said Jacob rising, and he and our sons disappeared to get on with the day's work.

Belle, who looked tearful, excused herself and the rest of us were left to discuss what kind of dress my mother-in-law could be persuaded into. She said she could not possibly wear what she called a 'sausage dress', not liking the new straight high waisted dresses we all wore. But encouraged by her granddaughters, she then said she might consider it, so I took that as an affirmation. I had already decided to ask Eliza to take her measurements and just get it made up for her, with perhaps a turban style hat.

I took her hand, "now dear mother-in-law, what colour would you fancy?"

This was a challenge, since she had staunchly worn black every day since the deaths of her son and husband, eighteen years before.

"A always liked greens, but green is unlucky at a wedding..."

"What about a greenish blue, like a turquoise?"

And so turquoise was decided upon, the girls would all be in white muslins of course, and I was still thinking about my own dress as I walked through the kitchen to start on with my dairy work.

In the calm privacy of the dairy, I shed a few tears thinking of my poor son Robert, and wondering what to say to him when I eventually saw him at dinner; I was aware of Belle's silent cold looks too. I leaned against the cool wall and thought of my first deep kisses in there with my dear, departed husband, so many years ago. My thoughts were jolted by Janet's coming in with a pile of clean cheese cloths and I could not disguise my tears.

"Don't fret Mistress, they'll all come round soon enough, sometimes it's hard for bairns ter see a parent replaced. But it happens every day, so sooner they learn that's t' way of life, t' better, A say."

I nodded thanks to her, tied on my apron, tucked my hair out of the way and proceeded to strain the whey. I worked hard for more than two hours, gradually forgetting the upsets of breakfast time and day-dreaming of the night before, I think I must have been smiling when Jacob came in and hugged me from behind.

"Happy?" he asked.

I nodded and said, "yes, very." I leaned against him but could not touch him as my hands were covered in watery milk still.

"A want ter mek thee happy always, my Lydia."

He kissed me on the side of my neck, and as I wiped my hands and pushed the deep bowl to one side, he turned me round to face him. Lightly he lifted me onto the work table, pushing up my skirts, he gazed into my eyes. He did this so easily, getting me at just the right angle, I knew he must have done this before. But I had decided not to let my mind run on such things, though I did wonder if he himself had been conceived in this very spot, as his own mother had been a dairy-maid.

Then I gasped out loud with pleasure, "shh," he laughed putting his finger to my lips.

The window was behind me, and I knew he would be able to see over my shoulder, if anyone was coming across the yard towards us. Even so, it was a hurried and passionate encounter.

As he fastened his breeches and I slithered of the table, I said, "Mr Curzon, please to remember I am Mistress of this farm, I'll thank you not to pleasure me in the dairy... not too often at least!" And I giggled a naughty laugh as if I were a young girl again.

"A've been longing for thee all morning my Lydia. Cannot stop thinking of thee."

And my God he did look so beautiful standing before me.

CHAPTER 15

In which there is a trip to the drapers and
also quite a shock later on.
The next day.

The next day Robert appeared at breakfast (having eaten
his dinner and tea in the kitchen on the previous day).
He did not speak, nor look at myself or Jacob. Eliza had
assured me he would soon come round, and Jacob had
told me to 'let him be'. So I did.

Straight after breakfast, I gathered the older girls
around me and amidst a flurry of gloves and bonnets,
the four of us set off on horseback for the two-hour ride
to Guisborough. And God had sent a most pleasant day
for us, blue skies and fluffy clouds and good dry ground.

On arrival in the market square we put our horses to
be baited, and though I was desperate for a cup of tea,
and a bracing port, I was quite out-voted, for Penelope
and Olivia (Belle barely spoke a word, start to finish)
wanted to go straight to Mcrae's. And so we all crammed
into that tiny shop, piled high with exotic silks, vibrant
cottons, Indian shawls and heaps of other wonders.

"Mrs Mcrae, I hope I do find you well," I grasped
her small hand.

"A've not been so well this last year, ter be honest, but
A'm better than A was, so A mustn't complain, thank
you Mistress Curzon. And tha's looking well thyself?"

"Indeed, I am well Mrs Mcrae, for I am to be married again in a few weeks' time, I am to marry my late husband's cousin, Mr Jacob Curzon, and this is his daughter Penelope. I think you will remember my girls, Belle and Olivia?"

She smiled her sweetest smile and nodded to them all, in truth she did look rather pale, though I thought little of it at the time.

"Well Mistress, what good news that is, A know my John will be as pleased as anything to hear of it, for he's good friends with thy intended, from market days and that." Then she added confidentially, "they always gets a bit political on them days, when they've had a drink or two."

I smiled, I had not known this and resolved to ask Jacob of it.

"So what has tha in mind for thy dress Mistress? We've some lovely imported silks just in."

She called her daughters through, to get the fabric bolts down. They were both pretty girls, with golden skin, not so dark as their African father, with deep brown eyes and black curly hair tied up high on their heads.

"A'm not up ter climbing ladders no more," she apologised, but I was hardly listening, for I was too busy admiring the myriads of coloured silks spread upon the counter.

Mr Mcrae imported stuffs from all over the world and I had heard, some were so unique, they were not even available in London.

"Tha'd suit a yellow, or an apricot and very fashionable now."

"This one's very lovely Aunt Lydie." Penelope pointed to a luteous yellow silk, delicately embroidered with tiny sprays of flowers in cream and silver.

"It is an expensive one Mistress, but tha would not need much of it if tha has a straight style."

"What my mother-in-law calls a sausage dress."

Mrs Mcrae laughed at this. Of course Penelope was right and I chose the yellow silk straight away, and together we decided on a peacock colour for mother-in-law. Lastly, the Mcrae girls got down rolls of white muslins, especially exciting for Olivia who had never had a new dress before, only hand me downs or dresses re-made from something else. Belle touched a pretty stiffened muslin embroidered with dainty white feathers.

"Do you like that one Belle dear?"

Quickly, she let go of it, "I don't care, I'll have whatever the others want," and she turned to stare out of the window.

"Well A like that one too, tha always has such good taste Belle," said the ever amiable Penelope.

So the lengths of silk and muslin were cut, enough for a dress for little Octavia too, packaged up and put to our account.

At last we got back to the Fox Inn and in a cosy private room we had a delicious dinner of chops, devilled kidneys and apple pie with thickest cream, several cups of tea and I had two good glasses of reviving port.

* * * *

We sat to a late tea, at home, everyone there except Robert; mother-in-law and myself at one end of the table, Jacob at the other, and our children down either side.

Grace was said, then mother-in-law added, "where's our Robert, he's usually one of t' first in ter get his tea?"

Now, I most definitely saw Belle raise a questioning eyebrow to Jack, to which he replied with the smallest nod and stared at his plate. There was a strangeness that Jacob picked up on at once.

"Do either of yo two know where Robert is?"

"I promised not to say," said Jack not raising his eyes.

"And I promised also," said Belle.

"Look, if tha knows where thy cousin is, tha'd better bloody say now," Jacob was uncharacteristically sharp.

Still neither of them said anything.

Finally, Ben spoke, "I'll tell yer where he is, I don't care, its bloody good riddance as far as I'm concerned, I hope he bloody stays away."

"Where is he Ben?" I said fearfully.

Ben wiped his mouth on the back of his hand, "he's sailed on the 'Fortitude', on the four o-clock tide."

"What?" I could hardly believe my ears.

"He's sailed for Greenland on a whaler."

"What's that, where's our Robert gone?" Mother-in-law was a little deaf now.

"Oh," I said on the edge of tears, "he's gone on a whaling ship."

"Eh, the naughty lad; he sat talking ter me this morning for an hour or more and he niver said owt, though he did ask about me brothers, who all went ter sea." She shook her head but did not seem to be unduly shocked.

"But he's so young," I said tearfully, "he's not yet sixteen."

"But that's when they go Lydie," she laid her hand on mine. "They need ter go young, so as ter learn, two of me brothers went at fourteen."

I fumbled for my handkerchief and Jacob challenged Jack again. "Jack, tha'd best speak out, with what tha knows, how did he get there?"

Jack sighed and said, "I rode into town with him after dinner and then brought his horse back, when he'd gone on the ship."

"What about his stuff? What did he have wi' him?"

"I lent him my book money, to get what he needed."

"And I lent him my dress money," piped up Belle.

"Tha's a bloody fool son," snapped Jacob.

"No I'm not Father, he's my cousin, he's gone to sea and I wanted him to have the proper things he needed." Jack spoke sullenly.

Jacob nodded and laid his hand on Jack's arm, "sorry son ter speak sharp, A were just worried for him."

By now I was overcome with tears.

"Don't tek on Lydia, don't tek on," he said.

But when he saw clearly that I was taking on, he got up and limped the length of the table and put his hand on my shoulder. "Is all this bloody carry on my fault?"

Mother-in-law stepped up now and said, "nay Jacob it is not; Lydie's done right ter tek thee and find happiness. Tis what our Benjamin would have wanted for her, A'm sure of it. And why not? If A were fifty year younger A'd have teken thee meself and no questions asked."

"And A'd have been proud ter tek thee Mistress," replied Jacob gallantly.

Now, I could not help smiling through my tears at this.

"That's better Lydie, thing's done now, for tha cannot go sailing after him. Besides, A think he'll do grand on t' whalers, mek a man of him, A'm sure of it," she said.

"Aye it will that," agreed Jacob.

CHAPTER 16

In which a nine-year courtship takes place entirely
in a cupboard.

All of us children loved to play hide and seek, other
games were tried, but none had the lure of this one,
especially in the Winter when it was too cold to play
outside. We were not allowed in the best parlours but
that still left the Great Hall, where we ate our meals, the
main staircase, the servants' staircase, the six bedrooms
and above them a dozen shadowy attic rooms, hardly
used and mainly empty, and we used to run through all
of them, hurtling up and down. Many a time we fright-
ened ourselves to death, making ghost noises and
jumping out of cupboards or from behind doors. As we
got older, the game got rougher and wilder, sometimes
the boys would throw themselves over the bannisters
and drop to the floor below in the most dangerous way,
so as not to be caught. For when you were, found, you
had to run as fast as you could to touch the big front
door of the house before the seeker touched it. If the
seeker got there first, then you had to shout, "caught
and shamed," and kneel down and kiss the seeker's feet.
Often as not the little ones fell over and cried, or the
servants complained to my Papa and we had to stop,
but generally we played for a couple of hours before
things got too out of hand.

One day, when I was eight, my Uncle Louis came to visit us. He was a most exciting person, for he was a soldier in a fine red and gold uniform. He brought us presents, mine was a little beaded purse which had come all the way from the Americas. Mama said Uncle Louis had always been a wild one, and on the first morning of his visit he arranged a pretend battle for the boys with shiny toy swords, in the Great Hall. I could hardly believe it, but my cousin Penelope wanted a sword as well, and fought along with all the boys. First Uncle Louis showed the different sword moves and then the battle began, it was a bit scary but my cousin Jack was wonderful with the sword, I could not take my eyes off him. As usual my little sister Olivia got upset and had to sit on Mama's knee; my Mama just laughed at it all and our nursemaid Mary, said that Uncle Louis had always been a caution.

Anyway, after the dinner, we told Uncle Louis of our favourite game, and he said we would all play and he and my Aunty Chloe would be the seekers. But as Uncle Louis didn't know the house very well, we were all to shout, "tis my delight those French to fight," to give him a bit of a clue as to where we were hiding.

It was during this game that my cousin Jack showed me the secret cupboard; we ran into the hallway and he grasped my wrist and said, "quick Belle, in here."

To my astonishment, he reached up high on the dark panelling and pressed some sort of catch and a concealed door swung open to reveal a narrow cupboard, about the height of a man, and quite empty except for a low shelf. Jack pulled the door shut, slid the bolt and we sat on the shelf, it was completely dark except for a small shaft of light which came through a crack near the top of the door. I was giggling with the thrill of it, "Ssh," he said, giggling himself.

"I didn't know there was a cupboard here," I whispered.

"No-one knows except us, I found it quite by chance the other day, I noticed the panelling was carved a bit different and when I touched it, why then I could feel the catch holding the door shut."

I marvelled at my cousin's cleverness, of course he was the eldest, but he always seemed to notice special things and be one step ahead of everyone else. My dear Papa had been teaching us all Latin for the last two years and though my brothers Ben and Robert, struggled with it and Penelope refused to learn it at all, Jack loved to learn and remembered all the words of it easily. Often he and my Papa would take their books to the dinner table with them and still be reciting Latin as they ate their dinners! I tried my best, for my Papa firmly believed girls should have the same education as boys, and he and my Mama both read books in Latin, to each other in the evenings. During this time, I noticed that Jack had begun to drop his Yorkshire words and speak, as my Mama would say, as a gentleman.

Over the years Jack and I sat for many hours in that cupboard, talking and whispering about everything and nothing. If one of us was sad, then we would sit in silence and just hold hands.

One day, when I was twelve and Jack fourteen, we were in the cupboard during the hide and seek game, while the others were all thundering about above our heads.

Then it seemed to go very quiet and Jack put his arm about my waist and said, "will you kiss me Belle?"

"Of course Jack, for we are cousins." I kissed him on the cheek, an innocent childish kiss.

"May I kiss you in return Belle?"

I turned my face to him, he pressed his mouth so softly against mine and our fate was forever sealed. For I knew for certain that we had always loved each other, more than just cousinly affection. We sat in the darkness some time holding hands and with my head against his shoulder. Then we could hear Ben, (who was the seeker) and Robert above our heads, shouting and running.

My twin brothers hated each other and Ben shouted, "I'll bloody get yer this time, yer can't get away from me."

"I'll die first, yer'll never get me, yer fucker," shouted Robert.

I was just about to comment on their simply awful language when it sounded like Robert missed his footing on the stairs above us, and we heard Ben throw himself on top of him. Then the worst thing that had ever happened in our games, happened. Jack and I slunk out of the cupboard into the hall, closing the door behind us, and saw my brothers fighting, rolling down and crashing into our poor Grandmama who was just passing the foot of the stairs. Fortunately, Eliza was also there and leapt forward to break her fall. Our Grandmama was a frail old lady of seventy-eight and now she lay flat out on the floor, half on top of Eliza, in a pool of water for Eliza had been carrying a bucket of soapy water when she had so adeptly leapt forward.

Jack and I both gasped in horror and ran to help our Grandmama to her feet; amazingly there were no bones broken, but we could feel her shaking in our arms.

Then my Mama appeared, in a furious temper, "you wicked, wicked boys, you shall be punished for this." She caught them both by the scruffs of their necks and stood them up side by side, facing the wall. "Put your hands on the wall and stay there till your Father comes." Then she turned to Jack and said, "Jack, fetch your Uncle and tell him to come at once, for his sons are to be thrashed."

I could see she was quite beside herself.

Robert began to cry, still with his hands and face pressed against the wall.

"Cry baby, cry baby," mocked Ben.

Where upon Robert turned and hit him, Ben grabbed his hair and banged his head hard against the wall.

At this awful moment my Papa came in, he was furious; all the more shocking because he never lost his temper with us, believing that all problems could be solved with reason and moderation.

"Husband, your sons have knocked their Grandmama to the floor with their disgusting fighting."

"Eh, no harm done, A'm sure it was an accident," said our Grandmama weakly, leaning heavily upon my arm.

My brothers stood shame faced before their father, who spoke quietly to them but with a terrible anger in his tone, "boys this fighting must stop from this day forward, for it breaks my heart to see you so. Your Uncle Jacob and I grew up as brothers and we never raised a hand to one another, nor ever would think of it, then or now. For your own good, you are to be beaten, in the hope that we shall see no more of this."

Olivia started to cry loudly, for she always took Robert's side, and clutching my Papa's waist said, "oh please, please do not beat Robert, he is truly sorry I know he is."

But my Mama pulled her away quite roughly, and held her firmly by both her hands. My Papa led the boys into the summer parlour and moments later we could hear the sound of his horse whip.

"A'll get a mop, Mistress," said Eliza wearily and limped into the kitchen.

Jack was taller than Grandmama now and put his arm strongly about her waist to lead her into the winter parlour.

She sat heavily in the elbow chair, and said, "in truth our Jack, A'm a bit shaken, shall thee get me a brandy lad?"

I put her warm shawl about her shoulders, while he poured the drink, just as if he were a grown up man.

"I am so sorry for this Grandmama," said Jack, "I feel this to be my fault."

"Nay lad, why's tha thinking that?"

"Because Grandmama, I am the eldest and I should have stopped the game when it turned badly."

"Nay lad, don't fret on it, 'tis not thy fault."

"But this must be the last time we play hide and seek, what say you Belle?"

"Definitely, for it has ended very bad today."

So that was the last time we all played hide and seek, but it was not the last time my brothers fought, and it was not the last time Jack and I spent time in the cupboard.

That cupboard was the greatest solace of my childhood, if ever one of us was troubled, we would look at each other across the tea table and with the smallest glance and nod, we would find our way secretly, to the cupboard.

When I was fourteen I started my monthly courses; I knew what it was for I shared a room with Penelope, (they all lived with us now, after Uncle Jacob's terrible accident) and she had started hers already, but I was still very shocked by it. When I woke up and saw it, I felt I could not move, Penelope hugged me and went off to fetch Eliza.

Moments later Eliza bustled in with a bowl of warm water and a bundle of rags. "Don't worry Miss, we'll soon get thee sorted out."

"But there's so much… is it always like this?"

"Yes, it'll be a few days and come every month."

"What every month forever?" I was horrified.

"Pretty much, till tha's an old woman and can't have no more bairns, then it stops."

I cleaned myself half-heartedly, while Eliza folded a wedge of linens and pinned them to a long strip tied around my waist.

"There tha'rt Miss, all set up, that's all there is to it."

My stomach churned and I wanted to cry.

"I hate it Eliza," I said brokenly.

"Well, there's certainly nowt ter like about it, that A will say, but if tha's a woman it's ter be borne Miss," She looked at my devastated face and hugged me in her friendly arms, "tha'll get used ter it, honest tha will."

Of course I did not believe I should ever get used to such a horrible thing.

Grandmama was especially kind to me that day, so Eliza must have told her of it; my Mama just asked me if I had everything I needed and if I wanted a brandy for the pain. But my Mama was very taken up at the time with my youngest sister Octavia.

I hardly ate any dinner and when Jack looked across at me I nodded and a few minutes later, when I slipped out into the hallway, he was already waiting for me in the cupboard.

"What is it my Sweeting, you look so pale and so sad?"

All morning I had so longed to be with him, but now I was self-conscious and unsure of what to say.

"I...don't feel well," I knew my voice was shaking to the edge of tears.

"Oh," he said realising at once, "oh...is it...are you a woman now?"

I nodded, unable to say anything. I was surprised how easily he had guessed, though Jack's family always talked very freely about intimate matters.

"I expect that must feel a bit strange," he put both his arms around me and kissed the top of my head. "I know my mother is in bed with it a day or two every month, but I think my sister not bothered by it too much."

I had not known that about Aunty Susannah, though I did remember, sometimes when we were little, my Mama would not allow us to go up to Aunty Susannah's, saying she was 'indisposed', of course I had no idea what she meant at the time.

"I think I'm going to cry," I said.

"Well then you must, it is good to let tears out and not hold them back."

I sobbed in his arms then, and again two years later when my dearest, dearest Papa suddenly died and again later still that same year, when Aunty Susannah died of the childbed fever. Jack was at the Cambridge University then and rushed back to catch his mother's last hours. He wept then too, with me.

I can hardly find words to tell how much I had loved Aunty Susannah; when I was a little girl I am rather ashamed to say, I used to wish she was my Mother. My own Mama was always busy with her horses or feeding a baby, there seemed hardly any times when I was little that she wasn't nursing a baby. Our home was always full of squabbling brothers, crying babies and barking dogs. In fact, if we had been her dogs we might have got more attention. My Mama adored babies and gave them all of her time and mostly seemed to forget about the rest of us. Aunty Susannah, on the other hand always had time for us. Olivia and I used to walk up to Hill Cottage often, sometimes one of my brothers came too and she would hold us to her clean apron and call us her Lambkins, then we would sit quietly around the fire in her dainty parlour while she read us a bible story in her charming strong Yorkshire accent. After this we had tea or milk in tiny bowels and the most delicious warm buttered scones or her special little Queen Cakes, baked with lemons and currants. Everything seemed so peaceful and orderly, even if baby Hugo started to fuss while the story was being read, she would catch his eye and put her finger to her lips and he was at once hushed and good. Her dog always lay calmly at her feet.

When we left she would hug us all and say, "come again soon and God bless."

Jack came home from Cambridge again, a few weeks after his mother's death, for the Christmas break; it was a desolate time for us that Christmas, with each of us having lost a parent, and he a stillborn sister as well, who he had never even known.

But he kissed me repeatedly in that cupboard, in a special grown up way, "Belle can I ask you something?"

"You can, and you know what my answer is."

For the understanding between us now needed few words, we were soulmates and had been since as far back as either of us could remember.

"Then Belle, we shall be married when I have taken Holy Orders and found a living. I think it may be many years off yet," he sighed, "can you bear that?"

"I can...may I call you my love now? Just when we are in the cupboard though."

"Yes my love, my darling," he clasped me to him and kissed me, and my heart thrilled.

* * * *

I did not see my love again until Easter (though we wrote many letters) and just after Easter I was angry beyond belief for my Mama had agreed to marry my Uncle Jacob. I knew not how she could forget my very dearest Papa so quickly; she who had thrown herself upon his coffin when the lid was to be nailed down and wept and called him her love over and over again, till my brother Ben and Aunty Susannah had to drag her off. Now, she was behaving like a complete trollop, sharing my Uncle Jacob's bedroom before they were even married, and I had heard the two of them giggling like children, in the corridor and when I peeped around the corner, I saw my uncle push her against the wall and kiss her and I had to turn away when I saw him put his hand up her skirts. Privately I had wept with anger and temper too, and I knew my brother Robert felt the same, he said he could not look at our Mama.

"Can you not be happy for them my love?" asked Jack mildly, on the day it was announced, as we sat wedged onto that narrow bench in the cupboard.

"I can only see they have forgotten my dear Papa and Aunty Susannah very quickly."

He sighed and paused before answering, "minutes before she passed, my mother made Father promise to marry again, though he begged her not, she insisted that he promise to take another wife."

I was astonished, "how could she love him so, yet want him to have another?"

"Twas <u>because</u> she loved him so, and knew him so well, she knew he could only be happy if he was married and thus wanted him to have her blessing I suppose."

"They seem hardly cold in their graves..."

"None of us know how short our lives may be, or when God may call us. I think my father and Aunt Lydie must feel they have to cling to happiness where they can."

My sixteen-year-old self knew he was right, but the child in me still burned with anger.

Jack kissed the inside of my wrist and went on, "I would wish most for my own mother of course, but that cannot be, so Aunt Lydie is the one I could love best as my stepmother. I have only happy memories of her kindness and good fun with us...when Father had his accident and Mother was distraught, it was Aunt Lydie that kept we three going with her care and kindly ways. She helped me so much last year, when I was nervous about going to Cambridge, and got everything packed up just right for me, when Mother was too ill to do it."

Of course all this was true and instead of feeling ashamed of my Mama, I felt a little ashamed of myself.

"Do you know my love, my very first memory in life is sitting on Aunt Lydie's knee and her singing a funny song that she must have made up, all about stars and every time she said 'star', I had to hold my hands up above my head like stars." He squeezed my waist, "I think you were there beside me even then, for she must have been with child with you, about that time."

I could hear the smile in his voice, and I knew my mama had many little songs and peepy games to amuse babies.

"But they behave without modesty, sharing a bed before they are married." Of course I could not tell him of what I had witnessed in the corridor.

"It is not for us to judge others for that, it is for God...but tell me true, Belle, have you never longed for the comfort of that union yourself?"

Though Jack and I could talk of all things, he had never said anything so intimate before, if there had been any light in the cupboard he would have seen me blush to the roots.

Unable to reply, I leaned my head on his shoulder, "you are always so reasoned and wise my love, how is it you never feel anger?"

"Of course I feel anger sometimes Belle," he rubbed my hair affectionately and twisted his fingers into it as he went on talking, "cruelty angers me, for there is much suffering in life that we must bear as best we can, but cruelty for the sake of it...that I cannot stand to see."

"Like to animals?"

"Yes...and helpless little children too. Like when my brother Hugo first arrived I was angry then."

"But why, how could a new-born babe anger you?"

I felt him turn to me in the dark, "Belle did you not know? None of us knew Hugo when he was born, he was a few weeks old when he first came to us."

I gasped, "but how? Is he not your brother?"

"He is our half-brother, he is my father's son, born out of wedlock...I thought you would know this? Anyway, the day he arrived, Penelope and I were out, not far from home gathering kindling sticks. This woman, of a low slovenly kind, came towards us carrying a baby, he was crying badly and she shook him too hard and shouted at him to be quiet. I hated her for her unkindness, and it was that which made me angry, for I was only young and had never seen such a thing before and of course there was naught we could do to help the poor little baby. Anyway, she asked us where Jacob Curzon lived and we pointed to the direction of our cottage, so when she was out of sight, we ran home. Well, Penelope wanted to go inside to see if our mother was alright with the horrible woman, but I thought it best to wait outside, so we hid down the side of the cottage until she'd gone."

"What happened then?" I was deeply shocked, yet gripped by his story.

"So we went in and there was our mother holding the baby, she looked scared but said she was alright and that we were going to wash the baby, for our poor Hugo was filthy dirty and bad smelling. So that was it, he was cleaned up and fed and stayed with us from then on."

"But how could I not know this?"

"We were all just children then. I hardly understood it myself, he was a dear baby and we all loved him...my mother loved him as much as any. Nothing was ever said, but Penelope and I always knew he was our brother, even on that first day."

"But what did poor Aunty Susannah think?"

I felt him shrug, "she did not speak to my father for many weeks, but I suppose she came round to it in the end and I do know she loved Hugo as much as me and Penelope."

"But I remember Aunty Susannah feeding him at her own breast, how could that be?"

He shrugged again, "animals can feed another's young. I suppose it's the same with women." He paused and then said, "you know my love, I feel certain my mother would have been pleased to see our parents marry, for Aunt Lydie was very dear to her."

I felt I had been a child, but now I had made a step into adult life. I resolved to apologise to Uncle Jacob for my rudeness, when for my whole life he had always been kindly and good humoured towards me. But I did not get the chance that evening or the next day, for my brother Robert had resolved to run away to sea without any of the adults knowing. Ben, Jack and I were sworn to secrecy, Jack said he would take him into town and bring his horse back. We all knew that going to sea, he'd need extra, heavy clothes and money, so I gave him my dress allowance and Jack gave him some of the money my Papa had left to him for his studies. I wanted desperately to go with them to see him onto the ship, but my mama was taking us girls into Guisborough to buy dress materials that day and I could not get out of that. Then Robert said it was unlucky for sailors to have farewells anyway, and that after he had signed up he would walk onto the ship on his own.

Early, on the morning that he was to leave, I hugged him tight, "please write if you can brother, I shall miss you so much."

I pressed a little piece of carved, black jet into his hand for luck.

"He'll be back in August, won't you?" (For that is when the whalers returned).

"Probably, don't know yet, kiss Olivia for me after I've gone."

We had decided that Olivia should not be let into the secret, because she always got so upset about things, and my Mama might have found out about it.

Ben seemed indifferent to his going, but at the very last minute he turned to Robert and said, "watch out for them whales Bruth," and clapped him on the back.

I was like a cat on hot bricks all that day at the draper's in Guisborough, wondering if he had actually sailed away on that great ship.

Later on, at the tea, my mama was really upset when she found that Robert had gone, and Uncle Jacob clearly blamed himself for the whole thing. So I thought I'd better wait a time before making my apologies.

But I got my chance later that evening, when I saw my Uncle Jacob and Jack in the middle of the stable yard, seeing to one of the cart horses.

I went straight up to them and said, "please forgive me Uncle Jacob, for I have been surly and rude with you, forgive me for I was in the wrong..."

He looked at me astonished and at once held out his arms to me, "Belle, Belle tha's done no wrong ter me, dun't think on it." He looked at me so sadly, "we all grieve thy father, but all t' grief in t' world'll not bring him back. We that's left living have to blunder on as best we can, A'll niver be half t' man thy father were, that A do know."

With that he hugged me tight and I kissed his cheek before I went back inside, glancing first at Jack, who gave me his most dazzling smile to thrill my heart.

CHAPTER 17

In which Lydia and Jacob are married.
1799.

Wedding plans continued apace, of course I missed my son Robert all the time, but there was nothing at all I could do about it other than pray for his safe return. If I managed to put him from my mind, I was filled with a girlish excitement about my darling Jacob and my amazement that we were actually to be married. Straight away I had written to my brother Louis, (who was in a temporary posting at York), to ask him to give me away and he had quickly replied;

> *Dear Sister,*
> *Shall be glad to give you away, can be there any time after May 20th. Do you need me there when you tell Ma? If so me and Chloe will be there about half after two on 20th. Me and Chloe have got a bit of surprise good news!!!!!*
> *We send love to Jacob and all the children.*
> *Your devoted brother,*
> *Capt. Louis George Franklin.*
> *Thousand kisses and good blessings from your most devoted cousin and sister-in-law Chloe Alice Franklin.*
> *xxxxxxxxxxxxxxxx*

Of course I wrote back and said that I did need support in telling my Mama, in truth I was dreading it. I also secretly hoped that their 'surprise' would involve a baby for there had been no mention of that in their nine years of marriage.

"Tha's not a child Lydia, tha can do as tha likes," said Jacob.

"Surely she'll be glad tha's ter wed again, for he's thy first husband's cousin, and not a stranger," said Mother-in-law.

Mary, however, well knowing the sharper side of my mother's tongue, was more sympathetic and said, "best ger it ovver with then tha'll know how she is, for good or bad Mistress."

But I had decided to wait for Louis' return before broaching things with Mama, aware that Jacob's being a humble carter and being a bastard would go much against him.

We booked the church for May 25th, a Saturday, and of course we had to promise the Vicar to mend our ways on our poor church going in the past. Next was a trip to Mrs Wilson's in Whitby with all four girls to get our dresses, made up from the lovely stuffs we had chosen. I had been going there for my dresses since I was a child, and though she no longer sewed herself, she ran a 'tight ship' with apprentices and outsourcing the sewing to a team of very competent ladies. My Aunt and my Mama always used to say that Mrs Wilson was not the cheapest, but she was definitely the best. Naturally, she was most excited to have a wedding to plan for, though there was precious little time in which to make up six dresses. We were all most carefully measured, and although I was confident they would be exactly right, we booked in for a final fitting in May. She marvelled at the wonderful yellow silk I had chosen and said she had heard many a time of Mr Mcrae's shop and his fabulous cloths from the East.

As we left, I asked her most particularly not to mention our wedding to anyone in case my mama found out about it, before Louis' visit.

"Discretion is my middle name Mistress Curzon," she assured me. And I hoped she meant it.

Jacob drove us all back to the farm on the cart, he seemed to have had a very great deal to drink and explained it was all to do with a surprise he was planning for our wedding day; later as he undressed to change his shirt, I saw a tight bandage on his upper arm.

"Have you hurt your arm Darling One?" I asked.

"No 'tis a surprise Darling for our wedding day, but tha mustn't see it yet."

I could not imagine how his arm could be a surprise, when I had seen it many times already, but I had little time to think on this, as he then drew me on to the bed and loved me quickly before it was time for the tea.

My poor little Octavia put her foot right in things at the tea table: never having been to the dressmaker's before she talked most excitedly of it to Jacob, "and my dress has got feather's all over it and a coral sash, Uncle Jacob..."

"My, shall tha look like a little peacock, walking down t' aisle?" he teased.

"No, no Father." Penelope always laughed dutifully at her father's jokes, "they're tiny white feathers embroidered on t' white cloth."

"Ah, A'm gerring t' picture now, tha'll look like a little angel then?"

Octavia giggled, "and Mama has a most beautiful yell…"

Quick as thought, Penelope clamped her hand over Octavia's mouth, "no, no Tavvy, Father must know nowt of t' bridal dress, for it brings bad luck."

Octavia burst into tears of shame at her mistake and at once Jacob reached out and lifted her onto his knee.

"Nay Tavvy don't cry, A din't hear what tha said, Uncle Jacob's going deaf in his old age, honest, A din't hear nowt," he said, kissing the top of her head.

Olivia knowingly whispered to me, "Uncle Jacob is always so kind to us all."

* * * *

In no time at all, our beautiful dresses had been collected and the dreaded day of May 20th had arrived, when my mama was to be told of our plans.

It started badly for Louis and Chloe had not yet arrived by three o'clock as Jacob and I stood in front of my mama like two disobedient children.

She glared at me, "you are telling me that you are to marry the Curzon's carter Lydie, in God's name why?"

Jacob stepped up and said, "Mistress Franklin, A love Lydia and intend to help her care for t' children and work t' farm till young Ben comes of age." But he spoke his words bleakly.

She stared at him incredulously, "anyone can talk of love, do you have anything whatsoever to offer my Lydie, or do you intend to live off her money Mr Curzon?"

And so it went on, I was embarrassed by my mama, and hated her. Later, I felt guilty for feeling so, for I only saw her once more after this, as she died shortly after our wedding; from a growth, which according to her maid Lizzie, she had had for some time and I had known nothing of.

At long last, Louis and Chloe arrived.

"Good God that bloody coachman wants shooting, it was the bloody ride of death coming from York, and now hours late we've had to walk all the way up from the White Horse, not a carrier in sight and my poor Chloe in her condition."

Chloe, huge with child laughed, "oh Louis we were only half an hour late and I am perfectly fine, for 'twas only a short walk dear."

"Ma," he kissed her cheek. My mama clutched him to her but he shook her off and went to hug me and shake hands with Jacob and clap him on the back.

He must have read a lot in our faces, for then he launched in with, "well Ma, grand idea Mr Curzon taking on our Lydie eh? How many children is it now Lydie? Seven is it?"

"Eight," of course Louis well knew how many children I had.

"Eight, good God, the man wants a bloody medal taking on eight, we'd best settle it all with a good drink before he sees sense and changes his mind."

Here Louis went to the drinks table and started filling glasses with Madeira wine. One of the glasses fell on the floor and smashed, nonchalantly he kicked it under a chair, carried on pouring and handed out the drinks.

"To our Lydie and Mr Curzon," he said knocking back his drink in one and pouring himself another.

Chloe lowered herself heavily into a French armchair and smiled brightly at us all.

"Oh Chloe, this is a nice surprise," I said sitting beside her and glancing at her stomach, "and how are you keeping?"

"Very well indeed cousin, I thank you." In truth Chloe looked wonderfully well and not a day over nineteen, which she was when I had last seen her, nine years since.

"Dear Chloe, you must rest a little after such a dreadful journey."

"No Aunt, I am well rested for I slept most of the way in the coach."

"What on the rough roads?" I was surprised.

"Mmm," she said. "To me it was like a gentle rocking, though one lady was sick twice and two of the gentlemen had made their wills before the journey and kept their pistols at the ready all the way." She smiled happily.

Another round of drinks was poured, which I was glad of, for my nerves were in shreds by now.

"To thy lovely wife and the future little one," said Jacob raising his glass, then he clapped Louis on the back and rather vulgarly added, "about bloody time man, what's tha been doing all these years?"

Louis merely laughed. "She's a grand girl is my Chloe, been half way around the world and never complained once."

"But Louis dear, I liked everywhere we've been, it has all been most interesting, there was nothing to complain of."

Louis snorted, "bloody awful food, I've spent months on end while we were away, longing for a good joint of beef and batter puddings. Couldn't eat a bloody thing in India."

Though Louis certainly did not look starved, and had grown even stouter since I had last seen him!

"It was really very nice," said Chloe confidentially, "we had two cooks in India and they cooked the most delicious spiced dishes every day, with great big flat breads and chutneys, which are a sort of pickle, like Peg used to make. But poor Louis could have no beef as the ladies could not cook it for us, because to them eating a cow was like us eating one of our own dear horses. And they were such very kind, well-mannered brown ladies."

"Natives cooked your food Chloe?" asked my mama in a horrified tone.

"Bloody flies everywhere," added Louis.

"Well now that is true Louis dear, but we had two sweet native boys with great big fans, who worked all day long to keep us cool and keep the flies away. Such darlings, I should like to have brought them back with us."

My mama merely gasped.

Thinking it propitious to change the subject, I asked Chloe when her baby was expected. She did not seem to know and appeared puzzled by the question.

"You seem quite... big Chloe, do you think it will be soon or might it be twins?" In truth she seemed enormous to me.

Mama was glaring at me for speaking so coarsely in front of the men. But as we were all family, I could see no wrong in it.

"Twins?" she looked at me in amazement.

"How many little hands can you feel moving about?"

"Oh three, definitely three."

Whereupon Louis burst into a great roar of laughter, "by Gad, my Chloe never was much good with the school room sums. Bless you Darling!"

She stared at him blankly for a moment and then smiled at herself, "I suppose it must be four then, ooh I should love to have twins, two babies when we have waited so long without any."

* * * *

And so our wedding day arrived, and a glorious fine day it was. We were to be married in the little village church, not more than a mile away. Jacob slept the preceding night up at Hill Cottage on his own so that I would not see him until he stood at the altar.

As arranged, Ben and Jack carried their Grandmama to the most charming stylish carriage, which had been hired for the day. I might add she looked quite splendid in the peacock dress and turban, with pearl bracelets and a diamond brooch in her headdress, even though she insisted she felt like a blue sausage.

Eliza assured her she looked smart as a pin. The girls and I rode in the carriage with her and were driven by our eldest sons. The other children and servants travelled in the farm cart, which had been decked out with white flowers and ribbons.

Outside the church, I took Louis' arm with one hand and my bunch of orange and yellow pansies from our own garden, in the other. Waiting at the alter with Jack at his side, stood Jacob, grinning broadly as we walked towards him, he looked as fine as could be in a yellow waistcoat and high cravat with closefitting buckskin breeches and tall boots. He had had his hair cut in a short and tousled style, and altogether looked as beautiful as a god, standing there.

And so we became man and wife, in God's own bond of love.

Of course Janet and Eliza had made a splendid wedding feast for us back at the farm, Louis and Jacob had a very great deal to drink, and in truth I did not stint myself, but I fear my son Ben drank the most, even though he was still only fifteen!

Perhaps you are wondering what wedding gifts we exchanged? I bought Jacob the, "The Interesting Narrative of Olaudah Equiano," which I knew he greatly coveted and two other leather bound books; he bought me a most lovely, brand new, diamond and amethyst ring, of a most fashionable cut and setting, which fitted perfectly above my wedding band. Finally, he took the bandage off his upper arm to reveal a tattoo of a heart with my name inside. I don't think I had ever been more astonished in my whole life for I had never seen a tattoo, nor even heard the word before that day! Apparently he had had it done at the Angel Inn by an old sailor who had been to the South Seas with Captain Cook and learnt the skill there.

I kissed it tenderly as he said, "always in my heart and always on my arm, forever my Lydia," then he took me ardently as his lawful wife.

And just to complete the very lovely day, a couple of minutes before midnight, in our own guest room, Chloe gave birth to twins. They were named Sophia (after her mama) and Clement. Where they got Clement for a name from, I know not; myself, I could only think of 'oranges and lemons'. As usual, Mrs Vye said what lovely names they were.

So after that there was much more celebratory drinking long into the small hours of the night. And of course my brother was as pleased and proud as could be.

CHAPTER 18

In which the Curzons throw the grandest Christmas party.
1799.

We were coming towards the end of the century, I had been married nearly six months and yes, of course I was with child yet again, and despite my age of thirty-six, I was really keeping very well and out riding every day.

"T'will be t' last Christmas o' t' century. A cannot believe A've lived this long." Jacob laughed. "Divil looks after his own eh my Lydia?"

"Oh Jacob dear, do not speak so, you must live a whole lot longer, now we have a little one on the way, besides you are only fifty."

"Come on Lydia, me father were dead at thirty odd and me mother at thirty-five. Thy own father, hardly more than a lad and thy mother not much older than me and... and," he looked at me sadly, "and our Ben."

"Oh, Jacob," I was crestfallen, thinking I might lose him.

"No worries," he grinned now, "A've a grandfather living yet and he's well in 'is nineties."

Now I was astonished, for I knew naught of this.

"You never said you had a grandfather Jacob."

"Well tha niver asked did tha? Any road A think he's still on t' go, Eliza's niver said owt and she keeps up wi' that lot more than me."

"Where does he live Dearest?"

"About ten mile off, he lives wi' two of his daughters."

"Then we must visit, next year, perhaps when we have the baby, that would be so incredible to have four generations all together, what do you think?"

Jacob snorted, "A don't think so Lydia, they're not t' kind of people that tha knows, nor even t' kind A know now. A've not seen any of them for thirty year."

I decided to pursue the matter on another occasion, as there was something else praying on my mind, "Jacob I've been thinking…"

"What my lovliest?"

"We are too much on our own, our daughters should be meeting young men…"

"Aye, A suppose so, Belle's seventeen now and Penelope almost eighteen, maybe we should be matching them up."

He sounded reluctant, but what father does not rue losing a loving daughter to another man?

"Do you think we could have a Christmas party?"

"Aye, well why not? A know a few good families who've sons as might do."

"I think we might fit fifty in the Great Hall, plus the twelve of us, do you know fifty people that might like to come?"

"Oh aye, no problem, A'll mek a bit of a list now and get out tomorrow and start asking folks, for it's less than four weeks ter Christmas now, what day was tha thinking of?"

"Christmas Eve?" I said tentatively.

"Grand idea, some of 'em'll be going ter church late on so they'll not stop too long. If they come about six eh?

What'd be proper Lydia? Tha knows more about manners than me."

"No you're right, six o'clock is an ideal time to start a party."

Now, he was sorting out writing things and starting to write a list. Myself, I resolved to ride into town the very next day to arrange for my old dancing master to come out to teach the children to dance, and also find someone to play our little used harpsichord on the night. For I have to say we were not a very musical family, though Olivia could play a bit, as could Hugo. The only really musical one was Robert, who could pick out tunes by ear, but of course he was not there and it cut me deeply that he would not be part of our Christmas party. I had hoped he would return last August, but one of the crew of the "Fortitude" told Jack that Robert had docked at Dundee and sailed off, on another ship. So naught was known of him now.

Next day, at breakfast we announced the party and there were shrieks of excitement all round, even from Ben and Belle who tended to be low key about most matters. I thought it best to say at the start that there would be no new dresses, and that we would all be wearing our wedding clothes, for as such a large family, we were quite stretched already.

Over the next three days, Jacob struggled valiantly with the guest list; every family he visited insisted he take a drink or two and many of them asked if they could bring extra relatives who were staying for Christmas. So in the end the guest list seemed to stand at ninety-three, and Jacob assured me that at least eight of them were young single men, suitable for our main purpose, whereupon he climbed onto the bed, missed his tea and slept off the drink until the next day.

Myself, I had tracked down my old dancing master, who had seemed as old as the hills when I was a young girl of seventeen, but now seemed only about the same age as my husband. So, he agreed to come to the farm and stay for three days, as soon as Jack was home for the Christmas break and bring with him a Miss Turner (who I had not yet met) to play the harpsichord. Whilst in town, I popped into the draper's and bought a bundle of coloured ribbons so that our girls would at least have something new for the night of the party and also, yards and yards of cheap red ribbon for the decorations.

Lastly, I had to tackle Eliza with my menu list.

"Dear God," said Eliza looking at all the pies, cakes and meats, to be prepared.

"We'll all help with the baking, and Mary can make some sweets."

"Mistress, if they only has two sweets each, that's over two hundred ter be made and she's t' little ones ter look after as well."

"Well Eliza, they're all coming now, we cannot be turning people away."

She tutted and shrugged, but I knew from experience she would rise magnificently to the occasion.

To pacify her I added, "you concentrate on the food Eliza, with Janet, and Betty and Clara (our yearly hired girls) can do all the scrubbing and cleaning."

"And t' laundry?"

"And the laundry Eliza."

"Well…" she said doubtfully, but I knew she was largely placated. And no-one could put on a better feast than our dear Eliza.

Betty was more useful than I had imagined, adeptly sponging all our wedding clothes and carefully removing the stains, which it shames me to say, I had not yet done, even though it was full six months since our wedding. Then she set about starching and pressing the white dresses for the girls. Belle and Penelope sewed themselves charming little headbands covered with ribbon and with silk flowers sewn on. Penelope's was lavender and darkest red to nestle in her chestnut curls and Belle's was all in shades of pink to wind through her abundant dark hair like a Grecian headdress, which, of course was so very fashionable just then. Mother-in-law produced three beautiful antique fans, in carved ivory and painted vellum for the girls. Then, much time was spent practising fluttering and simpering behind their fans, Penelope tended to get the giggles but Olivia proved the most adept and despite being the youngest, seemed quite the most flirtatious, peeping artfully from behind her yellow, flower painted fan.

Two weeks later, the dancing master and Miss Turner arrived to coincide with Jack's return. I insisted that they rest after their journey and take refreshments before the lessons began, indeed, the dancing master seemed most precious and drained. I worried about how to feed him during his stay, as he had very conspicuous false teeth and I feared my children giggling mercilessly at him if he sat to table with us. As it turned out, he ate in his bedroom, taking only sponge biscuits dipped in strong wine, for the entire three days, so that was actually quite a relief. On the other hand, Miss Turner, a lady a little older than myself, proved a 'good sort' and the easiest of guests; she ate everything put before her with great enjoyment, adored all the children and entertained them with a selection of jolly songs, banged out on the harpsichord. As to her bedroom, she squealed with delight, thought it as big as a ballroom and said she would be so thrilled to sleep in it, as it looked like something out of "The Mysteries of Udolpho".

That very evening the dancing lessons began, Jack and Belle together, Ben with Penelope, and Olivia with a reluctant twelve-year-old George. Cotillions and reels were learnt; setting, moving up and down the sets, forming a ring, linking arms, clapping, bowing and curtseying were all rigorously practiced. Though none of them showed much enthusiasm for it, I was convinced they would love nothing more than dancing when they were part of the excitement of a proper Christmas party. On day two of the lessons, Olivia burst into tears and ran out of the room, George shrugged and said, "what have I done?"

"Olivia dear, what is it dear?" I said, chasing after her.

"George is treading on my feet on PURPOSE, and he's really hurt me," she sobbed.

"Olivia dear, you must learn the steps." I took out my handkerchief for her and put my arm around her. "Next year you will be fifteen, and two of my cousins were married at only fifteen…"

She stared at me in wonder, through her tears, "oh Mama, shall I be married next year?"

"No dear, for your uncle and I think fifteen too young to marry, but it may be that if a suitable young man wishes to court you…"

"Oh Mama, I should so love that."

"Well then, you had better learn to dance, for how sad would it be if a delightful young man asked you to dance and you did not know how?"

Back in the Great Hall, the dancing master was saying, "you must all try much harder, still you do not know your steps, still you are lumbering and not gliding, where is delicacy, where is refinement?"

Ben snorted and Jack turned away to conceal his laughter.

I looked desperately at Penelope and very valiantly, she said, "A shall dance with George myself, and if he treads on my feet just once, A shall slap him hard."

Thus Ben partnered Olivia, showing himself a very competent dancer I thought, and George was rather entranced to dance with his grown up, nearly eighteen-year-old cousin and behaved himself quite properly, from then on.

On the final day of the lessons, Ben turned away from Olivia and held out his hand to me, "Mama?" then swept me into the Cotillion, and so also swept me back into my youth.

I was quite breathless at the end (for as I said, I was with child) as Ben bowed low and I gave a deep curtsey.

"Oh Mama, what a good dancer you are," laughed Olivia clapping her hands.

Jacob looked at me quite boldly, "by A wish A could give thee a turn about t' floor, but me leg's too bad Darling."

"Can you dance Dearest?"

"Oh aye, A din't used ter be a bad dancer at all, years back, me and Benjamin was often at a Christmas or a Twelfth Night do and there were always dancing."

Now, the dancing master having completed his task, had his things packed as quick as thought and was fussing about his hired horse. Jacob paid him and invited him to take a drink, which he refused, saying he must leave at once.

After he had gone, Jacob laughed out loud glancing across at Ben and Jack, "we've a right molly-boy there, eh lads?"

They both grinned broadly but for myself I had no idea what he meant and had not time to ask for I was up to my eyes in baking by this time.

"Dearest, do you think two hundred is enough?"

"Two hundred what?"

"Mince pies."

"Darling, A could eat two hundred of thy mince pies meself, what about guests though?"

* * * *

Miss Turner stayed on with us, as the party was only the day after and she was a great help twisting together the great swathes of holly and ivy. We had to make up the wreaths and garlands in the barn, as the servants considered it unlucky to trim the house before Christmas Eve.

That evening she played patriotic songs and Jacob and the elder boys sang "Rule Britannia" twice over in powerful, manly voices; they smiled and laughed as they sang but it made me want to weep, for I still greatly feared the French coming and killing us all. The thought of my family being hurt in any way, cut me so and I had to take out my handkerchief.

"Come on Darling, tha's done too much today, tha needs ter rest up fer tomorrow." Jacob put his arm about my thickened waist, to help me along to our bedroom.

"Tha needs ter rest Mistress, get a bit of a lie in tomorrow. We've everything in hand now, keep thyself fresh for t' party like," said Eliza, who could often be very thoughtful.

The next day passed so quickly, as a day of party preparations always does. The beautiful green garlands were fixed up in the Great Hall, scenting the room with their Christmassy green smell, and the red ribbons were looped in along them. I twisted up a kissing ball of mistletoe and ivy with two little green pottery birds peeping out of it, to hang from the entrance hall lantern. Hugo fixed it for me, as stretching up my arms above my head was yet another thing I was not allowed to do in my condition.

"Eh, A'm not sure about that," said Jacob jokingly, looking up at it.

"Oh why not Dearest?" for I had been so pleased with it.

"Best try it out A'm thinking."

He pulled me tightly to him and kissed me deeply under the pagan green ball.

Releasing me, he laughed and said, "aye, it works grand, just grand."

Over his shoulder, I saw Belle staring at us, she seemed to have appeared out of the hallway panelling, but of course that could not be so. She looked rather flushed and I hoped she was not taking a fever.

"Belle dear, I need you to help set the big table with me."

"Yes Mama," she said meekly.

Together we put every knife, fork, spoon, plate and glass that we had, on the long table in the Great Hall, which had already been pushed against the wall and covered with two old red velvet curtains. Eliza and Janet brought in four great hams, two pressed tongues, fifty small pigeon pies and the same of rabbit, six huge pork pies, six roasted ducks and six chickens. A good selection of pickles, mustards and other condiments stood at one end and in the middle, a large plum cake all frosted to look like snow, ginger cakes, syllabubs and two of my favourite brandy tarts, plus of course the two hundred mince pies. Green pottery bowls held oranges and apples. I felt so proud of how well the cheeses I had made that year looked, all ready to be eaten with the plum cake and ginger cakes. Beneath the table were stashed thirty bottles of brandy and twenty of Geneva with port wine and Rennish wine too. A great Imari, antique bowl of warm punch stood near the Christmas cake; strong, for it was mainly brandy and wine, floating with oranges, lemons and bottled cherries and giving off a rich spicy scent.

This was not finished until nearly five o'clock so then we had to rush upstairs to wash and change. My dear husband looked just as fine as he had done on our wedding day; for myself, although my beautiful luteous silk was a loose style, it only just fitted now. Jacob had had to let out my stays for me again, kissing me softly between my shoulder blades as he did so. Betty had thoughtfully sewed a ribbon loop onto the train of my dress so that I could hold it up easily for the dancing.

Jacob admired the feast set out on the long table, "eh, our Eliza, tha's done us proud on this one, done us proud."

She carefully covered up the food with two spotless sheets to keep it fresh, her cheeks flushing with the compliment.

Then he caught sight of Penelope, "why daughter tha looks t' most beautiful lass in all t' world, more beauteous than sun and stars together." Now he was emotional.

"No Father," she laughed, "A've tried me best but in truth A'm too short and too plump."

"Nay," he shook his head, "tha looks lovely, if only thy mother could see thee now, she'd be that proud. A fine young woman tha looks."

She hugged him affectionately.

All our children looked their very best; it was difficult to choose the most handsome between Jack and Ben, so tall now, in their fashionable coats, very close fitting breeches, bright waistcoats, high collars and tight cravats; Jack sporting his fine gold fob watch. Both young men, leaning against the great fireplace and sharing some joke, for Ben had the same lively humorous sense as my brother Louis.

Belle, and I speak as a biased mother, had truly lived up to her name, never more so than today. She had trimmed the hem of her white muslin dress with three rows of twisted muslin, each wound around with a different shade of pink ribbon, matching in with the pretty pink Grecian head band, taming her abundant dark hair. About her neck was a black band and on her wrist a little gold bracelet, tied with more ribbon and hanging from it her dainty handkerchief. All carried with her tall and graceful elegance.

But there was no more time for sentimental thoughts, for now there was the clatter of horse's hooves outside the front door and the chatter of our arriving guests. At once the valiant Miss Turner started up on the harpsichord with some cheery tunes to precede the dancing and

Jacob and I positioned ourselves beside the front door with our daughters, to show them off to best advantage.

Jacob must have said more than thirty times, "Welcome, this is me wife Lydia, our daughters Penelope and Belle."

Hands were shaken, cheeks kissed and every suitable young man (and there were several) got a chance to get a look at our girls before going into the Great Hall.

At last, all had arrived and I was glad to move away from the front door and out of the December chill.

Everyone was in their finest clothes, drinking furiously and shouting to make themselves heard, until Jacob clapped his hands and announced that the dancing was to commence with a French Cotillion. At once they backed away to make a space in the centre of the room, and partners were chosen while Miss Turner filled the room with a dramatic musical flourish until the two rows of dancers were ready. Penelope was one of the first to be asked up by a jolly young man with a shock of orange hair; then a most elegant gentleman who would not have looked out of place in the Assembly Rooms of Bath partnered Belle.

Jacob forbade the boys to dance with their cousins and made them dance with any young ladies, who through plainness or shyness did not have a partner. This was not done without some reluctance, but Jacob insisted upon it.

In fact, he proved an exemplary host, no lady, young or old was left uncomplimented or with hand unkissed; no gentleman without a kindly word and a joke and no glass was ever left empty for more than a minute.

Hugo's task, which he did with the greatest charm and grace was to wait upon his Grandmama and a group of elderly guests, ensconced close to the fire. All of whom she knew well from the 'old days' and were having a high old time reminiscing and working out who was related to who. I smiled to overhear her whisper to an old man with a huge white beard and wig, that though she had no favourites amongst her eleven honorary grandchildren, that if her arm was twisted she would have to choose dear Hugo.

"Lydie dear," she said turning to me, "we keep too much to ourselves, we should do this every year," and all warmly agreed with her.

After nearly a full hour of dancing, Eliza and Janet uncovered the magnificent supper to gasps of delight.

The young man so enamoured with Belle, turned out to be a Mr Hartley Fairfax, a relative of the Fairfax's of Lockwood Beck Farm. He was new to the area and was in the process of having a house built for himself in the gothic style and had also bought a row of tenanted cottages nearby. Though he paid Belle every attention possible, she hardly glanced at him; I put this down to shyness for she had met few young men before.

After supper there was more dancing and young Mr Harrison, as he turned out to be, hardly left Penelope's side. He was either whispering in her ear and making her laugh or they were dancing together. I think I had forgotten to tell the girls that it was not good manners to dance with the same young man more than twice, but too late now.

Miss Turner proved tireless and after the more formal dancing, she launched into some country dances which the older guests could join in with, as well as the various children.

Towards the end Jack was at my shoulder, "dearest Aunt Lydie," his hand was held out to me, and he proved himself the most accomplished of dancers as he turned me around the dancefloor.

Our most very splendid evening finished as midnight was approaching, as Miss Turner banged out "Hark the Herald Angels" and "While Shepherds Watched". Finally, in a magical stillness, Jack sang solo the Latin "Adeste Fideles" just as my first husband had sung every Christmas of our marriage. Mother-in-law read my thoughts and squeezed my hand as he sang, but I had to swallow very hard to keep my composure.

Before we knew it, everyone was singing "We wish you a Merry Christmas," downing the last of the drinks, hugging and kissing and desperately searching for bonnets and cloaks. One of our guests kindly gave Miss Turner a ride back to town in his covered carriage.

My final triumph was when Mr Hartley Fairfax asked if he might visit Belle, of course Jacob and I said yes at once. Belle was not there at the time, but how could any woman not be pleased by such a charming, prosperous man? AND just as nearly everyone had left and I was frozen near stiff standing at the cold front door, Mr Harrison appeared, hand in hand with Penelope and asked if he might court her, as she was the most beautiful girl in the room. He'd clearly had a good bit to drink, and when we agreed to his courtship he swept Penelope under the mistletoe ball and kissed her in the most immodest way, wished us all a Merry Christmas and staggered out to find his horse. I knew not whether to be shocked or not, Jacob assured me, "he's a reet good lad is that one," and Penelope looked pleased enough.

Then, Eliza started fussing about my condition, and insisted I go straight to bed and she would bring me a hot posset. I could not argue with this for I felt beyond exhausted; and we left our poor servants to the clearing up and our sons to a heavy drinking session at the fireside.

As we lay in our bed that night, tired but too stimulated to sleep, Jacob said, "a success eh wife?"

"Oh yes, everyone seemed to enjoy themselves so, and we have two suitors for our girls, can you believe it." I sighed with triumph.

"A should bloody think so, they're both bloody beauties, A'm surprised there weren't more asking for 'em. And how's our little one with all this excitement?" He laid his hand tenderly on my stomach.

"Jacob dear, you would not believe this," I laughed to think of it, "but at one point I leant against the harpsichord and it was vibrating against me, and I will swear to God our baby was trying to dance. Do you think such a thing is possible?"

He said that he did, for the covering of the womb was not very thick and it would only be like pressing your hands over your ears, when you could still hear pretty well.

I had not thought of it this way, "my love you are so wise."

"A think not, but A do try."

Whereupon he rolled me over and rubbed my aching back until I fell to sleep.

CHAPTER 19

In which Lydia's matchmaking has mixed success.
The next day, (Christmas Day 1799).

Next day I got up rather late, to a quiet household, our older children were all at church, the younger ones in the nursery. Only Mother-in-law was sitting by the fire in the little winter parlour drinking tea, I fetched another cup and joined her. We had much sport discussing the fun of the previous evening, she laughed a great deal hearing of the antics of Penelope's suitor and said she had known Mr Harrison's grandfather when he was young, many years ago. But she surprised me, when I told her of Mr Fairfax's request to court Belle.

"And what did our Belle say to that?" she asked. I explained she had not been there at the time and she shook her head and said, "best ask Belle first, afore owt's settled."

I could not imagine why any girl would not welcome the advances of such a charming elegant young man, but I had no time to question, for at that moment, Eliza came in to ask me about the goose, which was proving particularly challenging this year and I had to go through to the kitchen, to see about it.

Much later we all sat down to a good dinner in the Great Hall; despite Eliza's worries, the goose was magnificent, served with three kinds of stuffing and all the usual accompaniments. Her grand finale was a huge plum pudding aflame with brandy and just as Jacob was saying he'd never survive till Twelfth Night with all this feasting, there was a sharp knock on the front door.

Eliza went through and returned a minute later, "it's that Mr Fairfax, Mistress," she sniffed.

I jumped up and ran into the hallway. "Why Mr Fairfax, what a very great pleasure."

He was carrying two exquisite nosegays, one of which he thrust into my hands; winter roses, sprigs of herbs and bright berries, all knotted in orange ribbon.

"A small thanks for your most delightful Christmas party and welcoming me as a newcomer so very warmly."

"Our pleasure indeed, Mr Fairfax."

He paused, then said, "I know you will all be busy as a family today but might I give this to Miss Curzon?"

Here he held up the second nosegay, which was even prettier, with stiff white lace enclosing delicate pink roses and pale pansies all tied and looped with silver ribbons.

"Why of course Mr Fairfax, I am sure Belle will be delighted."

I called Eliza and asked her to show Mr Fairfax into the winter parlour, and to bank up the fire and bring a tray of refreshments.

"Yes Mistress." For some reason she stared at our guest quite sullenly.

Back at the dinner table, I said, "come Belle, Mr Fairfax is waiting to see you in the winter parlour." I gave a smile of triumph to Jacob.

At once Jack got up and disappeared into the kitchen, which I thought little of at the time.

"Come Belle, do not keep him waiting, you can finish your plum pudding later."

A deep flush spread over her cheeks and she rose slowly from her chair and meekly said, "yes Mama."

I sat down again with a smirk of satisfaction.

Shortly after, as the table was being cleared, there was another knock at the door, and Jacob, who had peeped out of the window, grinned and said, "thy turn now Penelope."

"Really?" she smiled with delight.

Mr Harrison did not wait to be announced but walked boldly in, greeting us all in his easy friendly manner and presented me with a little chip wood box, stuffed with candied fruits and paper lace, thanking me for the grandest party.

"Come in lad," said Jacob shaking his hand, "get bi t' fire and warm thyself, shall it be a brandy?"

But Mr Harrison was hardly listening and went straight to Penelope's chair, helped her to her feet and kissed her hand.

"A small gift Miss Curzon," he said thrusting a roll of paper into her hand.

Carefully she unrolled it and looked up at him questioningly.

"After meeting thee last night, A could not sleep for thinking of thee, so A wrote thee a song."

A smile spread slowly across her face, in exactly the way her father smiled.

"May A play it for thee?" He indicated the harpsichord.

"Oh please do," she replied going over to it and standing by the stool.

Mr Harrison sat down, turned back his coat cuffs and glancing up at Penelope almost bashfully, played a most lilting melody and sang:

When first I saw Penelope,
How she did so enamour me.
I could not sleep, nor take no rest.
To North or South or East or West,
Dear Penelope is my best.

When first I saw Penelope,
I knew I never would be free,
To walk or run or roam or ride,
Without her always by my side
However much I truly tried.

They were both laughing as he sang on;
I've seen Penelope today,
And she has heard me sing and play,
I hope she'll look down from above,
And shall agree to be my love,
Forever my own turtle dove.

He finished with a huge flourish on the keys, stood up and bowed to his love.

We all clapped vigorously, indeed I had never seen so novel a courtship!

"Get t' lad a drink wife, he deserves one after all that effort," laughed Jacob.

We had run out of clean glasses and as the servants had worked so hard over the last few days, I went into the kitchen myself to fetch one.

There was Eliza, stripping the meat off the remains of the goose, she looked at me accusingly, "our Jack's reet upset."

"Why, what has happened?"

She stared at me as if I was a complete idiot, and snorting slightly said, "he's out in t' yard," indicating the half open back door.

I went straight to him and there he stood with his head resting against the wall, flushed with anger and not seeing me, he banged his fist hard against it.

"Dear Jack, what is it? Please tell me that I may help." I put my arm around him, but he drew away a little.

"I'm sorry Aunt Lydie, I'm just being childish." I saw tears in his eyes and dark blood oozing along the line of his knuckles.

"Are you remembering your dear mother at Christmas time, is that it?"

"No, Aunt Lydie, it's not, though I know I should be thinking of her, for she would tell me not to let anger get the better of me."

"What is it then?"

"I cannot tell you Aunt, but I have given myself to anger, when I should not. For I am a man now and should not behave in such a selfish way. I have been away many months, and it is wrong of me to expect things to be the same on my return. I am being unfair to another."

I had not the least idea what he was talking about, but I tied my clean handkerchief around his poor bleeding knuckles.

"I'm so sorry dear Aunt, I cannot tell you and it is best forgotten. May I have your confidence of seeing me so?"

"Of course you have Jack."

He allowed himself to be hugged and he blew his nose. I took his arm and we went back into the kitchen to find a clean glass for Mr Harrison. Eliza glared at me, but I had no time just then to concern myself with the whims of my servants.

* * * *

That evening my husband and I sat in our bedroom in our comfortable bed robes. We had a little fire against the cold and rested our feet upon the fender. Just as Jacob was about to say something, there was a tap at the door, thinking it was Janet with our hot stones for the bed, I called, "come in."

But it was Belle, "Mama may I speak with you please?"

"Of course dear, how went it with Mr Fairfax, he stayed a good long time, he seems a most charming man."

She said nothing but glanced at Jacob, whereupon he said he thought he'd left his book in the parlour.

"Sit down dear," I indicated the elbow chair, "and tell me what is troubling you, for I do not see a happy courted one in your face."

She sat down and stared at the floor, "Mama, I fear you will be angry."

"No dear," for God's sake, had I turned into my own mother?

"It's about Mr Fairfax…"

"He seems a most pleasant man, is he not to your liking?"

"It's not that, he is a nice man, but I cannot accept his advances."

"But why? I think he is ideal for you..." then I realised I was interrupting and not listening properly.

She looked up at me with her lovely dark eyes and sighed, "please do not be angry Mama... I love someone else and I have promised myself to him."

"Who is this man?" for I had no idea Belle had met any other suitors.

"It is Jack, Mama."

"Jack," I repeated as if I had never heard the name before, "what Jack Curzon?"

She nodded and looked at the floor again.

"You cannot marry Jack, for he has his studies to complete and then it may be many years before he gets a living and only then could he even think of marrying."

"I knew you would be angry Mama, that is why I have not told you of it before. I wanted to tell you but I feared your anger."

"How long has this been going on?"

"Five years."

"Five years?" my voice had risen in annoyance, "you were both only children five years ago, what kind of nonsense..."

I stopped myself suddenly, remembering the scene with Jack in the yard. How could I have been so stupid, not to have seen this going on right under my nose?

"No Belle, I am not angry in the least, you know I love Jack as much as any of you." Now, I chose my words most carefully, "but you must see it is not practical, he is not in a position to marry and it is a sad courtship that sees no nuptials in close sight."

"I am determined Mama, it is not a course I can turn from, not only because of my promise, but because of the love in my heart for him and only him."

"So, are we to let the fine Mr Fairfax escape from us?"

"Yes Mama."

"Have you told him this?"

"Yes, I have, but he seemed to think me playing artful and laughed and said he would write to me."

"Well if he does, you can write back firmly and plainly, so the thing is clear understood."

And thus I saw handsome Mr Fairfax slip away from us with his fortune and his half built white gothic house at Lockwood Beck.

Instead, I saw my most beautiful daughter, my first-born, alone and yearning for many years and then in some draughty vicarage. Though I own she would make a far better vicar's wife than I ever could have done, had her father followed his chosen path.

"You will have to have much patience and tenacity for this way you have decided upon, Belle."

"I believe I have it Mama."

"Your Uncle and I will help you all we can when Jack has taken Holy Orders, but in truth we will not have much after Ben reaches twenty-one and takes over the farm, we'll be quite stretched ourselves."

"I know Mama; I thank you for your kindness."

We hugged each other but there was a stiffness there.

"Everything sorted eh?" said Jacob coming in, he had clearly been listening from behind the door.

"Yes, Uncle Jacob, I thank you, and wish you good night." Quietly she left the room.

"Did you know aught of this?" I asked him crossly, when I had explained the situation.

He looked thoughtful and said, "years ago A saw them coming owter t' hall cupboard hand in hand, they didn't see me of course. A wondered if there were summat going on then."

"What cupboard, there isn't a cupboard in the hall."

"Yes there is, it's hid in t' panelling under t' stairs. Benjamin showed it me when we were just lads; t' Master and Mistress were away for a few days, so he let me come in t' house for a look around. He called it a priest hole; one o' t' Curzon's turned a Catholic, couple of hundred years back and they'd ter hide priest in there if t' king's men came for them."

"Oh," I said, lost for words by the whole thing. "But did you know Jack wanted to marry her?"

"Course not, else A'd have said wouldn't A, but if he loves her what else can he do? He's not been brought up ter tek advantage of a lass."

I shuddered at the thought, and he went on, "he's ter tek Holy Orders so he can hardly keep her as his mistress can he? Bloody Hell no. So all he can do is wed her."

I frowned, quite defeated by the whole thing.

"Come on now, lovliest wife, A'm thinking our little bairn needs ter be tucked up with his mama and getting a bit of sleep now. Shall A fetch some hot stones? A caught Betty bringing some up and A told her ter wait, A didn't think yer'd want to be interrupted like."

"Do you know, my Love, you are always so thoughtful and tactful."

He smiled and helped me into bed.

I think I have never known a more exhausting Christmas, before or since.

CHAPTER 20

In which Eliza trys to speak her mind.
Still Christmas Day 1799.

That Christmas day, I got crosser and crosser as the day went on. To start with I'd had hardly a wink of sleep the night before, we three servants were up till the small hours clearing up after the party. Though I say it myself, the food I did was the best it could be. And I will say the Mistress was good in that way, for every time one of the guests complimented her on the food, she said it was nothing to do with her, and all of my doing, which meant I got more than a few tips off some of the gentlemen. But I was that tired with it and to top it all young Master Ben and our Jack sat up late drinking and just as I finally thought I could get off up to bed, Master Ben's asking for cheese on toast. If our Jack had asked, I'd have said no, but of course I couldn't refuse the young Master, (for he'd be my employer, soon as he was twenty-one) and after they'd had it, they said it was that good, could they have some more and by this time it's nearly three o'clock. I didn't even undress that night, just lay in my bed in my clothes, for I'd to be up at six to put the goose on to roast. I was worrying about that, for there's always so much fat on a goose, which is nice for your potatoes but quite difficult to manage as it all runs out of the bird. But I'm ahead of myself, what had really annoyed me last night, was a Mr Fairfax, a Mr Hartley Fairfax, making sheep's eyes at Miss Belle from the moment he arrived at the party. Danced with her most of the night too, which even I know isn't proper. Of course our Jack couldn't dance with her, for our Jacob made him and Master Ben dance with all the ugly girls who couldn't get a partner, which was kindly of our Jacob but not much fun for the two lads. Anyways, to top it all, I was just helping old Mrs Folds find her bonnet and everyone was going home, when I heard Mr Fine Fairfax asking if he could court Miss Belle. And I could hardly believe my ears, when our Jacob and the Mistress both said 'yes' but clearly they had no idea that our Jack and Miss Belle have been courting together for years. But I've said this times many, once folks start reading books and that, all common sense goes right out of their heads. Our Jacob was fine till that Susannah taught him to read and as for the Mistress, she's always got her nose in a book, some of them in foreign words too. Though, I think the old Mistress has got a bit of an idea about our Jack and Miss Belle, she asked me about it once when I was helping her dress, but I said I didn't want to speak out of turn and she says, "quite right Eliza." But I've known a good many years there was something going on between the two of them, for they'd been meeting up in that cupboard in the hallway, the old Mistress once called it a 'priest hole', though for the life of me, I could not imagine what a priest would be doing in it, for none of the Curzons were Romans to my knowledge. Anyways, I could hear the two of them in there some days, because the cupboard backed onto the game pantry, and when I was in there seeing to the game birds and rabbits and so forth I could hear them

on the other side of the wall. None of the other servants
ever went in there, so knew naught of it. Of course
they'd speak too soft for me to hear their words, but my
heart ached for Miss Belle when her father suddenly
died and I could hear her sobbing her heart out in there
with our Jack. She'd no comfort from her own mother,
as the Mistress spent weeks shut up in her bed chamber
with her dogs and her grief, and barely spoke a word
to anyone. How those two dogs relieved themselves,
I never did find out, for the door was often bolted all
day long. So Christmas day, I finally got that goose
served and for all my worrying it looked as good as
could be. I did it with a pork and marjoram stuffing, a
chestnut stuffing and a sage and onion stuffing, I did
plenty of slivers of potato fried in the goose fat, which
crisped up beautifully, to decorate it with and a great
pile of ordinary roasted potatoes. So when I'd brought
in the best flaming plum pudding you've ever seen, the
Mistress and our Jacob said I was not to lift a finger
again until the morrow. They meant it kindly, but of
course I'd all the farm servants' dinners to do next.
Then would you believe, Mr Fine Fairfax turns up with
bunches of flowers; where he got fresh flowers from at
this time of year, I've no idea. I had to take him a tray of
Madeira wine, Christmas cake and mince pies, (lucky
there were any left, for, I will say the Mistress makes an
excellent pastry, having naturally cool hands). So I take
it all into the winter parlour and there he is, fawning
over Miss Belle. Pretty as a picture she is, the colour of a
beetroot and staring at the floor, but I know men, and
they find that sort of thing encouraging. I should have
liked to have slapped them both and shouted out, "what
about our Jack?" but instead I just pretended to fuss

with the fire so I could listen in a bit longer. And Mr Fine Fairfax was a right show-off, going on about his carriage and his new house, and our Jack is the best of lads, handsome as his father, kindly and loving, working so hard with his studies and that. The old Mistress has said to me many a time, there's no lad, more goodly and honest than our Jack. When I gets back to the kitchen, Betty whispers that Jack's run through into the yard with a face like thunder, so I takes a quiet peep around the yard door and our Jack's leaning on the wall crying. Well no lad likes to be caught crying so I thought I'd leave him be a minute or two, so I carried on stripping the goose. Next thing the Mistress sweeps in, for she's wanting a glass, as there's another gentleman caller here now, would you believe. I was that angry by this time, I spoke plain to her and said our Jack was upset, she looked at me in such amazement, I could barely credit it. Now she goes off into the yard and before you know it, she's back in, arm in arm with our Jack and her handkerchief tied around his hand. I had to sit down now and take a good glass or two of port, just to calm myself, I was that over wrought with it all. Betty said she'd finish the washing up and I was to sit by the fire and rest up a bit. (I will say she's shaping up well is Betty). Goodness, then I nodded right off to sleep, for I'd hardly sat down once in the last two weeks and my legs were killing me. When I did wake up, I was annoyed with myself for falling asleep, for I like to keep a close eye on young servants, but I have to say everything looked neat enough and nothing amiss. Janet said that Mr Fairfax had just left and Miss Belle had run up to her room looking as if she were going to cry. Well that was my cue, I swigged down what was left of my port and ran up the back stairs, for I was furious now and ready to speak my mind to her, for playing false with our Jack. I knocked sharp on her door and walked straight in. When I saw her, well I do own, my heart did soften up a bit, for she was sitting on the bed, crying her eyes out, but I said I wanted to speak plain to her and sat down next to her. Before I could say another word, she threw herself into my arms, sobbing loudly.

"Oh Eliza," she says, "I don't know what to do, Mr Fairfax wants to court me and now Jack won't speak to me..." Then she couldn't go on for weeping.

"Look Miss, A know what's going on wi' thee and our Jack, A know yer've been meeting up in t' cupboard like, for years now."

She looks at me in astonishment, "but how could you know that Eliza? We were always most careful, though we will not be going in there again, for Jack will not even look at me now, he is so angry."

"Well Miss, A swear on me life A never eavesdropped nor owt, but that cupboard backs on ter t' game pantry and A've been aware of t' two of yer in there many a time ovver t' years. And A'm not blind Miss, A've seen t' way he looks at thee, and it's not t' way of cousins, that's for sure."

"What am I to do Eliza? My mama is going to make me accept Mr Fairfax's courtship, I know she'll make me marry him and Jack will go back to Cambridge and forget all about me, for there's lots of pretty girls there, that throw themselves at the students, hoping for a husband."

"Miss, there'll not be a single one half as pretty as thee, that A do know." When God gave out good looks, He gave a double portion to her, that's for sure.

"I'm so unhappy, this is the worst Christmas I've ever had, I wish myself dead."

Now I knew you had to be careful with this sort of thing with youngsters; there was a young lass in the town as hanged herself because she thought she'd been deserted by her lover and it turned out he hadn't let her down, but the poor lad had been taken by the Press Gang. Of course closer to home, many years ago, young Robert Curzon drank himself to death after his wife died. So I acted careful now, indeed seeing Miss Belle so distressed made me want to cry myself, she always was my favourite (after my cousin Jacob's three of course). I dried her tears on my apron and hugged her tight.

"Eliza, I have never told anyone this but I have promised to marry Jack, when he has taken Holy Orders and has a living. How can I do that with Mr Fairfax so eager and Mama thinking he's so marvellous?"

"First, does thy mama know what's going on between thee and our Jack?"

She shook her head.

"So tha must tell her straight off and even if she's angry, A know our Jacob'd niver mek thee do owt against thy will."

She sniffed on the back of her hand.

"Come along Miss, wash thy face and go and tell thy mama now, its best ter get difficult things owter t' way, then they're not hanging ovver thee like a nasty cloud."

"Will Jack forgive me? I did not mean to wrong him ever."

"Course he will Miss, there's no lad more steady and loving than our Jack, he's just feeling hurt, but it's nowt ter stand between yer. In fact, his anger shows his true love for thee otherwise he'd not be so bothered, would he?"

She washed her face and disappeared off to her mama's room. I didn't know what the Mistress would make of it, but later that evening, Jack and Belle were nowhere to be seen, so I do own, and may God forgive me, I went in to the game pantry and put my ear against the wall and smiled to myself for it was not the words of quarrelling I heard.

Two or three days later I was dusting the summer parlour when the old Mistress came in on our Jack's arm, chatting away.

"Shall A light a fire for thee Mistress?"

"Nay, Eliza, for we'll only be in here a few minutes". Then she adds conspiratorially, "our Jack's going to choose a ring for our Belle, though he's not going ter ask her formal like till Easter. Spring's a good time for an engagement dun't tha think Eliza?"

"Definitely Mistress."

Then she gives our Jack the key to the fancy cabinet where the Curzon jewel box is kept. I pretended to carry on dusting, but really I was sneaking a peep into the box. Of course I'd seen it a time or two before but it had always fascinated me.

"Nowt too bold Jack, A'm thinking Belle'd want summat dainty. What's tha think Eliza, for tha's Jack's family too?"

So now I had a good excuse to go over and take a proper look. There must have been twenty rings in there, all in neat rows between long velvet strips. Jack was hesitant, so the Mistress picked out a pretty ring of dark pink stones alternated with pearls.

"These are pink garnets, Belle's fond of pink and it's not too showy, but it'll show thy intention clear. What's tha think Eliza?"

I said I thought it just right.

Jack flushed and said "thank you so much Grandmama, do you think she will like it?"

"Nay lad," she tapped him lightly, "A cannot do thy courting for thee, tha knows if it's right one or not," she laughed.

"Thank you Grandmama, I think that it is," and he kissed her hand.

So the ring was put into its separate little box inside the main jewel box at the ready for when Jack came back for the Easter break.

When I was young, more than thirty years since, when I do admit to be truthful, I had hopes for myself and our Jacob, but of course, it came to naught for he never noticed me in that way. In fact, he once told me he thought of me more like a sister than a cousin; though he meant it kind, it was not what I wanted to hear and I wept over him many a night after that. In truth it seemed over the years that he would rather lay with any woman, so long as it wasn't me. Anyway, at this time, when we were young, our Jacob and Master Benjamin took me into the town a time or two to see plays at the theatre and one was "All's Well That Ends Well." I liked that title (though I could not make head nor tail of the play itself) and always remembered it, so on this day I can truly say "all's well that ends well."

CHAPTER 21

In which the eldest daughters become betrothed,
and a new member arrives in the Curzon family.
1800.

And so after the Christmas party, everything quickly
settled back to normal routines, as it always must when
running a farm. Even though it was such an important
New Year, we celebrated quietly and for Twelfth night
we were invited to a take a good dinner with old Mr
and Mrs Harrison. They had two daughters, as well as
Penelope's intended. The whole family were as musical
as their son, and we were thoroughly entertained after
the dinner with fiddle and pipe playing and the singing
of many comic songs.

Mr Harrison's courtship of Penelope proceeded
apace, he proposed in March, with the wedding set for
June, by which time my forthcoming confinement
would be well over.

Belle and Jack openly wrote copious letters to each
other, with great ease now, for at last we had a proper
post office in the town. When Jack came home for the
Easter break, he was summoned into the summer
parlour by mother-in-law and the Curzon jewel box
was produced; it seemed a pretty pearl and garnet ring
had already been chosen previously, and after church on

Easter Sunday and in front of the whole family settling down for dinner, Jack dropped on one knee, asked Belle to marry him and slipped the ring upon her finger.

"Did she say yes?" questioned Ben, "what did she say?"

"I said 'yes' a year since," she said smiling quietly.

Not wishing to steal their moment, I suddenly stood up and sat down again, for I felt most strange.

"What is it Lydia?" asked Jacob anxiously.

"I don't quite know; I just feel strange."

He got up, limped down the length of the table and put his arm about my shoulders and said softly, "is it thy time Lovie?"

I laughed and frowned at the same moment, "oh Jacob, that's what you always say to the horses and cows." He looked slightly hurt, but helped me to my feet again.

"Best lie down Mistress," fussed Eliza, "A'll fetch thee a hot drink."

I made it to the end of the corridor to our downstairs bedroom with Jacob's arm about my waist, but as I approached the bed, I found myself standing in a pool of water.

"Bloody hell wife, we'd best get that Mrs Vye sent for."

Janet appeared with my coffee.

"Janet, Mrs Vye, quick as tha can, then rags and towels and a bit of warm water."

"Yes Master."

I clutched the bed post, while he rolled off the fine bed coverings, spread towels for me to lie on and helped me onto the bed.

A pain was coming now, but as I gasped, Jacob pushed me onto my side, and placing his hand on my back, the warmth of it shot through me and my pain soaked away.

"Is it coming?"

"Tha tell me Darling, tha's one as knows."

Eliza bustled in with all the necessaries, followed by Belle and Penelope, who said, "Aunt we would like ter be with thee to assist."

"But you are both so young and not yet married," I protested.

"We have discussed it Aunt and we wish ter do it" she said firmly. "Besides, we are both betrothed, and also have seen all sorts of baby animals born."

"Can't do no harm," said Jacob, gently pushing up my knees. I badly wanted to push. "Belle get behind thy mama and hold her shoulders up, that's it lass, kneel on t' bed. That's it, look now our Penelope, there's his little head coming now."

Despite the intensity of my feelings, I was amused to see Penelope's face, for she looked as if her eyes might pop right out of her head. Next thing our baby shot into the world, shiny, red and screaming. Jacob held her up. "It's a girl, my Lydia, a girl."

Penelope clapped her hands in delight.

"Our Penelope, shall tha cut thy sister's cord," He tied it and handed her the scissors.

"Father, will it not hurt?"

"Nay lass, for that bit's all dead and useless now."

The darling baby was put in my arms "Oh Jacob," I said in wonder and love, "you wanted a son."

"No A didn't, A wanted a girl."

"But I th…"

223

"No, A wanted a girl," he said firmly, "A wanted two lads and two lasses, and that's what A've got now."

Then I remembered that the still born baby he had lost, eighteen months since, had been a girl.

Eliza was there now with a heap of baby clothes, "eh Mistress tha's not been half an hour start ter finish. Shall A tek her ter wash and dress her Mistress?"

Our baby protested loudly at this, despite the hushings and kissings of her sisters. Janet poked a little fire into life, for there had not been time before and my afterbirth was put in a covered dish.

Jacob cleaned me most tenderly and intimately, I caught Eliza staring hard at him, but I could not guess at what she might be thinking.

"Can we call her Lydia?" asked Jacob.

"Absolutely not, I hate my name."

"Ahh, it's such a pretty name, A thought that first time ever A met thee. A'd niver heard it afore and liked it so much."

"What was your mother's name dearest? You've never said."

"Martha-Jane, she were called Martha-Jane."

"I like that...she looks like a Martha-Jane," I said, staring at my baby and looking up into Jacob's proud face.

"Then Martha-Jane it is, me mother had thick dark hair like that."

"I thought the pains would be worse Mama?"

"Eh, tha should have heard her, t' night tha were born Belle, screamed bloody house down for hours, eh my Love?"

"Oh Jacob," I said crossly, slapping his arm lightly.

But both Belle and Penelope looked mildly shocked.

THE FARM ON THE MOORS

Soon after, all our children trooped in to see their new sister. Belle took the baby and showed her first to Jack, "our sister," she said.

"Our sister," he said, touching her tiny hands as he gazed into Belle's eyes. My heart ached for them, knowing it would be so many years for them to wait to hold their own baby. My heart ached for my Robert too, who could know naught of his fourth sister. Still nothing had been heard from him; Jacob assured me often that 'no news was good news,' but I longed for words, just to know he was still alive.

At last, Mrs Vye arrived, and the younger ones were sent out of the room, "dear me Mr Curzon, beaten me to it again." Hanging up her cloak, she went on, "A know tha delivered that great big lad of thine, and then a girl…" she looked about the room.

"That was me, Mrs Vye," laughed Penelope.

"And tha's another son, han't tha?" she frowned, "tha must've delivered him, for A know A did not." She was not really listening for she was examining me, but an awful silence fell, for of course none of us knew how dear Hugo had made his way into this world.

"We have called her Martha-Jane, after Mr Curzon's mother, Mrs Vye." I said brightly.

"Now that is a nice name," (which is what she always said, whatever name we chose), "so all's well down there, and…" she peeped in the covered bowl, "everything just as it should be, I compliment thee Mr Curzon. Tha'll be teking my job next," she joked.

"Nay, A think not, horses and cows is more my line."

CHAPTER 22

In which Lydia plays matchmaker again.
1801.

My cousin Ann was a pretty sweet girl, now twenty-six, I feared she might never find a husband, not that she lacked either looks or inclination, in truth I think she would have liked nothing more than a good husband and a few children. Her problem being, that she was slightly deaf, due to many colds and earaches in her childhood; fine if you faced her and spoke up, but she could not take part in a lively conversation of quick repartee. And a bit of flirtatious banter is always required in a courtship.

She lived, as she had always done in the house next to ours on Baxtergate with my cousin Margaret who had turned, I fear, into a snappish spinster. Their parents, my beloved Aunt and Uncle had been dead years now and had passed, as many very loving couples do, within a few days of each other. The two sisters lived quietly alone with just one servant. Ann's days seemed to consist of needlework sitting in a chilly parlour, or staring out of the front window at the busy street. They clearly had little money, the bulk of my Uncle's estate, having been left to his only son, who was currently away, involved in these tedious French wars.

"Bye, she's a sharp one is that cousin Margaret," said Jacob mildly after we had dropped in for tea one day.

Margaret had been annoyed by our darling little Martha-Jane who had left sticky marks on the window glass when she was looking out at horse in the street. Margaret had told her to stop touching the window and as Martha-Jane turned around, she lost her balance (for she was only fifteen months old) and grasped the curtain in her dear little hand. And, I hardly need add, the curtain rail came down, the curtain fell on top of Martha-Jane and she roared her head off.

"Really Cousin, can you not control your child better?" Margaret had said tartly. "I feel a little discipline would not go amiss."

Poor Ann, clearly mortified silently mouthed, "sorry" to me.

"A'd we best mek tracks wife?" Jacob had said, gulping down the last of his tea and picking up our youngest, who was still wailing pitifully. "A'll get young Ben ter call in tomorrow ter fix up t' rail like, he's grand with owt like that, no problem."

"Hmm," snorted Margaret, "It will have to be the morning, for I always go to the subscription library on a Wednesday afternoon."

"Morning it is Margaret, no problem."

* * * *

"Ann did look sad today, do you not think, my love?" I said much later on, as we lay in our bed.

"Aye, she's not got much of a life 'as she; mind A don't suppose it's much a ball of laughs for thy cousin Margaret either." Jacob always saw both sides of any situation. "Why not ask her out here for a couple of weeks, give her summat different ter look at owter t' window. At least we're not boring, we could give her a bit of fun eh?" He added, "A wun't be keen on having cousin Margaret out here though, A'd feel A'd ter mind me place all t' time. She's such a tartar, bit of t' ilk of thy mama, not wishing ter speak ill of t' dead."

"I shall write to her to invite her, and Ben can take it in with him tomorrow. Would you bring her back on the cart, when you go in next week? I don't think I could face another visit there just yet."

He nodded, "be glad to Darling," and he tenderly kissed me goodnight.

So that was settled, and Ann arrived the following week, with a small shagreen trunk and hatbox. She looked around, mesmerised and delighted, for it was several years since she had visited us at the farm.

She was an easy guest, requiring little entertainment, spending her days in the nursery playing with Martha-Jane who was at an enchanting age learning to talk and run around, and valiantly tackling the mountains of mending and sewing required by our very large family. At the end of two weeks she had made six beautifully stitched shirts for George, Frederick and Francis, (all away at boarding school now) and three pretty new caps for our girls. I felt I had put upon her kindness enough and after a brief discussion with my dearest husband it was decided that we should all have a day out in Guisborough and get some shopping.

"There is the most interesting book shop there now, and of course Mcrae's draper's, I'd like to buy Ann a pretty dress length, for she's dressed very dull. What do you think, my love? Nothing too expensive though."

"Grand idea, we can still afford a bit of cloth eh."

For things were harder now than they had been for farmers due to this endless war, some country folk found it difficult to manage at all. As for us, we still had a prosperous well run farm but we also had a large family and had to be much more careful now than twenty years ago, when we mostly bought pretty much what we liked. Generally now, it was a case of reusing and mending where we could.

"John Mcrae's looking a bit more himself now, but he was owter sorts some while after his wife died…"

"That's good to hear," though to be honest, I was hardly listening, as I was making a shopping list. Olivia needed new stays, for we had none fit to hand down, Mary needed tapes, pins and a length of calamanco, Mother-in-law needed her glasses repaired and I needed to get birthday gifts for George and Octavia. So that was actually quite a number of things to do on our little trip.

So off we set, the following day, Jacob, myself, cousin Ann, Olivia and Belle. We had to travel quite slowly, for Ann was not an experienced rider and it was a fair way, thus our first port of call on arrival was the Fox Inn, where we took the most excellent dinner and more than a few drinks too. Then to the oculist, and after that we spent ages in the bookshop where there were many things to tempt, but we decided we had to postpone the buying of any more titles for the moment. I chose a huge box of sweets for George's birthday as he was a lad fond of eating and lastly to the drapers.

Mr Mcrae was serving in the shop himself and I said I hoped he was keeping well and introduced Ann. Straight away his two daughters were brought through to help Olivia choose a serviceable set of stays. Both of them wore extravagantly pretty dresses, I imagine they saw themselves as advertisements for their father's shop. Meanwhile Mr Mcrae showed us many bales of dainty printed cottons and Ann, most appreciative of the attention, chose one, all in shades of blue with small touches of green. When Mr Mcrae turned to cut the fabric she stared at him quite hard as she put her gloves back on.

"Mr Mcrae, our little Octavia is going to be six soon, do you have something pretty for her, not too expensive I'm afraid?"

Rose, the elder daughter, pointed to some little straw bonnets, trimmed with baby rosebuds.

"Ah them's sweet, Lydia," smiled Jacob, who had just joined us, "she'd be so bonny in one of them. Our bairn should have one too."

"Are you sure dear?" I asked thinking of the money.

He nodded, and after we had everything packaged up and put to our account, Jacob stayed behind in the shop a minute or two, I assumed to catch up with his friend Mr Mcrae. But when he finally came out, he had a little parcel in his hand, which he quickly stuffed in his pocket and tapped his nose to indicate I should not ask about it.

So we had another drink and some hot chocolate to set us up for the journey home for the weather had turned quite chill. All felt we'd had a thoroughly good day out.

The next day, Jacob and I were sitting talking in the summer parlour, when we heard the sound of a horse arriving and then a bold knock at the front door.

Next thing Eliza came in, looking rather flustered, to announce a visitor, Mr Mcrae.

"He's a black man," she whispered to me.

"Thank you Eliza, we know who he is, please show him in," I said.

"Eh, John," said Jacob, rising to welcome him, "this is a surprise, but a good one, shall tha tek a drink." Already he was pouring them.

Mr Mcrae bowed to me, "please excuse me Mistress Curzon for imposing upon your time, but I know not how else to plead my cause."

He had a delicious deep booming voice and had not lost his rolling American accent one jot over the years.

"Nay man it's a treat ter see thee," said Jacob.

"Please do be seated dear Mr Mcrae, and pray tell of your cause."

I truly had no idea of what could be troubling him, I knew it could not be money matters for it was well known he was one of the most prosperous tradesmen in the area. I indicated the fireside chair opposite me.

He was dressed in a green figured wool coat of the very best quality, close fitting with a stand up collar, in the latest cut. His tall beaver hat with a toning green silk ribbon around it was still in his hand, his frizzed hair was caught neat at the nape; he looked as fashionable and fine as could be.

He sat opposite me with his elbows on his knees and stared at me, which of course gave me a chance to look at him. His coal black skin was as smooth as a twenty-year old's, though I knew he must be past fifty now, eyes so dark you could not distinguish the pupils, in all a most handsome man, with a most dazzling smile. Though he was not smiling now and looked more than a trifle nervous.

"Mistress Curzon, again I do beg your pardon for intruding in your most lovely home and upon your time...I have come about your cousin Miss Walker..."

Then, at long last, I realised what he was going to say.

"I have come to ask if Miss Walker has an understanding with anyone? Or if you would consider permitting me to court her. As you know it is nearly two years since my dear wife passed... and I do not wish to sound vulgar, but your cousin's great beauty has caught my eye."

Indeed, Ann did have a look of the first Mrs Mcrae with her small neat figure, golden curls and blue eyes.

"Well Mr Mcrae, what a surprise... I had no idea," I continued in my brightest tone, "perhaps you will let me discuss this with my cousin and she will write to you one way or the other. What say you husband?"

"Aye, aye that's well enough."

Mr Mcrae gulped down his drink, "I'll trouble you two very good people no more and I thank you for your consideration of this matter...and of your kindness to me."

He said this last phrase with meaning and sadly I knew he meant because he was a negro.

He shook my hand and Jacob walked him to the front door, saying with a bit of a nudge, "hope ter see thee here again, quite soon man."

Eliza closed the front door after him.

"Eliza," I said firmly, "please remember when a gentleman calls, always take his hat from him and place it on the hall table and return it to him upon his departure."

"Yes Mistress," she said with unusual meekness.

To be honest, we were often far too casual with our servants, sometimes they were too quick to express their opinions and forget their place, and as now, their duties.

Jacob was full of it as we went back into the parlour, he shut the door firmly in case Eliza should be lurking still.

"Well, well my Lydia, what's tha mek of that then?" He took me in his arms.

"Truly I had no idea, I thought we were just shopping yesterday."

"Sounds like tha bought more than tha expected eh, a good parcel of romance along with all t' rest."

I had to laugh, "now I think of it, they both looked at each other more than would be usual and he did glance at her left hand when she took off her gloves to look at the stuffs."

I cupped his face in my hands and kissed him, he dropped his hand over my buttocks and called me beloved wife.

"Will it be all right?" I questioned, suddenly feeling responsible.

"Oh aye, he's a reet good lad is John."

"Jacob, you say that about everyone."

"No A dun't, he is a reet good lad, and A'd lay me life on it."

Thus I went upstairs to fetch Ann, who was in the nursery, busy remaking one of Olivia's outgrown print dresses to fit Octavia.

"What is it Lydie?" she asked, as we went downstairs.

I just smiled at her, until we were back in the parlour.

"Well our Ann," said Jacob loudly, "we've had a bit of an offer for thee."

Feeling that made her sound like one of our cows, I said, "sit down Ann," and she sat in the same chair her suitor had sat in five minutes before. "Ann dear, Mr Mcrae has just called."

"Mr Mcrae?" I think she thought she had misheard me.

"Yes, Mr Mcrae from the draper's yesterday in …"

"Yes, yes Cousin, I know who Mr Mcrae is." She looked at me very directly and I saw the smallest flush rise in her cheeks.

"I don't know if you have thought of this, but he has asked if he might court you."

"Oh has he? Has he really? Is he quite serious?"

"I am most sure he is, but there are some things you must consider before you answer him."

"What things?"

"Well for a start he is past fifty, twice your age."

"I don't mind that Lydie, for he looks a great deal younger."

That was certainly true; I went on, "you know he has two daughters, not so much younger than yourself, Rose and, and…something or other. Jacob what is the other one called?

He shrugged, "A know one of them's Rose".

"And if things ran their full course, then you would be stepmother to them and that can be a challenge sometimes." Though on thinking about it, I always found my stepchildren a deal easier to manage than my own children.

"They seemed very nice girls to me."

"And the other thing is," I hesitated searching for the right words. "Mr Mcrae, well many years ago he was once a slave, bought and sold, in the Americas, for seven or eight years I believe, before he got his freedom and came to live here."

She frowned, "he surely cannot be blamed for that, it cannot have been his fault, and…and I should not shirk to know more of it."

There was naught else to say except, "Ann, he is a black man."

"Again Cousin, you cannot blame him for that, besides," and here she looked at the floor, "I rather think I do like his blackness."

"Settled then wife," said Jacob loudly, "we said tha'd write to him ter let him know one way or t' other. Ben's up that way on Friday, he can drop t' letter in for thee, if tha wants."

"Please," she nodded, "and I shall write to him now for I have already decided." Here she laughed a most girlish laugh and almost skipped back upstairs to her room.

"Will it be all right Jacob?" I asked anxiously. "What do you think her parents would have said, if they had lived to see this day?"

"A do know, they were both abolitionists and strong on it. Besides Ann's of age and can marry who she pleases. It's not like she's a young chick no more. One thing A will say, is dun't mention any of this ter cousin Margaret, not till it's more settled like."

I nodded thoughtfully.

"Any road wife tha's done reet well wi' matchmaking, our Penelope wed, Jack and Belle promised, Ann getting fixed up and A've a bit of a feeling about Olivia and Mr Fairfax."

"Really, my love, do tell." For only the previous week we'd all been to a party where Mr Fairfax had danced twice with Olivia and then taken her into the supper. But nothing had been said afterwards.

"Oh aye, A'm surprised he's not been a knocking at the door wi' a bunch or two of roses afore now."

"Oh do you think? I should be so pleased, he is so handsome and charming, it was a wrench to think he'd slipped between our fingers, when Belle turned him down, the Christmas before last. Such a fine catch."

* * * *

So two weeks later Mr Hartley Fairfax DID come knocking at the door, with the predicted bunch of roses, asking for Olivia. (He'd been away on business since the night of the party) and they were married the following year and then took a luxurious, six-month honeymoon in Bath, with no expense spared.

Ann stayed with us, never returned to Baxtergate and was married from our house, after a brief three-month courtship which took place mainly in our own gardens and parlours. Of course her groom provided her with the most gorgeous of bridal dresses, the heaviest quality cream silk embroidered with forget-me-nots and tiny rosebuds, made up with a long train. Quite the most exquisite dress imaginable. Whenever we saw Ann after the wedding, she was dressed in the finest of clothes, was worshipped by her husband and wanted for nothing. Most important of all she was clearly blissfully happy, and her husband's loud deep voice suited her exactly.

As predicted, Cousin Margaret was very cross about the whole thing.

And what with all this fervent matchmaking, I forgot to tell what was in the package that Jacob had bought at Mr Mcrae's. That same night as we prepared for bed, he had drawn it from his pocket.

"Dearest wife, A feel A never courted thee, for we were so quickly wed, this is ter show my very great love and eternal admiration for thee."

I tore open the tissue paper to reveal a bunch of scented velvet violets with green velvet veined leaves and fastened with a striped silk ribbon. I treasured them greatly and wore them always, pinned either to my best bonnet or pinned to my evening dress depending on the occasion.

CHAPTER 23

In which Martha-Jane sees a polar bear.
1803.

We dug out decent clothes from the back of the clothes press and Janet expertly pressed and sponged them for us. We rarely dressed up or went out anywhere now, but I have to say we looked smart as pins by the time we were ready on this day. Myself in a navy blue riding skirt with a short purple jacket and a dark blue bonnet with the velvet violets pinned on one side; Jacob in his dashing wedding outfit of four years before with a new beaver hat (from Mcrae's where we now got the most ridiculously large discounts on all our purchases). Our dear little Martha-Jane in a long red coat with a red striped dress underneath and what Jacob called her "Yorkshire Pudding" cap, which puffed up on her head over her straight dark hair. As to Octavia, she looked a picture in shades of green, her short jacket bound in tartan silk and fastening with fifteen tiny silk covered buttons and a neat little brown bonnet.

"My Mistress, tha looks fine today, wherever are yer all off to?" asked Eliza.

Before I could answer, Martha-Jane piped up, "going to see a baby poly bear."

"Dear me what a thing," laughed Eliza, kissing her. She always made a particular fuss of Martha-Jane, on account of her being a blood relative and as she quoted, at least once a week, "blood being thicker 'n water like".

"Yes Eliza, one of the sea captains has brought back a polar bear from Greenland, just a baby one I think and it swims in the harbour every day at three o'clock."

"Well A never," said Eliza clearly impressed, helping Octavia on with her gloves. Unfortunately, the gloves were too small and when Eliza tried to pull the fingers down, two of them burst open.

"Mama, my gloves are much too small," Octavia said crossly.

"No matter, we shall buy some more when we get into town; leave these ones with Eliza and then Mary can get them mended up for Martha-Jane."

Octavia rode with me, which meant Martha-Jane rode with her father and he had to put up with her wriggling and shouting, though he never seemed to mind in the least and just laughed about it.

We arrived in good time and took an excellent dinner of the tenderest beef with batter puddings and roasted beetroots. We had a couple of bracing brandies each, for riding with young children is always taxing. Our little ones had cups of small ale too. Martha-Jane could barely eat for excitement and asked over and over again when we could see the baby polar bear.

"Not while three o'clock Martha-Jane, A've told thee five times or more already."

"Dada, where is the baby poly bear now?"

"Sleeping in its little house."

"Where is its little house Dada?"

"Don't know Darling."

"How do you know it's there then Dada?"

Defeated, Jacob did not answer, but he caught my eye and smiled.

"Anyway," I said, "we have to get poor Octavia some more gloves first."

As it turned out, we had to purchase two pairs for Martha-Jane had lost hers somewhere between the inn and the market place. Search as we might we could not find them anywhere, I supposed they would make a lucky find for some poor person.

"See the baby poly bear now Mama?"

"No Martha-Jane. Not yet." I took Octavia's hand firmly, and went into the draper's. Leather gloves were expensive, but they had to be had, for we could not have our daughters looking like fisher folk urchins.

Quite a crowd had gathered by the quayside, and straight away our girls, newly gloved and hand in hand pushed their way to the front. I prayed God they would not slip through the rickety railings, for we could not get to them, with so many people in our way. Jacob clearly thought the same and called out to a somewhat shabby fisherman standing near them, "Bob, watch our lasses for us will tha," pointing to them.

"Aye man, will do."

Whereupon I saw him hold each of them firmly by their little collars and I gave a sigh of relief.

And right then, the baby polar bear was led out on a long chain, with a wide metal collar about its neck and shoved unceremoniously into the water. It dutifully swam up and down in short lengths, restricted by its clanking chain. The crowd clapped and a nasty boy threw a stone at it, which fortunately missed the poor creature. After a time, it was dragged from the water, it took two men to pull it out, for it was a heavy beast; growling and struggling it was heaved onto the harbour side and led away.

I turned my face into Jacob's shoulder, upset by the sight, "poor beast, it seems so cruel, on that heavy chain, alone and away from its own kind, I cannot bear to see it." Tears pricked my eyes.

Jacob put his arm firmly around my waist and stoically said, "such is life my Lydia, such is life."

This had not been a good experience for me, though it was educational, in that I had supposed polar bears to be white and fluffy, but this one was a straggly, dirty yellow.

Our little girls were quite enchanted and came skipping back to us. Jacob called out to the mysterious fisherman, "thanks Bob, see yer next week, A'll get yer a drink, eh?"

"Hold yer ter that man." He laughed, waved and disappeared into the crowd.

"What a dear little bear," said Octavia.

"Can I have a baby poly bear Mama?" pleaded Martha-Jane.

"No dear, polar bears are not pets."

"Want a baby poly bear," she repeated firmly, in fact she said it over and over again.

Jacob lifted her onto his shoulders and tried to divert her with the promise of the sweet shop. But by now she was whingey and tearful and when Jacob lifted her down to look at the neat rows of dishes filled with brightly coloured sweets, resting on paper lace, she sank to the ground moaning on about 'baby poly bears'.

An elderly couple walked past us and stared at Martha-Jane lying on the paving stones, crying.

"Wants her arse tanning does that one," said the man quite loudly.

"Nay husband," replied his wife, "tis not the fault of the child, 'tis the parents who should take the blame for her poor upbringing."

Jacob looked at me despairingly.

"Oh dear," I said, ignoring the rude couple, "I think Octavia will be the only one going in the sweet shop today."

Jacob, who never lost his temper with his children, raised a questioning eyebrow, but I could only shrug my shoulders, as I gave Octavia some coins to go in the sweet shop, to buy liquorice, lemon drops and barley sugars.

After Octavia was out of earshot, Jacob put his arm tightly about my waist, pushed back my bonnet and whispered in my ear, "can tha imagine those two old gits having a good…in the bedroom?"

I had to giggle, because of course I could not.

Luckily, Martha-Jane had worn herself out by the time we fetched our horses and slept heavily and awkwardly in Jacob's arms all the way home. But we were not to be spared and as soon as she was lowered from the horse, she opened her eyes, thought for two seconds and started to cry loudly for a 'baby poly bear'.

"Martha-Jane has been very naughty," said Octavia piously, walking into the hallway.

"Dear me, what is all this noise about?" asked a bewildered Mother-in-law.

"Want a baby poly bear," wailed our youngest, lying on the hall floor now.

"Well you cannot have one, so you might as well be quiet about it," I said, stepping over her and untying my bonnet.

"Ah don't be mean my Lydia, she only wants a baby bear."

I turned to snap at my husband but when I saw him doubled up with laughter, why I had to smile myself, for the whole thing was beyond ridiculous.

Janet tried to help Martha-Jane to her feet but she was screaming and stiff now. I could see Janet thought a good smacked bottom would be in order. Eliza would doubtless have agreed but for her blood tie to Martha-Jane and knowing that Jacob would never raise a hand to his children however provoked. And so, though usually quick to express an opinion, she confined herself to helping Octavia unfasten the many tiny buttons on her jacket.

"Leave her there Janet, there is naught any of us can do with her. I do need a good cup of tea, is it time Eliza?"

"Yes Mistress, it's all set, we were just waiting on yer."

"Thank God," I said taking my mother-in-law's arm, "I'll be bound you've never seen such a tantrum before?"

Here she laughed, "my own boy Robert was a one for shouting and screaming if he didn't get his way. But none of thy others were much for tempers were they?"

I shook my head, though to be honest, Benjamin and I had so many children so quickly, we were too busy to notice such things. If they were irked, I suppose they had to sort it out for themselves. Also, Benjamin was quite strict with them and would not have stood for any carrying on. As for Martha-Jane she was indulged and spoilt by all of us, being our last child, and now we were 'reaping as we had sown'.

We ate our tea to a background of sobbing coming from the hallway, until eventually Hugo took pity and went out to her, and through the open door I could see him kneel down on the hard stone floor beside her. Softly he asked questions about the bear, how big it was, what noises it made, what colour it was and so on. Slowly, between shuddering sobs, she began to talk and sit up. Gently he helped her to take her red coat off, which was when I noticed, with sinking heart, that her new gloves were nowhere in sight, so that was two pairs of good gloves lost today.

"Martha-Jane, does tha think that if A tied meself up in a white sheet tha could pretend A were t' polar bear?"

She stared at him in wonder, then she nodded vigorously, smiled through her tears and allowed herself to be helped up off the floor.

"Let's give it a go then and see if it works like."

Eliza fussed a bit about spoiling a good sheet, but soon produced one, for there were few who could refuse Hugo anything with his easy charm and winning ways. And the rest of our evening was entertained by him draped in a white linen sheet, crawling about the floor and growling, for a squealing, giggling Martha-Jane. It must be said he made a much fiercer bear than the poor cowering creature we had seen at the harbour side.

"Eh, he's a good lad is Hugo," said Mother-in-law fondly.

"Aye, he is that," grinned Jacob.

CHAPTER 24

In which Jacob makes plans.
1804.

After the dinner most days, Jacob and I lay on our bed to rest awhile, I suppose we were getting old now. Certainly I was starting to feel old, already I had plucked a nasty black hair or two out of my chin and several horrid white hairs out of my head. Both of us had lost a few teeth. Usually, during our rest we talked, sometimes we slept a little, occasionally we lay together, though not often, for there was always the danger of one of the younger children coming in, and we had already had one or two close shaves with that one.

I lay across Jacob's arm, with my eyes closed for the sunlight was piercing bright through the casement windows.

"What's tha thinking, my Lydia?" he asked idly.

"Not much Darling, only wondering if it's too late to plant out my rose cuttings, they took really well but I should have planted them out long since."

"Which are they?"

"The lovely dark peachy ones. I don't know the name."

My mama and my aunt had been such expert and tireless gardeners with our garden in Baxtergate. But it was quite an effort for me to keep up with my mother-in-law's delightful knot and rose gardens here at the farm, for sadly she had passed peacefully from us the previous year. Now she was no longer with me to advise, I had quite lost interest in it and would much rather have read a book than tend the plants.

"Truth, I am little interested in gardening."

"Really? A'd have loved ter have had a go at gardening, but nowt much grew up at t' cottage, it was too windswept and bleak. But A'd have loved a proper garden of me own."

"Why Jacob you could have worked on the gardens here, any time you liked."

Then I could have bitten my tongue out, but it was too late, for we may not turn back time. He pulled his arm from under me, folded his arms on his chest, his lips tightened and he let out a sigh.

"Lydia from being a child, A devoted most of me waking minutes to working on this bloody farm. After me father died, A were only ten, A'd ter work things way too heavy for me, till A could hardly stand, but that didn't mean A didn't have me own hopes and dreams, A allus had them. Me mother had ter tie old sacks on me 'cos A didn't have a coat for working outside in Winter and A'd no one ter teach me ter read till A were past thirty but A still dreamed of opening a book and knowing what it said." He looked at me with a coldness. "Spite of me bad leg, A've still worked as best A could, wi' t' pain, just ter keep things going till young Ben comes of age. But that dun't mean A ever thought of any of it as mine."

"Jacob, I'm sorry, you know I always say the wrong stupid thing. I'm so sorry."

He snorted and stared straight ahead of him. I put my hand on his arm, "please forgive me Dearest, or I shall cry."

Indeed, I did feel tearful, thinking of him as a child without warm clothes but he would not move nor look at me.

I thought for a minute, "Jacob, I've had an idea."

"Bloody Hell, A hope it's a better 'un than t' last 'un." Still he would not turn to me.

"No Jacob, listen to me, I think it's a good idea."

"Come, my Lydia, tell me." Then he shrugged my hand off him and leaned up on one elbow to look at me.

"Jacob, my darling one," Did his lips twitch slightly with laughter now? "Jacob it comes to me, that after Ben's coming of age next month, we should move back into town and live in our old house in Baxtergate. I'm certain Louis and Chloe do not wish to be there, for they're all over with army life, and if they did we could come to an arrangement, I'm sure. And it would be just ours together and have the garden at the back of the house and the bit at the front. I think it's all been let go now with only Lizzie there, but..."

"Lydia, tha's rambling now, but I do like t' idea, A will say."

At last he was smiling again, thank God.

"Should you mind, giving up farming and animals and everything?"

"Mind? A'd bloody love it, farming means nowt ter me, niver did. So long as A can keep me horse, A do love me horse."

"Truly?"

"Truly, A've wanted ter live in town all me life."

"You never said."

"No point, A had ter do farming, there was no choice, but now there is. Ter be honest, when our Hugo came along, things were that bad with me and Susannah, A thought of going ter sea; A'd a bit of money put by and A thought of teking a cottage on, in town, and going out on one of t' whalers. A was old ter be going ter sea but A still had all me strength then."

"I never knew that." I was very surprised now.

"Aye, Susannah always preferred town anyway. But A didn't want ter leave me children all that time so A stayed." He put his arm around me again, "A wanted ter go ter sea when A were a lad, just ter get away from here. A used ter live for going in ter town with Benjamin, we used ter drink and mess on wi' t' lasses, but what A liked most were meeting wi' people and seeing a bit of life. For me, A niver minded all t' smells and noise and that in town." He paused and went on, "is that what we're ter do next then? Move back ter town?"

"You decide."

He nodded, "A'd like that very much."

"And can you forgive me for speaking so stupidly?"

"On one condition...that we go in tomorrow and tek a good look at t' house, then we can mek plans proper." Hesitantly he added, "does tha think tha could mek enough of a gentleman of me, ter live in town?"

"No Darling, I do not, for I should not have married you if I did not think you already every inch the gentleman." And I kissed him on the cheek.

For once I had said the right thing and he looked at me very directly and smiled his broadest, lovliest smile.

So we set ourselves to visit my old home the very next day.

* * * *

When my mama died, she left Lizzie a small income as reward for her devoted service, and Louis and I agreed that she should continue to live on at the house as a caretaker. Since then Louis had been away on campaign in France with the dreadful war and I had hardly heard from him, though Chloe scribbled the occasional note, and what with one thing and another, I had rarely visited the Baxtergate house in the five years since Mama had died.

So that very next day, there we were at Baxtergate; we stabled our horses and went up the steps into my childhood home.

"Lizzie, Lizzie, are you there?"

Straight away she came out of the kitchen, wiping her hands on her apron, "why Miss," (she had never got used to calling me mistress), "what a surprise, and a good one… Sir," she nodded to Jacob.

"How are things Lizzie? Where are you sitting? In the kitchen?"

"Yes Miss, A just live in t' kitchen and me bedroom, for everything in t' other rooms is covered up or put away, though of course A keep it dusted and swept regular."

"I'm sure you do Lizzie, so let's go in the kitchen and have a talk."

We sat around the big scrubbed table; everything looked exactly as it had done twenty odd years ago, all the cups and plates in exactly the same order on the dresser. She made a good pot of tea in a chipped, brown teapot and we drank from old pottery mugs. I supposed all the pretty china to be packed away, now.

"A've no cake Miss, A din't know yer were coming."

"T'is of no matter Lizzie." Though as usual I was starving.

"Breads fresh though…" she said tentatively.

"Oh Lizzie, would you make toast?" Turning to my husband, I said, "no-one makes toast as good as Lizzie, I used to live on it as a girl."

She smiled and started slicing the large loaf of bread on the wooden bread board.

"Secret's in t' buttering, A allus butters twice, once when it's just made and t' butter soaks in and then again as it's served."

She toasted the bread with one hand and poked up the fire with the other. Jacob stared all around him, because he had never seen this room or any of the others, excepting the parlour before.

"Lizzie, Mr Curzon and I are planning to come back to live here, not right away but in a few weeks' time, after my son Ben reaches his majority…"

"Oh Miss," she clasped her hand to her chest, "A'm that relieved, for when A first saw yer, A thought yer'd come ter tell me yer were selling t' house and A were ter be turned out like."

"Good Lord no, we plan to make our home here for a good long time, with our children." I glanced at Jacob.

"Oh aye."

"A've a bit of money that thy mama so kindly left me, A could've taken a room somewhere, it's not that, but A think of this house as me home, A've been here nigh on forty year, for A were hardly more than A child when A came first off."

I was stuffing her most delicious toast into my mouth like a complete pig. I wondered if my mama was looking down on us from heaven, twitching and shuddering to see her only daughter, married to an illegitimate carter, slurping tea and toast at a kitchen table with a servant. But I cared not a jot.

Jacob stood up as soon as he had finished the toast and gulped down his tea, obviously anxious to look around and make plans, as he was always a great one for making plans.

"So Lizzie, I'll show Mr Curzon around and then we'll come down and make arrangements about what needs doing."

"Yes Miss, sorry Mistress," she corrected herself.

Jacob and I wandered into the parlour, the furniture shrouded in white sheets and everything just as I remembered it.

"A love that big window, lets in loads of light, more modern than t' farm eh?" He peeped under the dust sheets at my mama's fashionable furniture, "shall we keep all this Lydia?"

"Yes, or we could bring a few old pieces from the farm?"

"Nah, A'm not keen on all that old dark stuff ter be honest."

Inwardly I sighed, for myself I so loved all the beautiful old furniture, polished over the centuries to give it a rich patina. I loved the ancient dark panelled rooms of the farmhouse and pretty, stone faced casement windows, all wonderfully scented by lavender flowers brushed over the floors every week. In truth I should miss it all dreadfully, for when I was younger, I had assumed I would live all of my life there; but now I knew it was time for me and Jacob to step up and move our lives on. In some ways that was hard for me.

Then he was leading me upstairs, grasping the ban-
nister rail firmly to aid his bad leg. To the back of the
house was my old bedroom, looking bare for the bed
hangings had been taken down and folded away.

"This was my room Darling."

It seemed a million years ago that I was sitting on my
bed reading my first love letters from Benjamin, when
we were young and waiting for life to begin.

"We could get this boarding levelled off," said Jacob
touching the panelled walls, "and get a nice paper put
on ter freshen it."

"Paper?" I said blankly.

"Aye, A've seen them in t' decorator's shops. Printed
papers that's stuck on t' walls."

"Oh," I said doubtfully.

"A think that'd look bonny, summat colourful."

Now we were in my mama's room at the front.

"This is a grand room and no mestek, would this be
our room does tha think?"

I had no wish to sleep in my mama's bedroom, so
I said, "I like the back room best, it's quieter, remember
we're not used to the noise and smells of the town
anymore."

He nodded, feeling the panelled walls, "maybe a bit
of paper on these too?"

"Also," I went on, "this room being bigger, might be
better for our girls; for Belle, Octavia and Martha-Jane
will all have to share you know."

"Why what's upstairs?"

"I'll show you."

And we climbed up to the two large rooms above;
Louis' old room at the back would have to be for our
younger sons, when they were home from school and

army life, and for Jack or Hugo if they came to stay. The room at the front was Lizzie's and she would have to share with Mary, just like in the old days.

Jacob nodded thoughtfully, "we'll have ter get more beds in here, we cannot have them all in the one, not with them all being young gentlemen eh?" he laughed.

There were a number of strong wooden boxes on the floor; unwrapping one or two bits, I saw my mama's beautiful china and crystal. That would be a treat for my daughters to unpack and sort out, and perhaps put aside some nice bits for Belle who was now twenty-two and still in no near sight of a wedding ring. I did not think Olivia would want anything as her Mr Hartley Fairfax kept her well stocked with all the latest and prettiest household bits.

"Garden?" I said holding my hand out to my husband.

"Kiss first," his eyes smiled at me, remembering our little tiff of the day before, concerning gardens.

He pushed me gently against the wall, kissed me softly and then more passionately. "By God, tha's a fine woman my Lydia, the finest. A could tek thee now on that bed, but maybe not, A'd not want ter be shocking yon Lizzie."

So instead, we walked arm in arm, around to the garden; now it was Jacob's turn to feel sentimental.

"A remember this little garden so well, me and Susannah used ter sit on that far wall when we were courting. Many a time we'd stand behind that tree so as no one could see us from t' house like."

The garden was badly overgrown, I believe it had not been touched once in the last five years, but Jacob was clearly entranced.

He fingered and pulled at various plants. "A've a fancy for Tulips, Darling, there's that many varieties now, they'd mek a grand show. Are there any planted already, can tha remember?"

"No-o, there might be but I think not."

To be honest I rather disliked tulips, they were so stiff and shiny, I preferred more draped, scented things like Honeysuckle, Wisteria and Rambling Roses, but I decided to be tactful for once and say nothing.

That night as we prepared for bed, my mind was buzzing with a hundred things; preparations for our move and preparations for my Ben's coming of age celebration. The party was to be a family dinner for all of us and for Phoebe's family, so that we could get to know one another and ending with a formal betrothal between him and Phoebe. Her family, (her father a solicitor), clearly thought Ben a good catch and had always been most enthusiastic about the courtship, as well they might, with him inheriting a splendid house with plenty of good farmland. Though, my husband had privately said, he thought the years ahead would be hard for farmers, the awful war had changed everything now, for rich and poor alike.

Always, at the back of all my plans, my heart was wrenched by the fact that my darling son Robert, would not be there to share his twin's coming of age celebrations. He had written to Belle a year ago, from a place called Nantucket which I had never even heard of, but Jack said was in America, on the coast. The letter said that he was well and he hoped Belle was well and that he was still whaling and love to all especially Livvy, he had drawn some whales spouting and a little boat surrounded by huge waves underneath the writing, and that was it.

Indeed, I had sobbed mightily when Belle showed it to me; it did not indicate that he was even still alive, for the letter had taken over four months to arrive.

Jacob always insisted that "no news was good news," and that we would have heard if he'd been killed at sea. But a little bit of my heart was relieved, for at least on the other side of the ocean he was clearly a free man and no Press Gang to steal him and send him to his death on an English war ship.

While I was mulling all this in my head, I suddenly remembered my first husband's watch.

"Jacob, would you have Benjamin's watch altered, so I can give it to Ben on his birthday, for he's the eldest and should have his father's watch."

"Altered? What for? Is it not working like?"

"No-o," I smiled, "have you not seen inside it?"

He shook his head puzzled. I fetched the watch from my top drawer, where I kept it wrapped in one of Benjamin's handkerchiefs, still smelling so faintly of his cologne. I sat on the bed and snapped open the cover and lifted the secret panel. I turned the watch to show him the erotic roundel surrounded with the enamel stars.

"I gave it to him on our wedding day, as my marriage token."

"Bloody hell, Lydia," he laughed and laughed. "A've niver seen owt like. Course A saw him look at his watch times many, especially when it was coming up ter dinner time. But A niver knew that were inside."

My heart turned over to think of my Benjamin, keeping his word and looking at his watch every day at noon, to remember our loving hearts, as he had promised me on his wedding night.

"Well, it needs covering over or removing, I cannot give it to my son like that can I?"

Still shaking with laughter, he said, "by tha's a girl Lydia, what a girl." He touched the picture with his fingertips, then looked at me, "where's my erotic watch then? Tha didn't get me owt like that on our wedding day."

"Oh Darling," I said crestfallen, "I thought you would like those books, I chose them most carefully. Would you rather have had a watch?"

He shook his head, "no Sweetness, only joking, t' books were reet special ter me, made me feel like a gentleman ter have them for me own. Any road, A've me father's watch and wouldn't want another ivver."

He wrapped the watch up, put it on his bedside and promised to take it into town on the morrow.

"And A'm arranging a bit of a surprise for thee as well."

I thought no more of it, laid my head upon his shoulder and went to sleep.

* * * *

Once Ben's majority party was over, legal papers all signed and sealed, he became Master of all. Betrothed to the lovely Phoebe, (who now sported the largest, showiest ring in the Curzon jewel box), he was most moved and surprised to receive his father's gold watch, which he wore with great pride. I had his grandfather's watch, wrapped and at the ready in case Robert should ever return to claim his twenty-first gift.

Now, Jacob and I began to pack up in earnest, trunks of clothes and bedding, boxes of books and papers and Jacob's few woodworking tools; we were taking his beloved horse which we would have to share, and the two oldest dogs, who were only good for a quiet town life now. Also, we were leaving behind Hugo, now a huge strong lad of sixteen, well suited to farm work and destined to take over his father's job as carter.

On our last day at the farm, Jacob and I rode up to Hill Cottage for a final look around. I took two pannier baskets, though I knew there could not be much left up there now.

We walked straight in, and in the heavy sunlit air, it seemed like Susannah might still be there, perhaps this was where her ghost walked? Jacob went from room to room, seemingly without emotion. Penelope had had most of the china and good linens when she married, but in the corner cupboard there was still a pretty flowered, covered dish. It reminded me so much of happy tea times at Hill Cottage with warm scones or toast inside it. I wrapped it carefully and put it in the basket, along with a carved breadknife and an empty green velvet box. Upstairs, I discreetly packed a few, little used baby clothes, thinking perhaps Belle would one day need them, and a blue and white soap dish, still with a shred of dried up soap in it.

Down stairs Jacob was writing on a scrap of paper, "A'm just listing our names, someone might find it in years ter come."

Neatly he had written;

Susannah Mary Curzon, Jacob Curzon, Jack Curzon, Penelope Susannah Curzon, Hugo Curzon lived here 1780 till 1792.

He stepped up on the hob stone and pushed the rolled up paper, high up behind the corner cupboard.

"Maybe there'll be other Curzons live here one day, if t' farm stays in t' same family, tha niver knows."

He took my hand and we wandered out into the windswept garden. He lowered himself awkwardly to the ground beside a little yellow gorse bush, which must have been brought off the moors. He looked up at me with tears in his eyes.

"What is it my love?"

"A've niver told thee but our little Rebecca's buried here."

At the back of my mind, I remembered there had been a still born babe, shortly before Hugo arrived on the scene.

"She were still born, sixteen years since, we both loved her so, we buried her here so we'd always be close, and now none of us is here, except her."

I knelt on the dry ground and took him in my arms.

"How can yer love a bairn so, that yer've niver known in life?"

"Of course you can my dearest..." Memories came flooding back, "I had a miscarriage once that no-one knew of, save Janet and Eliza, for they dealt with my linens. Not even Benjamin knew of it. But it's always a little one missing in my heart...it was on the night of your accident."

"God Lydia, tha's a brave one and none of us knew of it." He sighed, "best not ter think of things too much, best ter get on with life today, as well as we can. We've much ter be thankful for, eh?"

I nodded and helped him to his feet. He brushed his hands together, blew a kiss towards the little grave, handed me onto my horse and together we rode back to spend our very last night at the farm.

Next day we piled our boxes, trunks and children onto the cart, my younger sons in a strop because I had had to tell them we could not afford to keep horses for each of them, now we were moving back to town.

Mary was as excited as any child, clutching her wooden box and a bundle, "Mistress, A cannot wait ter get back, A allus liked town life best. Eh and A cannot wait ter see Lizzie, just like old times again."

I felt much sorrow to be leaving the farm, even though I knew it was for the best. I looked sadly at the beautiful ancient house where I had loved both my husbands, and all my children had been born... But I bit my lip and shed no tears, for I did not want to show my feelings outside of myself.

We finally arrived at Baxtergate, hot, thirsty and cross (excepting Jacob and Mary who seemed to have a boundless supply of tolerance and good spirits).

"Don't go upstairs Darling, A want ter show thee t' surprise meself."

While the boxes were being unloaded, I wandered into the parlour and found it full of hot house roses in pinks and yellows, arranged with ferns. With all the furniture and ornaments arranged in the prettiest way.

"How very beautiful it looks," I said delighted, "thank you Lizzie."

"Master ordered them flowers for thee Miss, A mean Mistress, and he's a bonny surprise for thee upstairs as well, A know tha'll love it," said Lizzie.

At last, I was led upstairs into the large front bedroom, with my mama's pretty white painted furniture and two neat beds and every wall panel papered with a profusion of pink rosebuds. Indeed, the paper was pleasant enough and the girls seemed very pleased with it.

"Wait till tha sees our room Darling, tha'll be that surprised."

Surprised? More like a bloody shock! For my childhood bedroom had had its panelled walls flattened, and all four walls papered in a bright yellow paper, printed with a blue trellis and great twists of green ivy, and peeping out at regular intervals were feathered birds, each with lurid red eyes. My heart sank, "gaudy" was the only word that I could think of.

"Oh dun't tha like it? A thought tha'd love it." Jacob looked as crestfallen as a little child.

I pulled myself together, for there would be no turning back from this paper, "of course I like it Jacob, it's the best surprise." I kissed him fondly on the cheek, "I was only thinking we might get a new bed cover, perhaps a blue to tone in?"

Then Martha-Jane ran in, she shouted, "look at all the beautiful birdies," and jumped up and down on the bed, trying to reach the birds with her fat little hands.

Every morning for the rest of my life, I woke up to see those ghastly birds staring down at me with their horrid, beady red eyes; but I did so love my dear husband, lying beside me, so I tried only to look at him, instead.

CHAPTER 25

In which Martha-Jane gets a pet parrot.
1806.

That Summer was hot and dry, almost every day; too hot for me, but a blessing for Jacob, freeing him of some of the pain in his bad leg, which I know still hurt him a deal more than he ever let on.

Jacob had taken to the life of a retired gentleman with great enthusiasm; his natural intelligence and easy manner made him many friends. He had a strong interest in philosophies and experiments; most of all he was a fervent abolitionist, having papers and pamphlets sent up from London on the ups and downs of the anti-slavery movement. No sugar was allowed in the house now, excepting the expensive kind that came from India, refined with free labour. On our bedroom mantleshelf, amongst all the other bits and pieces, we had a blue and white pottery medallion, showing a chained man and the words, "am I not a man and a brother." It always broke my heart to look upon it, so hating cruelty and injustice myself.

As to the garden, well, Jacob did get that in very fine shape, and it was much admired by many a passer-by. The small garden in front of the house, was planted with a grass lawn and surrounded by bright tulips, standing stiffly in rows, and the garden behind the house was soon restored to the shady, scented haven of times past.

There was much enjoyment living in town apart from the gardening, with shopping and the subscription library. We all loved the little theatre behind our house and went whenever we could and often there was a good concert on at the Assembly Rooms. Indeed, we were generally most well entertained and amused.

This particular afternoon, Jacob was at a talk in the Assembly Rooms about ancient fossil discoveries on our very own coast, which seemed to be as old as the world itself. Myself I sat by our parlour window, with our new lace curtains fluttering in the soft breeze from the open window. My head ached in the heat, I was trying to read, "Victim of Prejudice," by Mary Hays which Jacob had thoughtfully bought me for my last birthday, but now I had let it fall to the floor and I drank my tea which had gone rather cold. Martha-Jane ever a noisy child was dancing around the room with an imaginary beau, singing to accompany herself. Though she was a good little dancer and had the sweetest of voices, it was grating upon me.

"Please Martha-Jane, would you play outside for a while, it is such a fine day and Mama has one of her headaches."

"Oh poor Mama, with a horrid headache," she pushed herself against me to kiss me.

"Martha-Jane, now you're squashing me, please play outside for a little time, though do be careful of Dada's special flowers."

"Mama, I shall," she said with unusual compliance, and trotted off to the front garden.

Though I could still see and hear her through the open window, I felt I could sleep a little and curled up in the big padded chair, pulled my light shawl around me and closed my eyes. I started to drift away, soothed by the gentle sound of bees buzzing in the garden, and the thin curtains moving in the warm air.

I heard the garden gate click and Martha-Jane's piercing voice, "I am Martha-Jane Curzon, who are you?"

There was a pause, and a low deep voice, which could have belonged to my first husband said, "I am your brother Robert."

My heart leapt into my throat and I leapt out of my chair and ran out of the house.

"Oh Robert, Robert my boy, you're alive."

I could not clasp him tightly enough, weeping and kissing him all at the same time.

"Mama," he laughed.

"Who is this man Mama? Is he really my brother, for I have never seen him before?"

"Yes, dear, he is your brother, come home from sea." I reached out for her hand and drew her into our embrace.

He pulled back and dropping his canvas bag on the ground, picked Martha-Jane up in his arms, "shall we go inside Martha-Jane, and you can get me a drink, for I'm parched after my ride."

"Ride?" I said, "but where have you come from?"

"Well, Mama, I docked two days since, and not knowing you were here, I hired a horse and rode straight out to Moorhome farm and I've been there with Ben and Phoebe."

I called Mary through to bring us tea and lemonade, upon which there was another round of weeping and hugging. When she finally let him go and went to fetch the refreshments, I could, at last take a really good look at him. Of course he was taller and stronger, with the body of a man, his dark hair was short and his skin as brown as a native's. But the main difference about him was that his entire face and the backs of his hands were heavily tattooed, with rows and rows of bluish dots arranged in lines and spirals. Answering my gaze, he explained he had spent several years in the Americas and sailed with a man who had been to the South Seas, and learnt the art from natives there.

"He did it for me at quiet times, when we were months at sea."

"How is it done dear? For I have heard it never washes off."

"They prick with a point of bone, and while it's open they push in soot or a blue liquid."

Martha Jane stared at him gently touching each of the dots, then tracing the swirls with her finger tips.

"Eh, Master Robert, that must've hurt a good deal, A'm thinking?" said Mary as she poured the tea.

"Oh aye, it did, but it was done bit by bit, over three years. But there's plenty of time at sea when you're waiting for a wind and such. And we passed a few voyages together."

Martha Jane began to touch his face again, he turned away from her.

"Stop it Martha-Jane, you're annoying me now, and I want to drink my tea."

"I am so sorry, brother Robert."

He did not cast her from his lap and she folded her hands meekly, staring fixedly at his face, while he drank his tea awkwardly, for she still was rather in the way.

There was so much news to relate, I hardly knew where to begin, "Did you know that Belle and Jack are engaged to be married? He's staying here this week and they're out walking now. They both swear they've been promised to each other for about ten years, so it's what you might call a very long engagement."

He smiled, "they were always very close as children, they used to disappear off together for hours on end."

"Did they?" I wondered how I could not have noticed this at the time.

"Aye, Jack once told me they had a secret hiding place, but he'd never let on where it was...but why so long? Surely Jack must be twenty-six by now or nigh on."

"So, he took Holy Orders at Cambridge just as your dear father did, and now he's a curate, but I think it will be some years before he can afford or come by a living, so God only knows when they can marry."

"I might be able to help them there, for I've made a fair bit at sea...in fact, wait for it Mama...in two weeks' time I'm to captain my own ship; well not all my own, but I've a quarter share in it."

This he said with such pride, I had to embrace him again.

"I've done well for myself Mama, but as I say, I've been out at the farm for a couple of days, and when I saw Ben with a wife and a baby, why I felt well behind on things."

"No dear, not at all, you've both taken very different paths in life."

"Anyway, we're fine now, me and Ben, no fighting or anything, all those fights we had seem so stupid now," he laughed, "in fact we got on real well."

"I'm so glad," I gazed at him with such love, but my reverie was soon broken by Jacob's return.

"By God, it's our Robert come back ter us." He held out his arms to him, "A'm that glad ter see thee safe and well."

"Not the black sheep then, Uncle Jacob?"

"Nay lad, A'm only jealous A niver went to sea meself."

"Really Uncle Jacob? I never knew you'd any thoughts of it."

"Oh aye, a time or two A've had idea of going out on t' whalers but one thing or another stopped me… mainly women truth be told," he laughed.

Brandies were poured and Jacob settled down and said, "now then, our Robert, start at t' beginning, tha went out on t' Fortitude, first off…"

"Aye, to Greenland, learnt the basics of whaling, I loved it from the first, the feel of the sea under us. But my God I was scared many a time, doesn't matter how much skill you've got, God tests yer to yer limits and always has the upper hand at sea. Scared as hell when we went out in those little boats after the whales but," he laughed, "it's a thrill like naught you'll ever know, my God it's a thrill. When it's done you can't wait to get out there again."

I saw Jacob transfixed with fascination and, yes, envy, but for myself, I could only remember Susannah telling how her first husband, out whaling, was caught by a harpoon rope, slipped into the waters and when her brother, who was a most skilled speksioneer, tried to help him; he was dragged down too, both to icy deaths at the bottom of the sea where they still lay.

Robert went on, "so we got to Greenland and it was beautiful, not a bit like I'd expected, cold and bleak, but beautiful in its way. All tiny flowers and birds I knew not the names of, and great lumps of ice, floating in the waters, as big as...as Miss Coates' house. (Miss Coates lived opposite us in a very large house). Beautiful they were, pure clean white, in fantastical shapes. Sometimes, near the ice you could hear like a ghostly cracking sound. Great walrus and seals and massive polar bears everywhere you looked."

"Have you seen a poly bear, brother Robert?" interrupted Martha-Jane.

"Yes, many of them, caught and killed 'em too."

"I've seen a poly bear."

Robert looked questioningly at me.

"One of the captains brought back a baby polar bear and it used to swim in the harbour on a long chain and we all went to see it one day and Martha-Jane was very taken with it."

"Aye, we bloody rued that day," said Jacob, "she niver shut up about it and wanted one for her own, A tell thee our Robert, tha's niver heard a tantrum like it."

"Nay Martha-Jane, they're horrible things, polar bears, why I've seen a man killed with a single swipe of a polar bear's paw. They're fierce, with nasty teeth and a nasty temper too. You don't want one of them anywhere near you."

"No brother Robert," she said wide eyed and thoughtful.

"Anyway I've brought you a gift much better than a bloody polar bear, I've got a parrot that talks, for you."

"Oh, oh where is it, the parrot that talks?"

"Yer'll have to wait a bit, it's still on the ship, so we'll fetch it up later. You don't mind having a parrot in the house do you Mama?"

"I don't think so Dear, in truth I know little of them."

"You have to keep them warm and not set the cage in a draught. It's a friendly little thing, it'll repeat anything you say to it and sit quiet on your arm."

Martha-Jane clapped her hands in delight.

"A'm looking at thy tattoos," said Jacob admiringly.

Here Robert put his sister onto the floor and stood up and raised his shirt, to show the squirling patterns across his back and chest.

"Tha'll laugh ter see mine," said Jacob rolling up his sleeve and showing the crude heart with my name in it, "hurt that much A had ter have five brandies afore A could tek pain of it."

"Too right, the pain was bad, though I never showed it in front of the men. You've just got to laugh it off, haven't you?"

And our family was almost complete, when Belle and Jack returned from their walk and Octavia from her music lesson. (Francis was away at school, and Frederick and George both in the army now). I had high hopes that Francis would following his father's footsteps and go to Cambridge, for he was a clever child.

I did not know if Octavia would remember Robert, but she insisted that she did.

Robert embraced them all, then delved in the pocket of his jacket, counted out some notes and pushed them into Jack's hands.

"Money what you lent me, plus a bit of interest."

Jack stared at the notes, astonished, "I cannot take this, Robert, there's a hundred pounds here, just give me and Belle what you borrowed."

But Robert pushed Jack's hands away from him, "you can take it Jack, you helped me out when I needed it, I've made some real money now and that's your share, for you and my sister."

Jack put his arm around Belle. I had never seen him touch her before, though I suppose they must have behaved as lovers when they were in that cupboard thing at the farm.

He looked at her, "Belle, if we took this, with what we've saved, we could buy that living at Cookering. What do you think?"

"Naught to think about Jack," interrupted Robert, "take it and move your lives along, it's yours and I'll not take it back for anything."

Jack smiled amazed and Belle leaned against him intimately.

"Robert I will, and a thousand thanks."

Suddenly I felt ancient, our children were grown up and moving on and making decisions. Jacob and I were just an old couple, in a settled life, idly wondering what our little grandchildren were all up to.

"Shall you come down and see my ship, you'll never guess what she's called."

"What?" asked Belle.

"I've a quarter share in her, well, all the others are married, so it couldn't be called after one wife and not another and we wanted a woman's name for luck, so it fell to me to name her and I'd missed my sister's so much, I named her the Olivia Belle."

Belle smiled in delight.

My heart turned over at the thought of my boy, alone at sea and missing his sisters.

"Can I come to see the ship and see my parrot, brother Robert?"

"You'll need a bonnet and shawl; it might be breezy at the harbour side."

"You'd better behave yourself Martha-Jane, if you're coming with us," said Belle, rather sharply I thought.

I stood up to join them but Jacob stopped me, "we'll come down later lad, A need ter rest me bad leg a bit now."

Robert nodded and after the fastening of bonnets and shawls off they all went.

"Let t' youngsters go on their own, they dun't need old folks like us holding them back, Darling." He pulled me to sit on his good knee, "eh, my Lydia, tis a long while since we've sat like this, eh?"

I nodded and put my arms around his neck, "I'm suddenly feeling old, my love."

"Nay niver Darling, still a beauty, still a beauty my sweeting."

He kissed me so tenderly.

I sighed, "how has life passed so quickly Jacob?"

* * * *

That evening I gave Robert his Grandfather's watch, which he should have had on his twenty first birthday and he was most moved to receive it. He said around that time, he had felt really homesick, wondering what we were all up to and missing home life.

We sat up late that night, listening to tales of sea-life and Robert's many adventures. At first it was all accompanied by loud squawks from Martha-Jane's new parrot, a darling thing which could say many words, some of them in strange tongues. But Robert explained that if we covered it up, it would think it night time and go to sleep. Incredibly this worked and we never heard another sound from it, even though we were all still in the room talking quite loudly, for many hours more.

Robert told us how difficult the whaling was at the start.

Jacob said, "surely all them years of hard work on t' farm, must've stood thee in good stead?"

"To be honest it did, and I was quite as strong as any of the lads, no it wasn't that..." he hesitated, "you'll think me a babby, but when I started out, it was the look on those whales when we went to strike them, some-times they'd come up towards us quite trusting and friendly and when we pierced them, the look of pain in their eyes, as they thrashed about, trying to cling to life, it used to wrench me. When we saw a male and female together, we'd take the female first off, knowing it's mate would never leave its side and then be easy pickings. Of course, I just had to get used to it, but you could see a look of knowing and intelligence in their fish eyes. Yer could not be fearful, for it would have let down the men who relied on yer and each other."

I turned away unable to bear thinking of any cruelty, Jacob patted my hand idly and asked about the different types of harpoon.

Robert explained in detail and then told of going out on the American whaling ships, and how he had met with Indians and men from all over the world, all labour-ing together. Some, he said were escaped slaves, seeking work and safety.

"My God they were strong, those slaves, twice the size of me, Mama, and one of them could do the work of three ordinary men."

"Really dear?" I said as positively as I could, though I was still thinking of the wretched whales, loyal to their mates till the last and the ship's deck swimming with their final bloods.

"So how were they commanded? Did they not all speak different tongues?"

"Aye, they did, but strange as it may seem, wherever I've been in this world, everyone can always speak a few words of English as well as their own tongue. And when things were quiet, we had amazing entertainments from them, songs and so forth; two who'd been slaves, used empty barrels as drums and it made a powerful sound, as I cannot describe. Hit deep inside you somehow, like the beating of those drums told the whole of life's story."

I could see Jacob was mesmerized, "did tha know thy mama's cousin Ann is wed ter a black man as used ter be a slave?"

Now it was Robert's turn to be surprised, "how did that come about then?"

"Tis a long story dear," I said, "years ago my cousin Penelope and her husband (your namesake) met Mr Mcrae walking on the beach and he told them how he'd been a slave and gambled for his freedom, then he'd sailed the world and eventually married a Whitby girl and set up this marvellous draper's shop in Guisborough with stuffs he imports from India and so on, things he's learnt about in his travels. So that's how we came to know of him. Anyway, after he was widowed, quite by chance, I took Ann over to see the shop. Well soon as they met…"

Here Jacob took up the story, "so t' very next day he's ovver at ours, asking if he can court our Ann. As it happens, A knew him pretty well from market days, when A'd had many a drink with him, for we'd both an interest in politics and such. And one night, a while since, he spoke to our abolitionist group about his life as a slave, and all its cruelties, A'll not repeat them here, for t' sake of thy mama."

Again, I felt emotional, "he's such a kind and gentle person, it cuts me to think of it. Dear Ann is as happy as can be married to him, and his grown up daughters so sweet, Rose and what's her name Jacob, I always forget?"

"Violet," he laughed, "tha allus forgets it."

"Mcrae eh?" said Robert, "all the blacks had English or Scotch names, they were not allowed to keep their own. Is he branded?"

"Aye, he's got 'McR' burnt large across his right breast."

"Oh," I cried out horrified for I had never known that, or thought of such an awful thing. I had to dab away tears. I know not why I was always so sensitive nowadays.

"Sorry Mama," said Robert, "I didn't think…shall I sing a whaling song to cheer a bit?

"Oh, please do Robert, for you have such a lovely voice. I have much missed your singing."

"Come Octavia, keep the time for me," he handed her a book to beat her hand on and began to sing in his deep strong voice.

We hoisted our flag to the top of the mast,
And for Greenland sailed away, brave lads,

Our ship sailed away so swift and fast,
All of our lads the finest, brave lads.

The lookout high up on the mast head he stood,
There's a whalefish, a whalefish my lads,
Our lads of iron in our ship of wood,
Blowing she is, give the chase our lads....

He sang all ten verses in his fine voice, and here it was Jacob brought emotional now and pinching the top of his nose.

I looked at him, he shook his head and said, "nay but A'm an old fool, but it's brought me a tear, for Susannah used ter sing that same song to our bairns when they were fretful. She'd learnt it from her first husband who were a grand singer A believe."

Jack stood up and put his hand on his father's shoulder, "I remember it well Father."

* * * *

Next day, Jacob and I went down to the harbour side. Robert carried a large, stoneware jar under his arm, which I recognized from the pantry at Moorhome Farm.

"Whatever is in there, Robert dear?" I asked curiously.

He laughed and told me that when he'd visited the farm, he'd related his many marvellous adventures to all, but that Eliza was quite unimpressed and merely asked how he'd been cleaning his teeth for the last seven years, when she knew for a fact, that he'd taken none of her homemade, charcoal toothpowder with him. As a result, she said she could not risk his teeth again, and had given him a seven-year supply of toothpowder in a stoneware jar! Jacob and I laughed much about this and realized how we missed Eliza with her many opinions and her unfailing devotion to our wellbeing.

The grand "Olivia Belle," was a fine ship indeed. All in shiny new wood, with new clean ropes and rolled up sails, awaiting its first voyage. In all my life I had never stepped on a such a vessel before, it felt strange and precarious, rocking slightly on the water, even though it was quite safely moored. I clutched Robert's arm nervously to steady myself.

How he laughed at me, "is this my Mama who used to ride that great spirited wild black horse without a thought?"

Truth be told, I became a little bored after I had seen the kitchen area and the cabins, it seemed unimaginable to me how so many men could live in such a small space for months on end. It was not even possible to stand up straight inside the cabins, except in the captain's quarters. Jacob, however was fascinated and spent a full two hours asking questions about cordages and rigging and so on. I did not like the slight rocking of the boat so I sat down upon a big wooden reel, wound around with thick rope. Near to me was a rather rough looking sailor, about my own age, scraping something clean. He stared at me quite boldly, so I turned to look away in the direction of the quayside, with its row of little shops and inns, catering for all the mysterious needs of the sailors and their ships. When I glanced back, he was still staring at me.

"Excuse me Mistress, is it Miss Franklin?"

Now I stared back at him, but could not recognize him at all. "Sir, I was Miss Franklin, now Mistress Curzon."

"A knew it were thee, straight off, tha dun't know me then?"

I shook my head puzzled still.

"A lived in thy yard for a couple of year when A were a lad and worked for thy mother as boot boy, Peter Thompson I am... A left ter go ter sea, just after thy cousin Miss Walker got wed..."

"Oh, oh of course."

I leapt up to shake his rough, calloused hand, feeling I had been rude not to recognize him.

"Did tha say tha were Mistress Curzon now?"

"Yes, my son is captain of this ship." I smiled with pride to say it out loud.

"Eh, he'll be a grand captain that A do know, for A've sailed wi' him afore, A've nowt but respect for him, and A'm not just saying that for thy benefit Mistress. Fancy him thy son, eh."

"And how as life treated you, Mr Thompson? You must only have been twelve or thirteen when you first went to sea?"

"Aye, twelve A were, but A've made it me life and a grand life it is too. A've a wife and eight children living, as well now..."

I laughed, "there I do top you Sir, for I have nine myself."

"Is Mary still with thee Mistress?"

"Why yes, and Lizzie too, though my mama died some seven years ago."

"Am sorry to hear that Mistress, A lost me own mother thirty years since and A can still see her face in me mind clear as day... shall thee remind me ter Mary? She were allus that kindly ter me in them days, for A'd no family of me own then."

"Of course I shall Mr Thompson and of course our Mary is still just as kindly as she ever was to us all."

Indeed, I was so grateful for Mary's kindness, I had resolved to give her a sum of money so that she and Lizzie could give up service and perhaps start up a little sweet-shop to see them through their old age, for Mary still made the most wonderful sweets. They were both nearly sixty and less able than they were. Frankly, I needed a strong young girl to scrub and clean for me now, and I thought perhaps I could save a bit of money by doing the cooking myself, with Octavia's help.

I saw my husband and son reappearing at long last and said, "so Mr Thompson, I do wish you most well for your voyage."

"Good ter see thee again, Mistress Curzon."

I nodded to him as my son reached out, to hand me over the little bridge that led from the wobbling boat to the welcome firmness of land. I was glad to be leaving the nasty smells of fish and seaweed too as we walked home.

There were two youngish lads on board sweeping and scrubbing the deck and Robert had one of them carry a small trunk back to the house and then things became much more interesting, for inside the trunk were many foreign treasures. We sat in the parlour and Robert unpacked coloured shells, gaudy feathers, rather crude carvings, decorated whale teeth and a horrid wooden mask with human hair stuck on it. He had collected the weird rather than the beautiful, in his travels. And the only thing I liked was a huge shell, all pearly inside.

"Press it to your ear Mama and you'll hear the sea, far away."

Belle chose some little Walrus ivory carved animals.

277

"You can have them on the mantle in the vicarage, eh?" said Robert.

"Robert, will you walk me down the aisle to give me away?" It seemed, at long, long last, wedding plans were going apace for Belle and Jack.

"Definitely not, that's for our Ben to do, he's the eldest, besides..." he glanced at me sheepishly, "I'll be sailing next week and won't be back for some time."

"Oh no, Robert," I moaned, "you've hardly been here any time." (And yes, I did sound exactly like my mama).

He went on, "I should have said this afore Uncle Jacob, but I'm planning on taking young Hugo to sea with me, for he's expressed a fancy for it. Is that all right with you?"

"Oh aye, of course it is, A've no wish for him ter waste his life at t' farm, like A did. He needs a chance ter mek summat of himself."

Octavia chose one of two inlaid boxes of coromandel wood, Martha-Jane wanted one too but Robert insisted that as she'd already had the parrot, he was going to give the other to Olivia.

Martha-Jane had to frown hard to control her temper as she was rarely thwarted.

Robert said, "I'm planning on riding out to see Olivia and me new niece for a couple of days and then collecting Hugo on me way back, and then we'll still have a few days to get ready for going to sea, afore sailing Wednesday next. I'm wanting to meet her Mr Fairfax; Eliza didn't have a good word to say about him, when I asked her."

Jack and Belle exchanged little secret smiles.

"What?" I said puzzled. "Robert, I must speak up for Mr Hartley Fairfax, he is devoted to your sister, why they spent a full six months in Bath on the most splendid and perfect honeymoon. A fine handsome gentleman and a most charming man. I cannot imagine what Eliza has against him."

Jacob laughed out loud and patted the back of my hand.

"What?" I said blankly.

He just smiled and shook his head.

* * * *

Later we lay in bed, so much had happened, we were almost too excited to sleep. Under the watchful red eyes of the wallpaper birds we talked for a long while.

"Told thee young Robert'd come back safe and sound din't A?"

"You did Dearest, you always did." I kissed his cheek.

"When tha talked of thy Olivia and Mr Fairfax, did tha sound a touch envious of them going ter Bath?"

"Well, anyone would want to go to Bath, would they not Dearest?"

"Maybe... A'll tek thee ter Bath any time tha wants, not away for six month though, A like me own bed too much, but we could go for two or maybe three week like."

"Truly, we could visit Bath?"

"Any time tha wants Darling."

I sighed and closed my eyes with a little smile of complete happiness and satisfaction.

So that was an exciting thing to look forward to, a trip to Bath....

CHAPTER 26

In which Rob and Penny buy a new house.
2018

"Have we ever been up this way?" asked Rob, turning the car towards a muddy farm track.

"I don't think so," replied Penny, "it doesn't look like a proper road really."

They drove to the top of a steep lane, and in front of them stood a neat row of four late Victorian cottages. Each with a little garden and a few cars parked in the front. The road ended there.

"They're nice aren't they, but I like that old one there better, looks like it's got a tale or two to tell."

Penny followed his gaze to the far right of the cottages, where a much older property stood. Her stomach lurched and she could hardly believe her eyes, for there was "Hill Cottage", much altered and extended, but there was no mistaking it. The ancient front door was still there, and the downstairs windows in the same place. Now there was another storey to it, with two windows above the door and a pan-tiled roof.

"It's had new windows put in," she blurted out.

Rob frowned at her, in disbelief. "Penny they must be two hundred years old, late Georgian, I'd say."

"Sorry." Penny didn't quite know what to say. She'd tried to talk to Rob about time-travel before now, and he'd just roared with laughter and asked her if she believed in aliens as well. She couldn't make sense herself, of her eighteenth century life; at first she'd tried to put it from her mind altogether, wondering if she'd been mentally ill. But now, as the years passed, she thought of it all more and more. For of course, it had all been such a very special interlude in her life and it was just so amazing that Rob had found her again in the twenty first century. And he loved her as much now as he had over two hundred years before.

"Shall we park up and take a look, there's a 'for sale' sign, looks like it's empty," he said.

A thrill shot through her as he reversed and pulled up the car. Could she really look at Hill Cottage again?

She turned around to check their two babies, strapped into car seats behind her. "Look at them Darling, both fast asleep, they'll be all right for a few minutes, won't they?"

They got out and closed the car doors as quietly as they could. Rob took her hand as they walked across a muddy pathway to the cottage and in at the little broken down gate. There were only some rough yellow gorse bushes growing in the front. He peered through the filthy windows and then they walked around to the back of the cottage, where there was a rundown vegetable garden edged in brick pathways and the remains of an outside toilet building. Old paint had peeled so badly, that the bare wood of the windows and door could be seen. Rob stared at it all, he seemed mesmerised, but their silence was soon broken by a voice behind them.

"Been empty twenty year, and now it's finally up for sale, there's none wants ter tek it on."

They turned to see an old man, probably well into his eighties standing behind them. "Been on t' market five year now and only a handful of viewings ter my knowledge. Too much work needs doing and youngsters can't be bothered wi' all that nowadays."

"Actually we are looking to buy ourselves, but we didn't know this was for sale, we've driven up here quite by chance." Rob turned to him, and in his usual friendly way added, "I'm Rob Curzon and this is my wife, Penny."

"Aye, pleased ter meet yer both, bit of a coincidence is that."

"What?"

"Well, it's called Hill Cottage as yer see, but A've lived up here all me life and when A was a lad, me grandad always called it Curzon Cottage. He was born in that cottage yon." Here he indicated the second of the Victorian cottages. "And he said when he was a lad, this was always called Curzon Cottage after t' family that lived there. They'd had a great farmhouse, a Moorhome Farm, at one time ovver that way, in t' valley, but t' father had been a gambler and lost it all, and t' lands too in t' 1870's, A believe. Re-mortgaging and that. So this place was all they had left ter live in. Some of t' stone from t' farm was brought up here ter build them cottages like, after t' new owner demolished it all, hundred and fifty year ago."

"Why did he demolish the farm house?" asked Rob.

I could hear the absolute amazement in his voice, for he had traced his family tree meticulously back, in both time and place, but until now, had never found any information about how the fifteenth century farm house was lost, or what happened to the branch of the family that lived there after about 1850.

"Well he was a lord that bought it all, and had his own stately home ter live in, just wanted t' land, for its bloody good farmland is that; well, all round here is. He built these here cottages for his workers."

"Is there any land with this cottage?" asked Rob hesitantly.

"Oh aye, that field up that way, and some beyond, about three acres A'd say."

Penny smiled, for they'd been looking at properties for more than a year now. Always, the suitable houses had no land or else the land was just right and the property horrible, for they both wanted something old with a bit of character.

Rob reached for his phone, "I'll give the agent a ring right now, and see if we can get a viewing some time."

"Nay lad, don't bother wi' that, A've still a key from when t' last owner lived there, course he weren't a Curzon, they were gone long since. A can let yer tek a look and yer can see what yer think, though A wouldn't have thought it'd be much in line fer youngsters like yo two. There's nowt modern in there."

"But that's why we like it," laughed Penny.

A few minutes later, a huge rusty key was turned in the lock, and the old front door creaked open. Sun blazed through the grubby windows and somewhere in the dust motes, Penny half expected to see Susannah step forward from the fireside. Indeed, the ancient stone fire place was much the same, the corner cupboard was still there to the left of it. The old scullery had been extended; there was a white pot sink and a green enamelled gas ring standing on the scrubbed wood worktop. Various pans and crockery from the 1950's filled the narrow wall shelves. Everything thick with years of dust.

Penny led the way in to what she remembered as Susannah's bedroom, when the cottage had been single storey and consisted of only two rooms. Now it was a cosy living room, with a most beautiful Georgian fire place, still with its original dog-grate, set in a deep brick alcove.

"Oh, I love it," cried Penny, "what a beautiful little room."

They went upstairs on their own, as the old man had said he wasn't too good on stairs.

"It's not really big enough is it with only two bed-rooms and there's no space for a bathroom at all." Rob spoke sadly, for he loved the feel of the place. He'd already got the details and price, up on his phone. He stared out of the little twelve paned window across the golden moorlands.

"How much is it?" Penny peered at his phone. "Ooh, that's our top price isn't it...I suppose it's all the land that goes with it."

"God, I'd love all that land, for a few cows and a couple of horses and chickens in that little yard bit at the back."

"I expect they'd take an offer on it if it's been up for sale for a long time, and we would be paying cash, then perhaps we'd have some money left over to build on a bathroom, or else we could have a tin bath in front of the fire, honestly I wouldn't mind that you know," laughed Penny.

Now they were outside again and Rob prodded the rotten window frames, "you know, these could be filled and painted, and if it was done soon, I think they could be restored and not need replacing."

"Could you do it yourself Darling?" asked Penny thinking of the money that could be saved.

"Course, just need some long ladders. The roof doesn't look too bad, it's very old but there wasn't any water coming in was there?"

Penny shook her head.

He turned to her, "am I being selfish? Just thinking of what I want, could you set up your little business here, it's quite isolated, would that matter?"

"No," she replied, "it's mainly on line anyway."

Now they had been lucky enough to come into some money, Penny had decided to give up her teaching job and work from home. Her dream was to make uniforms and costumes for historical re-enactments, and there actually seemed to be quite a market for this. She had found her full-time teaching job an absolute nightmare with a baby and a toddler to manage as well, in fact she had already handed in her notice, at the ghastly school where she worked.

"Rob, I love it, I wouldn't mind the mess or the work or anything, I really feel at home here, does that sound silly?"

"Have we looked at it properly, is it stupid to make an offer straight off?"

"Bye, yer don't mess about yo two, do yer?" grinned the old man.

And within a couple of hours, quite a low offer had been accepted on the cottage, and Rob and Penny were sitting outside The Angel pub having a celebratory drink and trying to control the babies who wanted to climb on everything and knock over the drinks. They drank a toast to the future and agreed they'd always been impetuous and laughed about it. Years before, they had married when they were students and had only known each other less than a year, then Penny had had a baby in her second year and another in the week before her finals and somehow still managed to graduate. Then, before they'd found jobs or come into the money, they had to live in Rob's mother's caravan for six months. But now they both agreed they were going to be mature and sensible about things and plan properly.

"Or at least we'll try," said Rob optimistically, even though he'd already phoned up about adopting some ex-battery hens and had also bought a reclaimed bath off ebay, just in the short time they'd been sitting outside the pub.

* * * *

Six weeks later they were turning the huge old key in the door of their very own cottage. They'd hardly started with the unloading, before various kindly neighbours came round with pot-plants and bottles of wine and a casserole, and it was only after several mugs of tea, glasses of wine and endless conversation that they could get on with things.

"It's all so dusty," said Penny, wrinkling up her nose and trying not to sneeze as she brushed down some of the high up cobwebs. "I'll have to get on the step ladder, I can't reach those ones on the beams."

When she was on a level with the top of the corner cupboard, she scooped up three dead flies in a tissue, from its triangular top.

"I don't think they've ever dusted up here, not ever."

She wiped it over with a damp cloth and was just about to climb down again, when she spied the twist of paper sticking up from the back. She pulled it up, along with a lot more dust and unrolled it. Of course it was brittle and yellowed with age but the writing was still legible.

"Oh look Rob, look, this is really interesting…"

He took the scrap of paper, read it and stared at her in amazement. "Does it really say what I think it says or am I just imagining it?"

Penny read out loud for him, "Susannah Mary Curzon, Jacob Curzon, Jack Curzon, Penelope Susannah Curzon, Hugo Curzon lived here 1780 to 1792."

She reached out to the cupboard top to steady herself, remembering at once dear little baby Jack, who must have had a sister called Penelope and a brother Hugo, later on.

"You all right up there, Love?" He reached up and helped her safely off the step ladder. "It's quite a shock when the past leaps up and hits you in the face like that. I'm not sure who this lot were in my family, it's so difficult when they all have the same names generation after generation…"

"Well we've not helped much with that have we," laughed Penny, who was still quite shaken by the little note.

"Guess not," grinned Rob, for their own children were called Suzie and Jake.

Later that night they lay in bed, both on their phones, as the hadn't got the broadband set up yet. Rob was trying to work out who exactly this particular branch of eighteenth century Curzon's were, while Penny checked her emails.

"Oh that would be nice, what a surprise," she said.

"What is?"

"My Auntie's finally found somewhere to live in Bath, for her new job and she's asked us if we'd all like to go and stay for a few days when she gets settled in. That'd be nice wouldn't it Darling?"

"Mmm," he replied unsure, thinking of his future commitment to his farm animals.

"We'd have to do it before the hens and things come," she said reading his thoughts.

"Go on then Pen, let's do it, let's get in a good holiday and then settle to farming life."

So that was an exciting thing to look forward to, a trip to Bath...

Lydia's favourite Brandy Tart.

For the pastry-
2oz butter
4oz plain flour
Pinch of salt
Teaspoon of sugar
Cold water

For the filling-
4 beaten eggs
¼ pint of cream
Handful of sliced almonds
Handful of dried fruit (apricots, raisins, cherries)
3 tablespoons of brandy
3ozs caster sugar

Rub the butter into the flour, salt and teaspoon of sugar and add enough water to make a pastry, shape, roll out thinly and place in a greased tin or shallow dish. Blind bake in a moderate oven for fifteen minutes.

Then place the fruit and almonds on the pastry base; mix together the eggs, cream, brandy and sugar, pour this mixture over the fruit and bake in a moderate oven for 20 minutes or until set.

Serve warm with pouring cream.

Susannah's Little Queen Cakes.

4ozs soft butter
4ozs brown sugar
4ozs self-raising flour
2ozs currants
2 teaspoons of fresh lemon juice
Grated rind of two lemons
Pinch of nutmeg
Icing sugar to dust

Cream the butter and sugar together.

Slowly add the beaten eggs and then the lemon juice.

Stir the flour, nutmeg and lemon rind together and then fold into the mixture.

Add the currants.

Place the mixture in a greased bun tin (lined with circles of greaseproof paper) to make 12 individual cakes.

Bake at 160 degrees for 30 minutes.

Let the cakes cool for two minutes, then turn out of the tin.

Dust the finished cakes with icing sugar and eat immediately.

Eliza's Unrivalled Cheese on Toast.

Lightly toast two slices of thick bread.

Put 4ozs of cubed cheddar cheese in a skillet and slowly heat it up.

As it starts to melt add a pinch of black pepper and a good pinch of mustard powder.

Stir in a dessertspoonful of milk (or thin cream).

When almost melted and browned around the edges, pour over the toasted bread.

Serve at once with sliced tomatoes or beetroots.

The Curzons in 1796

Benjamin Curzon m Lydia Belle 1781
|
Belle   Benjamin and Robert   Olivia
b 1782   b1783   b 1785
George   Frederick Francis Octavia
b 1787   b 1789   b1791   b 1795

Jacob Curzon m Susannah 1780
|
Jack   Penelope   Hugo
b 1780   b 1782   b1789